영미 명작 단편선

미국편

영미 명작 단편선 – 미국편

초판 2쇄 펴낸날 | 2024년 3월 25일

편저자 | 신현욱
펴낸이 | 류수노
펴낸곳 | (사)한국방송통신대학교출판문화원
03088 서울시 종로구 이화장길 54
대표전화 1644-1232
팩스 02-742-0956
홈페이지 http://press.knou.ac.kr
출판등록 1982년 6월 7일 제1-491호

출판위원장 | 백삼균
편집 | 신경진 · 정미용
본문 디자인 | (주)성지이디피
표지 디자인 | 이상선

ⓒ 신현욱, 2019
ISBN 978-89-20-99243-8　93840

값 10,000원

이 도서의 국립중앙도서관 출판예정도서목록(CIP)은 서지정보유통지원시스템 홈페이지(http://seoji.nl.go.kr)와
국가자료공동목록시스템(http://www.nl.go.kr/kolisnet)에서 이용하실 수 있습니다. (CIP제어번호: CIP2019024250)

영미
명작
단편선

미국편

신현욱 편저

에피스테메
EPISTEME

영미 명작 단편선 – 미국편

차 례 ‹‹

책을 펴내며

방송대 영문학과에서 문학개관이나 단편소설 등의 과목을 운영하다 보면, 학기가 끝난 뒤 '발동이 걸려서' 더 읽어볼 작품을 추천해 달라는 분들이 많다. 이 가운데는 애초부터 문학작품에 관심이 큰 분도 있지만 영어공부를 하려고 영문과에 왔다가 뒤늦게 '이야기'라는 것에 재미를 느낀 분도 꽤 많다. 이야기에 맛이 들어 읽다 보니 원문 읽기의 호흡이 조금씩 길어지면서 영어공부가 덤으로 뒤따라오더라는 것이다. 성인 학습자들의 풍부한 삶의 경험은 작품의 이야기가 뿌리를 내려 잘 자라는 비옥한 토양이라는 인상을 받는다. 이분들의 요청에 부응하여 이야기의 즐거움에 더해 삶에 대한 통찰이 담긴 작품, 지금 여기 우리의 삶에 대한 고민을 풀어가는 데도 얼마간 기여해 줄 수 있을 작품을 골라 묶어보려고 했다.

한편, 이 책이 나오게 된 계기가 방송대 프라임칼리지에서 운영하는 두 편의 교양강좌 "원어로 읽는 영미 명작 단편선"인데, 수강생 면면을 보면 뜻밖에 일반시민의 비중이 작지 않다. 영미문학 작품을 원어로 읽어보고자 하는 일반시민 독자들의 관심은 인문학에 대한 사회적 관심과도 일정하게 연관되지 않을까 추측해 본다. 영미문학 단편소설을 읽으면서 인문적 소양을 넓히는 동시에 이를 해당 언어의 맥락에서 이해하고 소화하고자 하는 분들이 학교 안팎으로 많음이 실감된다.

여기에 묶은 미국 단편소설은 호손의 "The Great Stone Face", 오 헨리의 "The Gift of the Magi", 피츠제럴드의 "The Curious Case of Benjamin Button" 등과 같이 작품의 제목 정도는 들어본 적이 있거나 영화나 대중문화를 통해 직·간접적으로 접한 경험이 있는 조금은 더 친근할 법한 작품이다. 작가들이 자신의 사회적·역사적 환경에서 맞대면한 삶과 가치의 문제를 저마다의 독특한 필체를 통해 펼치는 이야기를 따라가다 보면 어느 새 독자들의 생각과 정서에 탄력이 더해지지 않을까 기대해 본다.

— 편저자 신현욱

영미 명작 단편선_1

The Great Stone Face

Nathaniel Hawthorne

Nathaniel Hawthorne(1804~1864)은 19세기 미국 고전문학의 주요 작가 중 한 사람으로 *The Scarlet Letter*(1850)를 통해 잘 알려졌으며 미국 초기 역사의 주요 단면들을 형상화한 작품을 많이 썼다. Hawthorne은 짜임새가 아주 촘촘하고 깊은 의미구조를 지닌 수많은 단편소설로도 잘 알려졌다. 그중에는 초기 청교도사회의 면면, 청교도와 그와는 다른 종교적 신념을 지닌 퀘이커교도의 인간관계 등 신대륙 정착지 내에서의 갈등, 과학적 탐구와 인문예술의 관계 등 묵직하고 진지한 주제를 다루는 단편소설이 꽤 많다. 그런가 하면 일상을 스케치하듯 그리는 가운데 삶에 대한 깊은 통찰을 담아내는 단편소설도 있다. "The Great Stone Face"(1850)는 후자에 속한다고 할 수 있으며 동화 같은 분위기 속에 삶에 대한 잔잔하면서도 깊은 지혜를 전하고 있어서 미국은 물론 전 세계 독자들에게 많은 사랑을 받아 온 작품이다.

The Great Stone Face

One afternoon, when the sun was going down, a mother and her little boy sat at the door of their cottage, talking about the Great Stone Face. They had but to[1] lift their eyes, and there it was plainly to be seen,[2] though miles away, with the sunshine brightening all its features.[3]

And what was the Great Stone Face?

Embosomed[4] amongst a family of[5] lofty mountains, there

---

1 have but to : =have only to. ~하기만 하면 되다
2 it was plainly to be seen : 그것을 분명하게 볼 수 있었다 *plainly : 분명히, 있는 그대로
3 with the sunshine brightening all its features : 햇살이 그 '이목구비'를 모두 비춰 주고 있는 상태 그대로 *feature : (이목구비 따위) 얼굴의 생김새 (복수형 features로 사용 시 용모, 얼굴이라는 의미가 있음), 특징, 특색. 여기에서는 사람의 얼굴 모양의 바위를 묘사하고 있으므로 '이목구비'로 하는 것이 자연스러움.
4 embosom : 둘러싸다(surround), 가슴에 품다
5 a family of : 일군의, 한 무리의

was a valley so spacious that[6] it contained many thousand inhabitants. Some of these good people dwelt in[7] log-huts,[8] with the black forest all around them, on the steep and difficult hill-sides. Others had their homes in comfortable farm-houses, and cultivated the rich soil on the gentle slopes or level surfaces of the valley. Others, again, were congregated[9] into populous villages, where some wild, highland rivulet, tumbling down from its birthplace in the upper mountain region,[10] had been caught and tamed by human cunning, and compelled to[11] turn the machinery of cotton-factories.[12] The inhabitants of this valley, in short, were numerous, and of many modes of life.[13] But all of them, grown people and children, had a kind of familiarity with[14] the Great Stone

---

6 so spacious that ... : 꽤 널찍하여 ~한 (계곡)

7 dwell in : ~에 거주하다, 살다

8 log-hut : =log cabin(house) hut. 오두막, 임시 가옥

9 congregate : <자> 모이다, 집합하다, <타> ~을 많이 모으다

10 tumbling down from its birthplace in the upper mountain region : 고산 간지대의 발원지로부터 요란하게 흘러내려 오는

11 had been caught and tamed by human cunning, and compelled to : 인간 의 꾀에 의해 붙잡혀 길들여져 ~하지 않을 수 없었다

12 cotton-factory : 목화(면화) 공장

13 (the) mode of life : 생활양식, 삶의 방식

14 had a kind of familiarity with : ~와 일종의 친밀함을 지녔다

Face, although some possessed the gift of distinguishing[15] this grand natural phenomenon more perfectly than many of their neighbors.

The Great Stone Face, then, was a work of Nature in her mood of majestic playfulness,[16] formed on the perpendicular side[17] of a mountain by some immense rocks, which had been thrown together[18] in such a position as, when viewed at a proper distance,[19] precisely to resemble the features of the human countenance.[20] It seemed as if an enormous giant, or a Titan,[21] had sculptured his own likeness[22] on the precipice. There was the broad arch of the forehead,[23] a hundred feet in height; the nose, with its long bridge;[24] and the vast lips,

---

15 distinguish : 구별하다, 식별하다
16 a work of Nature in her mood of majestic playfulness : 자연이 장엄한 장난기를 부릴 기분일 때 만든 작품
17 perpendicular side : 수직면
18 throw together : 서둘러 만들다, 뚝딱 만들다
19 when viewed at a proper distance : 적당한 거리에서 볼 때면
20 countenance : 생김새, 용모, 안색, 표정
21 Titan : 그리스 신화에 등장하는 원시 종족의 거인신으로 Gaia(Earth)와 Uranus(Sky)의 자손들임.
22 sculptured his own likeness : 자신과 닮은 모습을 조각했다
23 the broad arch of the forehead : 넓은 아치 모양의 이마
24 with its long bridge : 긴 콧날을 지닌

which, if they could have spoken, would have rolled their thunder accents[25] from one end of the valley to the other. True it is, that if the spectator approached too near, he lost the outline of the gigantic visage,[26] and could discern[27] only a heap of ponderous[28] and gigantic rocks, piled in chaotic ruin[29] one upon another. Retracing his steps,[30] however, the wondrous features would again be seen; and the farther he withdrew from them, the more like a human face, with all its original divinity intact,[31] did they appear; until, as it grew dim in the distance, with the clouds and glorified vapor of the mountains clustering about it,[32] the Great Stone Face seemed positively[33] to be alive.

---

25 would have rolled their thunder accents : (으르렁거리듯) 천둥 같은 말소
리를 냈을 것이다

26 lost the outline of the gigantic visage : 그 거대한 얼굴의 윤곽을 잃어버렸다

27 discern : 알아보다, 식별하다

28 ponderous : 크고 무거운

29 piled in chaotic ruin : 혼돈스러운 잔해로 쌓은

30 retracing his steps : 자신의 발걸음을 되짚어 오면

31 with all its original divinity intact : 본래의 모든 신성함이 전혀 손상되지
않은 채의

32 with the clouds and glorified vapor of the mountains clustering about it :
그 주변에 무리를 이룬 산악의 구름과 멋들어진 운무로 인해

33 positively : 확실히, 정말로, 몹시

It was a happy lot[34] for children to grow up to manhood or womanhood with the Great Stone Face before their eyes, for all the features were noble, and the expression was at once grand and sweet,[35] as if it were the glow of a vast, warm heart,[36] that embraced all mankind in its affections, and had room for more.[37] It was an education only to look at it. According to the belief of many people, the valley owed much of its fertility to[38] this benign aspect that was continually beaming over it,[39] illuminating the clouds,[40] and infusing its tenderness into the sunshine.[41]

As we began with saying, a mother and her little boy sat at their cottage-door, gazing at the Great Stone Face, and talking

---

34 a happy lot : 행운

35 at once grand and sweet : 웅장하고도 다정한

36 as if it were the glow of a vast, warm heart : 마치 그것(표정)이 거대하고 따뜻한 가슴이 뿜어내는 은은한 빛이듯이

37 embraced all mankind in its affections, and had room for more : 온 인류를 그 애정의 품에 품고도 남는(그 이상의 여지가 있는)

38 owed much of its fertility to : 그 비옥함의 상당 부분은 ~ 덕분이었다

39 beaming over it : 그(계곡) 위로 활짝 웃어 주는

40 illuminating the clouds : 구름을 밝게 비춰 주는

41 infusing its tenderness into the sunshine : 그 부드러움을 햇살에 스며들게 넣어 주는

about it. The child's name was Ernest.[42]

"Mother," said he, while the Titanic visage smiled on him, "I wish that it could speak, for it looks so very kindly that its voice must needs be pleasant. If I were to see a man with such a face, I should love him dearly."[43]

"If an old prophecy should come to pass,"[44] answered his mother, "we may see a man, some time or other,[45] with exactly such a face as that."

"What prophecy do you mean, dear mother?" eagerly inquired Ernest. "Pray[46] tell me about it!"

So his mother told him a story that her own mother had told to her, when she herself was younger than little Ernest; a story, not of things that were past, but of what was yet to come;[47] a story, nevertheless, so very old, that even the

---

42 Ernest: 남자 이름이자 'earnest'(진지한, 열심인)의 의미를 지님. ＊작품 속 등장인물의 이름 혹은 별명인 Gathergold, Blood-and-Thunder, Rev. Dr. Battleblast 등에서도 알 수 있듯이 인물의 이름은 특정인의 이름이면서 동시에 그 사람으로 대표되는 일반적인 속성과 자질을 의미함.

43 dearly: 몹시, 매우, 대단히

44 come to pass: 발생하다, 일어나다

45 some time or other: 언젠가

46 pray: 기원하다, 간절히 바라다 ＊<옛글 투 또는 반어적> 질문 부탁 등을 할 때 please와 같은 의미로 씀.

47 yet to come: 아직 오지 않았다, 아직 더 남아 있다

Indians, who formerly inhabited this valley, had heard it from their forefathers, to whom, as they affirmed,[48] it had been murmured by the mountain streams, and whispered by the wind among the tree-tops. The purport[49] was, that, at some future day, a child should be born hereabouts, who was destined to[50] become the greatest and noblest personage[51] of his time, and whose countenance, in manhood,[52] should bear an exact resemblance to[53] the Great Stone Face. Not a few[54] old-fashioned[55] people, and young ones likewise, in the ardor of their hopes,[56] still cherished an enduring faith[57] in this old prophecy. But others, who had seen more of the world, had watched and waited till they were weary, and had beheld no man with such a face, nor any man that proved to be much greater or nobler than his neighbors, concluded it to be

---

48 affirm : 단언하다, 확증하다
49 purport : 전체적인 뜻, 요지
50 destined to : ~할 운명인
51 personage : 저명인사, 명사
52 in manhood : 장년이 되면, 성장하면
53 bear an exact resemblance to : ~을 정확히 닮다
54 not a few : 적지 않은, 꽤 많은
55 old-fashioned : 구식의, 전통적인 사고방식을 지닌
56 in the ardor of their hopes : 열정적인 희망으로 * ardor : 열정, 정열, 열심
57 cherished an enduring faith : 오래 지속되는(영속하는) 믿음을 품었다

nothing but an idle tale.[58] At all events,[59] the great man of the prophecy had not yet appeared.

"O mother, dear mother!" cried Ernest, clapping[60] his hands above his head, "I do hope that I shall live to see him!"

His mother was an affectionate and thoughtful woman, and felt that it was wisest not to discourage the generous hopes[61] of her little boy. So she only said to him, "Perhaps you may."

And Ernest never forgot the story that his mother told him. It was always in his mind, whenever he looked upon the Great Stone Face. He spent his childhood in the log-cottage where he was born, and was dutiful to his mother, and helpful to her in many things, assisting her much with his little hands, and more with his loving heart.[62] In this manner,[63] from a

---

58 nothing but an idle tale : 그저 헛된 이야기일 뿐 ＊idle : 쓸데없는, 무익한, 근거 없는

59 at all events : 좌우간, 여하튼 간에

60 clap : 손뼉을 치다, 박수를 치다

61 the generous hopes : 통 큰 희망 ＊generous는 '후한,' '넉넉한'의 의미인 데 보통보다(필요 이상으로) 많거나 풍부한 경우에 씀.

62 assisting her much with his little hands, and more with his loving heart : 그의 작은(어린) 손으로 그녀(어머니)를 도와 많은 것을 했는데, 다정한 마음씨로는 더 많은 도움이 된

63 in this manner : 이런(그런, 어떤) 식으로

happy yet often pensive[64] child, he grew up to be a mild, quiet, unobtrusive[65] boy, and sun-browned with labor in the fields,[66] but with more intelligence brightening his aspect[67] than is seen in many lads who have been taught at famous schools.

5　Yet Ernest had had no teacher, save[68] only that the Great Stone Face became one to him. When the toil of the day was over, he would gaze at it for hours, until he began to imagine that those vast features recognized[69] him, and gave him a smile of kindness and encouragement, responsive to his own

10　look of veneration.[70] We must not take upon us to affirm[71] that this was a mistake, although the Face may have looked no more kindly at Ernest than at all the world besides. But

---

64　pensive: (특히 슬픔·걱정 때문에) 깊은 생각에 잠긴, 수심 어린

65　unobstrusive: 불필요하게 관심을 끌지 않는, 지나치게 야단스럽지 않은

66　sun-browned with labor in the fields: 들판에서의 노동으로 햇볕에 그을려 갈색이 된

67　with more intelligence brightening his aspect: 더 많은 지성이 그의 용모를 밝게 비춰 주는

68　save: ~을 제외하고(except)

69　recognize: 알아보다, 인지하다

70　responsive to his own look of veneration: 그 자신의 존경(숭배)의 표정에 반응하는 * responsive: 대답하는, 감응하는, 응답하는

71　take upon us to affirm: ~라고 주장하는 것을 의무로 생각하다 * take upon: ~의 책임(의무)을 지다, 맡다

the secret was that the boy's tender and confiding simplicity[72] discerned what other people could not see; and thus the love, which was meant for all, became his peculiar portion.

About this time there went a rumor throughout the valley, that the great man, foretold from ages long ago, who was to   5
bear a resemblance to the Great Stone Face, had appeared at last. It seems that, many years before, a young man had migrated[73] from the valley and settled[74] at a distant seaport, where, after getting together a little money, he had set up as[75]
a shopkeeper. His name — but I could never learn whether   10
it was his real one, or a nickname that had grown out of his habits and success in life — was Gathergold.[76] Being shrewd[77] and active, and endowed by Providence with that inscrutable faculty[78] which develops itself in what the world calls luck, he became an exceedingly rich merchant, and owner of a whole   15

---

72 tender and confiding simplicity : 다정하고 신뢰하는 순박함(천진난만함)
73 migrate : 이동 · 이주하다
74 settle : 정착하다, 이주하다
75 set up as : ~로 창업하다, 사업을 시작하다
76 Gathergold : '금모아' 씨
77 shrewd : 상황 판단이 빠른, 기민한
78 endowed by Providence with that inscrutable faculty : 신의 섭리의 의해
    그런 불가해한 능력을 타고난　＊endowed with : ~을 가지고 타고난

fleet[79] of bulky-bottomed[80] ships. All the countries of the globe appeared to join hands[81] for the mere purpose of adding heap after heap to the mountainous accumulation[82] of this one man's wealth. The cold regions of the north, almost within the gloom and shadow of the Arctic Circle,[83] sent him their tribute[84] in the shape of[85] furs; hot Africa sifted[86] for him the golden sands of her rivers, and gathered up the ivory tusks[87] of her great elephants out of the forests; the East came bringing him the rich shawls, and spices, and teas, and the effulgence[88] of diamonds, and the gleaming purity of large pearls. The

---

79 fleet : 함대, 선대(船隊)
80 bulky-bottomed : 바닥의 부피가 큰 * double-bottomed : 이중 바닥의
    * a flat-bottomed : 바닥이 납작한
81 join hands : 서로 손을 잡다, 제휴하다
82 adding heap after heap to the mountainous accumulation : 차곡차곡 쌓아
    가 산더미같이 축적함
83 Arctic Circle : 북극권 한계선(북극의 경계를 가르는 가상의 선으로, 북극을
    중심으로 원형으로 이루어짐.)
84 tribute : 헌사, 찬사
85 in the shape of : ~의 형태로
86 sift : 체로 치다, 거르다
87 ivory tusk : 상아 엄니(코끼리 따위의)
88 effulgence : 광휘, 광채

ocean, not to be behindhand with[89] the earth, yielded up[90] her mighty whales, that[91] Mr. Gathergold might sell their oil, and make a profit[92] of it. Be the original commodity what it might,[93] it was gold within his grasp.[94] It might be said of him, as of Midas[95] in the fable, that whatever he touched with his finger immediately glistened, and grew yellow, and was changed at once into sterling[96] metal, or, which suited[97] him still better, into piles of coin. And, when Mr. Gathergold had become so very rich that it would have taken him a hundred years only to count his wealth, he bethought himself[98] of his native valley, and resolved to go back thither,[99] and end his

---

89 behindhand with : ~에 뒤처진

90 yield up : 내다, 생산하다, 넘겨주다

91 that : =so that

92 make a profit : 이윤을 창출하다, 돈을 벌다, 이익을 얻다

93 Be the original commodity what it might : =whatever the original commodity might be. 원 상품이 무엇이든 간에

94 within his grasp : 그의 손아귀에 들어가면, 그의 손안에서는

95 as of Midas : 미다스에 대해서와 마찬가지로 * Midas : 미다스(손에 닿는 것을 모두 황금으로 변하게 한 Phrygia의 왕)

96 sterling : 영국 법정 순도의 금은을 함유한, 순수한, 진짜의 * a sterling article : 진짜, 진품 * sterling silver : 순은

97 suit : ~의 마음에 들다, ~에 편리하다, 적합하다

98 bethink oneself of : ~를 생각해 내다, ~가 생각나다

99 thither : 저쪽으로, 그쪽으로

days[100] where he was born. With this purpose in view,[101] he sent a skilful architect to build him such a palace as should be fit for[102] a man of his vast wealth to live in.

As I[103] have said above, it had already been rumored in the valley that Mr. Gathergold had turned out to be the prophetic personage so long and vainly looked for,[104] and that his visage was the perfect and undeniable similitude of the Great Stone Face. People were the more ready to believe[105] that this must needs be the fact, when they beheld the splendid edifice[106] that rose, as if by enchantment,[107] on the site of his father's old weatherbeaten farm-house. The exterior was of marble, so dazzlingly white[108] that it seemed as though the

---

100 end his days : 여생을 마치다
101 with this purpose in view : 이런 목적을 간직하고(고려하여)
102 be fit for : ~에 알맞다, 적당하다
103 I : 작품의 화자인데, 작중의 구체적인 인물이라기보다는 이야기꾼으로서의 작가의 목소리라고 볼 수 있음.
104 so long and vainly looked for : 그렇게나 오랫동안 아무리 찾아도 소용없던 (예언상의 인물)
105 the more ready to believe : 그만큼 더 기꺼이 믿다
106 edifice : (크고 인상적인) 건물, 조직, 체계
107 as if by enchantment : 마치 마법에 의해서인 듯
108 so dazzlingly white : 너무나 눈부시도록 하얀 (대리석)

whole structure might melt away[109] in the sunshine, like those humbler ones[110] which Mr. Gathergold, in his young play-days,[111] before his fingers were gifted with the touch of transmutation,[112] had been accustomed to[113] build of snow. It had a richly ornamented[114] portico,[115] supported by tall pillars, beneath which was a lofty door, studded[116] with silver knobs, and made of a kind of variegated[117] wood that had been brought from beyond the sea. The windows, from the floor to the ceiling of each stately apartment, were composed, respectively,[118] of[119] but one enormous pane of glass, so transparently pure that it was said to be a finer medium than

5

10

---

109 melt away : 점차로(서서히) 녹아 사라지다

110 those humbler ones : 더 소박한 그 구조물들(ones=structures) ＊이것은 Gathergold가 어린 시절 눈으로 만든 집을 가리킴.

111 play-day : (일요일을 제외한 학교 따위의) 휴일

112 gifted with the touch of transmutation : 변화시키는 손길의 재능을 부여받은

113 be accustomed to : 익숙하게 ~하다

114 ornamented : 장식된

115 portico : 포르티코(특히 대형 건물 입구에 기둥을 받쳐 만든 현관 지붕)

116 stud : 못, (특히 대가리가 큰) 장식 못, ~에 장식 단추를 달다, 장식 못을 박다

117 variegated : 얼룩덜룩한

118 respectively : 각자, 각각, 제각기

119 be composed of : ~로 구성된(이루어진), ~로 만들어진

even the vacant atmosphere.[120] Hardly anybody had been permitted to see[121] the interior of this palace; but it[122] was reported, and with good semblance of truth,[123] to be far more gorgeous[124] than the outside, insomuch that[125] whatever was iron or brass in other houses was silver or gold in this; and Mr. Gathergold's bedchamber, especially, made such a glittering appearance that no ordinary man would[126] have been able to close his eyes there. But, on the other hand, Mr. Gathergold was now so inured to[127] wealth, that perhaps he could not have closed his eyes unless where the gleam of it was certain to find its way beneath his eyelids.[128]

---

120 a finer medium than even the vacant atmosphere : 심지어 아무것도 없는 대기보다도 더 섬세한 매개체

121 hardly anybody had been permitted to see : 거의 누구도 ~를 보도록 허락되지 않았다

122 it : =the interior of this palace

123 with good semblance of truth : 상당히 진실된 모습을 띤　＊semblance : 외관, 겉모습

124 gorgeous : 아주 멋진, 좋은

125 insomuch that : ~할 정도까지

126 made such a glittering appearance that no ordinary man would … : 너무나 반짝이는 모습을 띠었기에 어떤 보통 사람도 ~ 없었을 것이다　＊침실이지만 보통 사람은 눈이 부셔 잠을 못 잘 지경일 만큼 화려하다는 의미

127 inured to : ~에 단련된, 익숙한, 이골이 난

128 perhaps he … his eyelids : 눈이 부실 정도로 화려한 이런 곳에서만 잠들

In due time,[129] the mansion was finished; next came the upholsterers, with magnificent furniture; then, a whole troop of[130] black and white servants, the harbingers[131] of Mr. Gathergold, who, in his own majestic person,[132][133] was expected to arrive at sunset. Our friend Ernest, meanwhile, had been deeply stirred by the idea that the great man, the noble man, the man of prophecy, after so many ages of delay, was at length to be made manifest[134] to his native valley. He knew, boy as he was,[135] that there were a thousand ways in which Mr. Gathergold, with his vast wealth, might transform himself into an angel of beneficence,[136] and assume a control

---

수 있다는 의미는 자신의 재산을 눈으로 확인해야만 안심하고 잠들 수 있다는 점을 풍자적으로 설명하고 있다고 볼 수 있음.

129 in due time : 머지않아, 곧

130 a whole troop of : 대단히 많은 무리의 ~ *whole : 대단히 많거나 크거나 중요함을 강조할 때 사용함.

131 harbinger : 선발대, 전령

132 in person : 몸소

133 in his own majestic person : 그 자신이 위풍당당하게 몸소 *in person (몸소, 직접)을 작가가 응용 · 변주한 표현으로 볼 수 있음.

134 make ... manifest : ~을 성취시키다, ~을 명백한 것으로 만들다

135 boy as he was : =though he was a boy

136 an angel of beneficence : 선행(자선)의 천사

over human affairs[137] as wide and benignant[138] as the smile of the Great Stone Face. Full of faith and hope, Ernest doubted not that what the people said was true, and that now he was to behold the living likeness[139] of those wondrous features on the mountain-side. While the boy was still gazing up the valley, and fancying, as he always did, that the Great Stone Face returned his gaze and looked kindly at him, the rumbling[140] of wheels was heard, approaching swiftly along the winding[141] road.

"Here he comes!" cried a group of people who were assembled to witness the arrival. "Here comes the great Mr. Gathergold!"

A carriage, drawn by four horses, dashed[142] round the turn of the road.[143] Within it, thrust partly out of[144] the window,

---

137 assume a control over human affairs : 인간사를 다스리는 일을 떠맡다
138 benignant : 인자한, 자애로운
139 living likeness : 꼭 닮음, 판에 박은 듯 닮은 것
140 rumble : 우르르거리는 소리를 내다, 덜커덩거리며 나아가다
141 winding : 구불구불한
142 dash : 서둘러 가다
143 round the turn of the road : 길모퉁이를 돌아
144 thrust partly out of : ~로부터 부분적으로 내밀어진

appeared the physiognomy[145] of the old man, with a skin as yellow as if his own Midas-hand had transmuted[146] it. He had a low forehead, small, sharp eyes, puckered[147] about with innumerable wrinkles, and very thin lips, which he made still thinner by pressing them forcibly[148] together.

"The very image of the Great Stone Face!" shouted the people. "Sure enough,[149] the old prophecy is true; and here we have the great man come, at last!"

And, what greatly perplexed[150] Ernest, they seemed actually to believe that here was the likeness which they spoke of. By the roadside there chanced to be an old beggar-woman and two little beggar-children, stragglers[151] from some far-off region, who, as the carriage rolled onward, held out their hands and lifted up their doleful[152] voices, most piteously

---

145 physiognomy : (어떤 사람의) 얼굴 모습, 생김새, 골상
146 transmute : 변형시키다, 변화시키다
147 pucker : 주름지게 하다
148 forcibly : 강력히, 강제적으로, 힘차게
149 sure enough : 아니나 다를까, 말할 것도 없이
150 perplex : (무엇을 이해할 수 없어서) 당혹하게 하다
151 straggler : 부랑자, 낙오자
152 doleful : 애절한

beseeching charity.[153] A yellow claw[154] — the very same that had clawed together so much wealth — poked[155] itself out of the coach-window, and dropt some copper coins upon the ground; so that, though the great man's name seems to

5 have been Gathergold, he might just as suitably have been nicknamed Scattercopper.[156] Still, nevertheless, with an earnest shout, and evidently with as much good faith as ever, the people bellowed,[157] "He is the very image[158] of the Great Stone Face!"

10 But Ernest turned sadly from the wrinkled shrewdness of that sordid visage,[159] and gazed up the valley, where, amid a gathering mist,[160] gilded[161] by the last sunbeams, he could still distinguish those glorious features which had impressed

---

153 most piteously beseeching charity : 아주 애처롭게 자비를 간청하면서

154 a yellow claw : 누런 갈고리 같은 손 *Gathergold의 손을 '탐욕'과 '공격성'이 드러나도록 이렇게 비유적으로 묘사하고 있음.

155 poke : (재빨리) 밀다, 찌르다, 쑥 내밀다, 삐져나오다

156 Scattercopper : 동전 흩뿌리는 이

157 bellow : 고함치다

158 the very image : 꼭 빼닮은 것

159 the wrinkled shrewdness of that sordid visage : 그 추악한 얼굴의 주름진 약삭빠름 *Gathergold 얼굴의 내·외적 특징을 효과적으로 집약하고 있음.

160 gathering mist : 몰려드는(끼기 시작하는) 안개(연무)

161 gild : 금빛으로 빛나게 하다

themselves into his soul. Their aspect cheered him. What did the benign[162] lips seem to say?

"He will come! Fear not, Ernest; the man will come!"

The years went on, and Ernest ceased to be a boy. He had grown to be a young man now. He attracted little notice from the other inhabitants of the valley; for they saw nothing remarkable[163] in his way of life save that, when the labor of the day was over, he still loved to go apart[164] and gaze and meditate upon the Great Stone Face. According to their idea of the matter,[165] it was a folly, indeed, but pardonable, inasmuch as[166] Ernest was industrious,[167] kind, and neighborly,[168] and neglected no duty for the sake of indulging this idle habit.[169] They knew not that the Great Stone Face had become a teacher to him, and that the sentiment which was expressed

---

162 benign : 친절한, 자애로운, 상냥한, 온화한

163 remarkable : 놀랄 만한, 놀라운, 주목할 만한

164 go apart : 따로 떨어져 나가다, (남들로부터) 멀어지다

165 according to their idea of the matter : 그 문제에 대해 그들이 생각하는 바에 따르면

166 inasmuch as : ~이므로, ~인 한, ~인 점을 고려하면

167 industrious : 근면한, 부지런한

168 neighborly : 사귐성 있는, 친절한

169 for the sake of indulging this idle habit : 이런 헛된 습관에 빠져 마음껏 즐기기 위해

in it[170] would enlarge the young man's heart, and fill it with wider and deeper sympathies than other hearts. They knew not that thence[171] would come a better wisdom than could be learned from books, and a better life than could be moulded[172] on the defaced[173] example of other human lives.[174] Neither did Ernest know that the thoughts and affections which came to him so naturally, in the fields and at the fireside, and wherever he communed with himself,[175] were of a higher tone[176] than those[177] which all men shared with him. A simple soul,[178] — simple as when his mother first taught him the old prophecy, — he beheld the marvellous features beaming adown[179] the

---

170 the sentiment which was expressed in it: 그것(큰 바위 얼굴)에 담겨 표현된 정서

171 thence: 거기에서

172 mould: (부드러운 재료를 단단히 다지거나 틀에 넣어) 만들다, 주조하다

173 defaced: 외관이 훼손된

174 than could be moulded on the defaced example of other human lives: 삶이 훼손된 다른 사람들의 사례를 참조해 형성될 수 있을 것보다

175 commune with oneself: 깊은 생각에 잠기다, 숙고하다 *자신의 내면과 깊은 교감에 이른 상황을 묘사하고 있음.

176 of a higher tone: 더 고결한, 더 격조 높은

177 those: =the thoughts and affections

178 a simple soul: 평범한(소박한) 사람

179 beam adown: = beam down. 빛을 비추다

valley, and still wondered that their human counterpart[180] was so long in making his appearance.

By this time poor Mr. Gathergold was dead and buried; and the oddest part of the matter was, that his wealth, which was the body and spirit of his existence,[181] had disappeared before his death, leaving nothing of him but a living skeleton,[182] covered over with a wrinkled yellow skin. Since the melting away of his gold, it had been very generally conceded[183] that there was no such striking resemblance,[184] after all, betwixt the ignoble[185] features of the ruined merchant and that majestic face upon the mountain-side. So the people ceased to honor him during his lifetime, and quietly consigned him to forgetfulness[186] after his decease.[187] Once in a while, it is

---

180 their human counterpart: 그것들에 상응하는 인간존재
181 body and spirit of his existence: 그의 존재의 육체와 정신
182 a living skeleton: 산송장
183 concede: 인정하다, 수긍하다
184 striking resemblance: 눈에 띄는(도드라진) 유사함
185 ignoble: 비열한, 야비한
186 consigned him to forgetfulness: 그를 망각으로 보내 버리다, 그를 잊게 되다 * consign ... to ...: ~를 ~에 넘기다(보내다)
187 decease: (법률 또는 격식) 사망

true, his memory was brought up[188] in connection with[189] the magnificent palace which he had built, and which had long ago been turned into a hotel for the accommodation[190] of strangers, multitudes of whom came, every summer, to visit that famous natural curiosity,[191] the Great Stone Face. Thus, Mr. Gathergold being discredited[192] and thrown into the shade,[193] the man of prophecy was yet to come.[194]

It so happened that a native-born son of the valley, many years before, had enlisted[195] as a soldier, and, after a great deal of hard fighting, had now become an illustrious commander.[196] Whatever he may be called in history, he was known in camps and on the battle-field under the

---

188 his memory was brought up : 그에 대한 기억이 불러일으켜졌다(환기되었다)

189 in connection with : ~와 함께, ~와 연계하여(되어)

190 accommodation : 거처, 숙박시설

191 curiosity : 호기심, 진기(신기)한 것

192 discredit : 존경심을 떨어뜨리다, 신빙성을 없애다

193 Mr. Gathergold being discredited and thrown into the shade : '금모아' 씨가 신빙성을 잃고 (눈의 띄지 않게) 그늘 속에 파묻혀 버리자

194 be yet to come : 아직 오지 않고 있다

195 enlist : 병적에 편입하다, 입대하다

196 an illustrious commander : 빛나는(걸출한) 지휘관, 사령관

nickname of Old Blood-and-Thunder.[197] This war-worn
veteran,[198] being now infirm with age and wounds,[199] and
weary of the turmoil[200] of a military life, and of the roll of the
drum[201] and the clangor of the trumpet,[202] that had so long
been ringing in his ears, had lately signified[203] a purpose of
returning to his native valley, hoping to find repose where he
remembered to have left it. The inhabitants, his old neighbors
and their grown-up children, were resolved to[204] welcome the
renowned warrior[205] with a salute of cannon[206] and a public
dinner; and all the more enthusiastically, it being affirmed that
now, at last, the likeness of the Great Stone Face had actually

---

197　Old Blood-and-Thunder : '노련한(경험 많은) 피와 천둥' ＊blood-and-
thunder는 '유혈과 폭력'이라는 뜻을 포함하고 있으며 (통속소설 따위에
서) 폭력과 유혈투성이, 선정주의를 의미함.

198　war-worn veteran : 전쟁에 지친 퇴역 군인

199　infirm with age and wounds : 노년과 상처로 인해 쇠약한, 늙고 상처 입어
쇠약해진

200　turmoil : 소란, 소동, 분투

201　the roll of the drum : 두두두두하는 드럼 소리

202　clangor of the trumpet : 트럼펫의 금속성 음

203　signify : (행동으로 감정·의도 등을) 나타내다

204　be resolved to : ~하기로 결의하다, 결심하다, 결정하다

205　renowned warrior : 유명한(명성이 있는) 전사

206　salute of cannon : 예포(禮砲)

appeared. An aid-de-camp[207] of Old Blood-and-Thunder, travelling through the valley, was said to have been struck with[208] the resemblance. Moreover the schoolmates and early acquaintances of the general were ready to testify, on oath,[209] that, to the best of their recollection,[210] the aforesaid[211] general had been exceedingly like the majestic image, even when a boy, only that the idea had never occurred to them at that period. Great, therefore, was the excitement throughout the valley; and many people, who had never once thought of glancing at the Great Stone Face for years before, now spent their time in gazing at it, for the sake of knowing exactly how General Blood-and-Thunder looked.

On the day of the great festival, Ernest, with all the other people of the valley, left their work, and proceeded to[212] the spot where the sylvan banquet[213] was prepared. As he

---

207 aid-de-comp : =aide-de-comp. 부관, 참모
208 be struck with : ~에 감명받다
209 on oath : 선서를 하고
210 to the best of their recollection : 그들의 기억이 미치는 한
211 aforesaid : 앞서 말한, 전술한
212 proceed to : ~로 나아가다, 진행하다
213 sylvan banquet : 숲속의 연회

approached, the loud voice of the Rev.[214] Dr. Battleblast[215] was heard, beseeching a blessing on[216] the good things set before them, and on the distinguished friend of peace in whose honor they were assembled. The tables were arranged in a cleared space[217] of the woods, shut in by the surrounding trees, except where a vista opened eastward,[218] and afforded a distant view[219] of the Great Stone Face. Over the general's chair, which was a relic from the home of Washington, there was an arch of verdant boughs,[220] with the laurel profusely intermixed,[221] and surmounted by his country's banner, beneath which he had won his victories. Our friend Ernest raised himself on his tiptoes, in hopes to get a glimpse of[222] the celebrated guest; but there was a mighty crowd[223] about

---

214 Rev. : Reverend(목사)의 약자

215 Dr. Battleblast : '전투를 알리는 취주' 박사

216 beseech a blessing on : ~에 대해 축복을 간청하다

217 a cleared space : 개간된 공터

218 where a vista opened eastward : 전망이 동쪽으로 열린 곳

219 afforded a distant view : 먼 경관을 제공했다

220 an arch of verdant boughs : 신록의 가지들로 이뤄진 아치

221 with the laurel profusely intermixed : 월계수가 풍성하게 혼합되어 있는

222 get a glimpse of : ~을 흘끗 보다

223 a mighty crowd : 굉장한 군중

the tables anxious to hear the toasts[224] and speeches, and to catch any word that might fall from the general in reply; and a volunteer company,[225] doing duty as a guard, pricked ruthlessly with their bayonets at any particularly quiet person
5 among the throng.[226] So Ernest, being of an unobtrusive[227] character, was thrust quite into the background, where he could see no more of Old Blood-and-Thunder's physiognomy than if it had been still blazing on the battle-field.[228] To console himself, he turned towards the Great Stone Face,
10 which, like a faithful and long remembered friend, looked back and smiled upon him through the vista of the forest. Meantime, however, he could overhear the remarks[229] of various individuals, who were comparing the features of the hero with the face on the distant mountain-side.

---

224 toast : 축배의 말, 축사

225 a volunteer company : 자원봉사자 단체(무리)

226 pricked ruthlessly with their bayonets at any particularly quiet person among the throng : 군중 사이의 어떤 아주 얌전한 사람에게마저 찌를 듯이 무자비하게 총검을 겨냥했다 ＊실제로 찔렀다기보다는 살벌한 분위기를 조성했다는 의미로 이해할 수 있음.

227 unobtrusive : 주제넘지 않은, 겸손한, 삼가는

228 he ... on the battle-field : 여전히 전쟁터에서 전투 중이어서 얼굴을 볼 수 없던 경우와 전혀 다를 바 없었다는 의미임.

229 remark : 소견, 비평, 의견

"Tis[230] the same face, to a hair!"[231] cried one man, cutting a caper[232] for joy.

"Wonderfully like,[233] that's a fact!" responded another.

"Like! why, I call it Old Blood-and-Thunder himself, in a monstrous[234] looking-glass!" cried a third. "And why not?[235] He's the greatest man of this or any other age, beyond a doubt."[236]

And then all three of the speakers gave a great shout, which communicated electricity[237] to the crowd, and called forth[238] a roar from a thousand voices, that went reverberating[239] for miles among the mountains, until you might have supposed that the Great Stone Face had poured its thunder-breath into

---

230 Tis : It is

231 to a hair : 털끝만큼도 틀림없이

232 cut a caper : 신나게 뛰어다니다, 까불어 대다

233 wonderfully like! : 놀랄 만큼 똑같다!

234 monstrous : 무시무시하게 큰, 거대한 *monster는 태어날 때부터 결함을 지녀 형태가 온전하지 않은 동물이나 인간을 가리키며 예외적으로 거대한 크기를 함축하는 경우가 많음.

235 why not? : 왜 아니겠어?

236 beyond a doubt : 의심의 여지없이

237 electricity : 전기, (사람에서 사람에게 전달되는) 강한 흥분, 열광

238 call forth : 불러일으키다

239 reverberate : 반향하다, 울려 퍼지다

the cry.[240] All these comments, and this vast enthusiasm, served the more to interest our friend; nor did he think of questioning that now, at length, the mountain-visage had found its human counterpart. It is true, Ernest had imagined that this long-looked-for[241] personage would appear in the character of a man of peace,[242] uttering wisdom, and doing good, and making people happy. But, taking an habitual breadth of view, with all his simplicity,[243] he contended[244] that Providence should choose its own method of blessing mankind, and could conceive that this great end might be effected even by a warrior and a bloody sword,[245] should inscrutable wisdom see fit to order matters so.[246]

---

240 went reverberating … into the cry : 큰 바위 얼굴이 사람들의 외침에 자신의 천둥 같은 숨결을 쏟아부었다고 생각될 정도로 산중에 수 마일을 울려 퍼져 갔다

241 long-looked-for : 오랫동안 찾아왔던(기대되어 왔던)

242 a man of peace : 평화주의자

243 taking an habitual breadth of view, with all his simplicity : 순박하지만 늘 폭넓은 시각을 지니고 있으므로

244 contend : (강력히) 주장하다

245 this great end might be effected even by a warrior and a bloody sword : 이 위대한 목적이 전사와 피 묻은 칼에 의해서조차 이뤄질 수 있을지 모른다 * effect : 어떤 결과를 가져오다

246 should inscrutable wisdom see fit to order matters so : 헤아릴 수 없는(신

"The general! the general!" was now the cry. "Hush! silence! Old Blood-and-Thunder's going to make a speech."

Even so;[247] for, the cloth being removed,[248] the general's health had been drunk,[249] amid shouts of applause,[250] and he now stood upon his feet to thank the company. Ernest saw him. There he was, over the shoulders of the crowd, from the two glittering epaulets[251] and embroidered collar[252] upward, beneath the arch of green boughs with intertwined laurel, and the banner drooping[253] as if to shade his brow! And there, too, visible in the same glance,[254] through the vista of the forest, appeared the Great Stone Face! And was there, indeed, such a

---

의) 지혜가 그렇게 상황을 처리하는 것이 적합하다고 한다면 ＊if가 생략되면서 조동사 should가 주어 앞으로 도치되었음.

247 even so : 과연 그랬다 ＊even : 바로, 정확히

248 the cloth being removed : 천이 제거되자 ＊비록 앞에서 장군의 동상에 대한 이야기가 언급되지는 않았으나 이 대목은 동상 개막식에서 덮어 놓은 천을 제거하며 개막하는 광경을 연상시킴.

249 drink somebody's health : ~의 건강을 위하여 건배·축배를 들다

250 a shout of applause : 박수갈채

251 epaulet : 견장

252 embroidered collar : 수놓인(장식된) 깃(칼라)

253 droop : 수그러지다, 축 처지다

254 in the same glance : 똑같은 눈길에, 눈길이 향하는 같은 방향에

resemblance as the crowd had testified? Alas,[255] Ernest could not recognize it! He beheld a war-worn and weatherbeaten[256] countenance, full of energy, and expressive of an iron will;[257] but the gentle wisdom, the deep, broad, tender sympathies, were altogether wanting[258] in Old Blood-and-Thunder's visage; and even if the Great Stone Face had assumed his look of stern command,[259] the milder traits would still have tempered it.[260]

"This is not the man of prophecy," sighed Ernest to himself, as he made his way[261] out of the throng. "And must the world wait longer yet?"[262]

The mists had congregated about the distant mountain-side, and there were seen the grand and awful features of the Great Stone Face, awful but benignant, as if a mighty

---

255 Alas : 아아, 슬프도다, 불쌍한지고

256 weatherbeaten : 풍파에 시달린, 단련된, 햇볕에 탄

257 iron will : 강철 같은 의지, 굳센 의지

258 altogether wanting : 완전히 결여된(lacking)

259 stern command : 엄명

260 the milder traits would still have tempered it : 그럼에도 불구하고 더 부드러운 특징들이 그것(엄명의 표정)을 누그러뜨려 주었을 것이다

261 make one's way : 나아가다

262 "This is not the man ... wait longer yet?" : 이런 대목을 보면, 이제 Ernest 는 거의 '큰 바위 얼굴' 감별사가 된 듯하다.

angel were sitting among the hills, and enrobing himself in a cloud-vesture of gold and purple.[263] As he looked, Ernest could hardly believe but that a smile beamed over the whole visage,[264] with a radiance still brightening, although without motion of the lips. It was probably the effect of the western sunshine, melting through the thinly diffused vapors[265] that had swept[266] between him and the object that he gazed at. But — as it always did — the aspect of his marvellous friend made Ernest as hopeful as if he had never hoped in vain.[267]

"Fear not, Ernest," said his heart, even as if the Great Face were whispering him, — fear not, Ernest; he will come."

More years sped swiftly and tranquilly away.[268] Ernest still dwelt in his native valley, and was now a man of middle age. By imperceptible degrees,[269] he had become known among

---

263 enrobing himself in a cloud-vesture of gold and purple : 금빛과 자주색의 구름옷을 (예복처럼) 걸치고 있는 *robe는 가운 식으로 만들어진 예복을 의미함.

264 a smile beamed over the whole visage : 얼굴 전체에 미소가 환하게 퍼져 있다

265 thinly diffused vapors : 얇게 퍼진 운무(수증기)

266 sweep : 넓게 퍼져 있다, 드리워져 있다

267 as if he had never hoped in vain : 그때까지 희망한 것이 헛되지 않았던 듯

268 speed away : 서둘러 달리다

269 by imperceptible degrees : 알아차릴 수 없을 정도로

the people. Now, as heretofore, he labored for his bread, and was the same simple-hearted man that he had always been. But he had thought and felt so much, he had given so many of the best hours of his life to unworldly hopes for some great

5 good to mankind,[270] that it seemed as though he had been talking with the angels, and had imbibed a portion of their wisdom unawares.[271] It was visible in the calm and well-considered beneficence[272] of his daily life, the quiet stream of which had made a wide green margin all along its course.[273]

10 Not a day passed by, that the world was not the better because this man, humble as he was, had lived.[274] He never stepped

---

270 unworldly hopes for some great good to mankind : 인류에게 어떤 위대한 이익이 되고자 하는, 때묻지 않은 희망

271 had imbibed a portion of their wisdom unawares : 모르는 사이에 그들 (천사들)의 지혜의 상당 부분을 흡수했다

272 well-considered beneficence : 사려 깊은 선행(자선)

273 the quiet stream of which had made a wide green margin all along its course : (그의 일상생활에 담긴 고요하고 잘 배려된 자선의) 요란하지 않고 조용한 흐름은, 흘러가는 곳마다 가장자리에 넓고 푸른 곳을 만들어 냈다 ＊which가 가리키는 것을 그가 일상에서 펼치는 '자선'으로 보고 그것이 강물처럼 흘러가는 듯 비유한 것으로 이해할 수 있음.

274 Not a day passed by, that the world was not the better because this man, humble as he was, had lived : 비록 소박하지만, 이 사람이 살아가기 때문에 그만큼 세상이 더 좋아지지 않은 날은 단 하루도 지나가지 않았다

aside from his own path, yet would always reach[275] a blessing to his neighbor. Almost involuntarily[276] too, he had become a preacher. The pure and high simplicity of his thought, which, as one of its manifestations,[277] took shape in the good deeds[278] that dropped silently from his hand, flowed also forth in speech. He uttered truths that wrought upon and moulded the lives of those who heard him.[279] His auditors, it may be, never suspected[280] that Ernest, their own neighbor and familiar friend, was more than an ordinary man; least of all did Ernest himself suspect it; but, inevitably as the murmur of a rivulet,[281] came thoughts out of his mouth that no other human lips had spoken.

When the people's minds had had a little time to cool,[282]

---

275 reach : 건네주다

276 involuntarily : 본의 아니게, 무심결에

277 as one of its manifestations : 그(그의 순수하고 정말 간명한 생각) 발현들 중의 하나로서

278 good deeds : 선행

279 wrought upon and moulded the lives of those who heard him : 그의 말 을 들은 이들의 삶에 작용해 그 형성에 강한 영향을 미친

280 suspect : ~이 아닌가 의심하다

281 inevitably as the murmur of a rivulet : 시냇물의 소곤거림을 막을 수 없듯 이(그렇듯이 필연적으로)

282 time to cool : 진정할 시간, 가라앉힐 시간

they were ready enough to acknowledge their mistake in imagining a similarity between General Blood-and-Thunder's truculent[283] physiognomy and the benign visage on the mountain-side. But now, again, there were reports and many

5 paragraphs[284] in the newspapers, affirming that the likeness of the Great Stone Face had appeared upon the broad shoulders of a certain eminent statesman.[285] He, like Mr. Gathergold and Old Blood-and-Thunder, was a native of the valley, but had left it in his early days, and taken up the trades[286] of law

10 and politics. Instead of the rich man's wealth and the warrior's sword, he had but a tongue, and it was mightier than both together.[287] So wonderfully eloquent[288] was he, that whatever he might choose to say, his auditors had no choice but to believe him; wrong looked like right, and right like wrong;

15 for when it pleased him, he could make a kind of illuminated fog with his mere breath, and obscure the natural daylight

---

283 truculent: 흉포한, 호전적인
284 paragraph: (신문의) 단평 기사
285 upon the broad shoulders of a certain eminent statesman: 어떤 저명한 정치가의 넓은 어깨 위에
286 take up the trades: 직업들에 손을 대다
287 it was ... together: 그것(혀)은 두 개('부'와 '검')를 합친 것보다 더 강했다
288 eloquent: 웅변의, 능변의, 설득력 있는

with it.[289] His tongue, indeed, was a magic instrument:[290] sometimes it rumbled[291] like the thunder; sometimes it warbled[292] like the sweetest music. It was the blast[293] of war — the song of peace; and it seemed to have a heart in it, when there was no such matter.[294] In good truth,[295] he was a wondrous man; and when his tongue had acquired him all other imaginable success, — when it had been heard in halls of state, and in the courts of princes and potentates,[296] — after it had made him known all over the world, even as a voice crying from shore to shore,[297] — it finally persuaded his countrymen

---

289 make a kind of illuminated fog with his mere breath, and obscure the natural daylight with it : 한낱 입김으로 환히 빛나는 안개와 같은 것을 만들어 자연 그대로의 햇빛을 흐리게 하다

290 magic instrument : 마술 도구

291 rumble : 우르르거리다

292 warble : 지저귀다, (바람이) 살랑거리는 소리를 내다

293 blast : 경적, 취주

294 when there was no such matter : 그런 일이야 없었겠지만, 그런 일이 없었을 때는 *구문의 의미가 다소 애매한데, '혀 속에 심장을 지니고 있는 일이라는 것은 있을 수 없는 일이었겠지만'의 의미로 볼 수 있지만, 앞 대목과 연관하여 '전쟁' '평화' 등과 같은 '그런 커다란 상황들이 없었을 때는'의 의미로도 볼 수 있음.

295 in good truth : 실제

296 potentate : 강한 지배자, 통치자

297 a voice crying from shore to shore : 해안에서 해안까지, 즉 전국 방방곡

to select him for the Presidency.[298] Before this time, — indeed, as soon as he began to grow celebrated, — his admirers had found out the resemblance between him and the Great Stone Face; and so much were they struck by it, that throughout the country this distinguished gentleman was known by the name of Old Stony Phiz.[299] The phrase[300] was considered as giving a highly favorable aspect to his political prospects; for, as is likewise the case with the Popedom,[301] nobody ever becomes President without taking a name other than his own.[302]

While his friends were doing their best to make him President, Old Stony Phiz, as he was called, set out on a

---

곡에서 울려오는 목소리 ＊이 대목의 의미를 더 확장하여, 대서양의 양쪽, 즉 유럽의 해안에서 그리고 신대륙의 해안에서 울려 퍼지면서 전 세계적으로 알려졌다는 의미로 볼 수도 있음.

298 Presidency : 대통령직

299 Old Stony Phiz : 늙은 바위 얼굴 ＊phiz : =physiognomy. 골상, 얼굴

300 The phrase : =Old Stony Phiz

301 Popedom : 로마 교황의 직

302 without taking a name other than his own : 자기 자신의 것이 아닌 다른 이름을 취하지 않고 ＊이 대목은, 차기 교황이 수락 의사를 밝히면서 자신의 본명 대신에 존경하는 성인이나 전임 교황의 이름을 선택하여 자신의 교황명으로 삼아 공표하는 상황을 들어, 이야기 속의 정치가가 대통령이 되기 위해 자신의 본명 대신에 좋은 이미지를 만들기 위해 'Old Stony Phiz'라는 이름을 앞세운 것임을 비유적으로 말하고 있음.

visit to the valley where he was born. Of course, he had no other object than to shake hands with his fellow-citizens and neither thought nor cared about any effect which his progress[303] through the country might have upon the election. Magnificent preparations were made to receive the illustrious[304] statesman; a cavalcade of horsemen[305] set forth to meet him at the boundary line[306] of the State, and all the people left their business and gathered along the wayside to see him pass. Among these was Ernest. Though more than once disappointed, as we have seen, he had such a hopeful and confiding[307] nature, that he was always ready to believe in whatever seemed beautiful and good. He kept his heart continually open, and thus was sure to catch the blessing from on high[308] when it should come. So now again, as buoyantly[309] as ever, he went forth to behold the likeness of the Great Stone Face.

---

303 progress : (진행) 과정, 공적 여행, 순행
304 illustrious : 뛰어난, 이름난, 빛나는, 화려한
305 a cavalcade of horsemen : 기수들의 기마 행렬
306 boundary line : 경계선
307 confiding : 신뢰하는
308 the blessing from on high : 하늘 높은 곳으로부터의 축복
309 buoyantly : 뜨기 쉽게, 쾌활히, 낙천적으로

The cavalcade came prancing[310] along the road, with a great clattering of hoofs[311] and a mighty cloud of dust, which rose up so dense and high that the visage of the mountain-side was completely hidden from Ernest's eyes. All the great men of the neighborhood were there on horseback; militia officers, in uniform; the member of Congress; the sheriff of the county; the editors of newspapers; and many a farmer, too, had mounted his patient steed,[312] with his Sunday coat[313] upon his back. It really was a very brilliant spectacle, especially as there were numerous banners flaunting[314] over the cavalcade, on some of which were gorgeous portraits[315] of the illustrious statesman and the Great Stone Face, smiling familiarly at one another, like two brothers. If the pictures were to be trusted, the mutual resemblance, it must be confessed, was marvellous. We must not forget to mention that there was a band of music, which made the echoes of the mountains

---

310 prance : 껑충거리며 뛰어가다

311 clattering of hoofs : 말발굽의 덜커덕거리는 소리

312 patient steed : 참을성 있는 (승마용) 말

313 his Sunday coat : 그가 가진 옷들 중에 제일 좋은 옷

314 flaunt : 자랑삼아 보이다, 과시하다, 드높이 휘날리다, 나부끼다

315 on some of which were gorgeous portraits : 그것들(깃발들) 중 어떤 것들
     에는 아주 멋진 초상들이 (그려져) 있었다

ring and reverberate with the loud triumph of its strains;[316] so that airy and soul-thrilling melodies[317] broke out among all the heights and hollows,[318] as if every nook of his native valley had found a voice,[319] to welcome the distinguished guest. But the grandest effect was when the far-off mountain precipice flung back[320] the music; for then the Great Stone Face itself seemed to be swelling[321] the triumphant[322] chorus, in acknowledgment that, at length, the man of prophecy was come.

All this while the people were throwing up their hats and shouting with enthusiasm so contagious[323] that the heart of Ernest kindled up,[324] and he likewise threw up his hat, and shouted, as loudly as the loudest, "Huzza[325] for the great man!

---

316 reverberate with the loud triumph of its strains : 크게 울리는 승리감에 찬 가락으로 떠나갈 듯 울려 퍼지다

317 airy and soul-thrilling melodies : 환상적이고 영혼을 황홀하게 하는 멜로디

318 the heights and hollows : 높은 언덕들과 골짜기들

319 find a voice : 기꺼이 말하고 싶어지다

320 fling back : 되던지다

321 swell : 부풀리다, 증가시키다

322 triumphant : 의기양양한, 승리를 거둔, 성공한

323 contagious : 전염성의, 만연하는

324 kindle up : 불이 붙다, 불타오르다

325 Huzza : =Hurrah. 만세!

Huzza for Old Stony Phiz!" But as yet he had not seen him.

"Here he is, now!" cried those who stood near Ernest. "There! There! Look at Old Stony Phiz and then at the Old Man of the Mountain, and see if they are not as like as two twin-
5 brothers!"

In the midst of all this gallant array[326] came an open barouche,[327] drawn by four white horses; and in the barouche, with his massive head uncovered,[328] sat the illustrious statesman, Old Stony Phiz himself.

10 "Confess[329] it," said one of Ernest's neighbors to him, "the Great Stone Face has met its match at last!"[330]

Now, it must be owned[331] that, at his first glimpse of the countenance which was bowing and smiling from the barouche, Ernest did fancy that there was a resemblance
15 between it and the old familiar face upon the mountain-side. The brow, with its massive depth and loftiness, and all the

---

326 in the midst of all this gallant array : 이 모든 위풍당당한 행렬 한가운데로
327 barouche : 4인승 4륜 포장마차
328 with his massive head uncovered : 그의 (육중하고) 거대한 머리에 아무 것도 쓰지 않은 채
329 confess : 인정하다, 시인하다
330 has met its match at last : 마침내 그 짝을 만났다
331 own : 인정하다, 자인하다

other features, indeed, were boldly and strongly hewn,[332] as if in emulation[333] of a more than heroic, of a Titanic model. But the sublimity[334] and stateliness,[335] the grand expression of a divine sympathy, that illuminated the mountain visage and etherealized[336] its ponderous[337] granite substance[338] into spirit, might here be sought in vain. Something had been originally left out, or had departed.[339] And therefore the marvellously gifted statesman had always a weary gloom in the deep caverns[340] of his eyes, as of a child that has outgrown its playthings or a man of mighty faculties and little aims, whose life, with all[341] its high performances, was vague and empty, because no high purpose had endowed it with

5

10

---

332 boldly and strongly hewn : 대담하고 힘 있게 깎아 새겨진
333 emulation : 경쟁, 겨룸, 모방
334 sublimity : 장엄, 숭고, 고상, 극치
335 stateliness : 당당함, 위엄 있음
336 etherealize : 영화(靈化)하다, 기화(氣化)하다, 영묘하게 하다
337 ponderous : 묵직한, 육중한
338 granite substance : 화강암 물질
339 Something had been originally left out, or had departed : 뭔가가 원래부터 빠졌었는지, 아니면 (있었다가) 사라져 버렸다
340 cavern : 동굴, 굴
341 with all : ~에도 불구하고

reality.[342]

Still, Ernest's neighbor was thrusting his elbow into his side, and pressing him for an answer.

"Confess! confess! Is not he the very picture of your Old Man of the Mountain?"

"No!" said Ernest bluntly,[343] "I see little or no likeness."

"Then so much the worse for the Great Stone Face!" answered his neighbor; and again he set up a shout[344] for Old Stony Phiz.

But Ernest turned away, melancholy, and almost despondent:[345] for this was the saddest of his disappointments, to behold a man who might have fulfilled the prophecy, and had not willed[346] to do so. Meantime, the cavalcade, the banners, the music, and the barouches swept past him, with the vociferous[347] crowd in the rear,[348] leaving the dust to settle

---

342 And therefore the marvellously ... had endowed it with reality : 재능은 있으나 높은 이상이나 목적의 부재가 삶에 미치는 영향을 설명하고 있음.

343 bluntly : 무뚝뚝하게, 퉁명스럽게

344 set up a shout : 아우성치다, 함성을 지르다

345 despondent : 낙담한, 기운 없는, 의기소침한

346 will : 뜻하다, 의도하다, 바라다

347 vociferous : 큰 소리로 외치는, 소란한, 시끄러운

348 in the rear : 뒤쪽에

down, and the Great Stone Face to be revealed again, with the grandeur that it had worn for untold centuries.

"Lo,[349] here I am, Ernest!" the benign lips seemed to say. "I have waited longer than thou, and am not yet weary. Fear not; the man will come."

The years hurried onward, treading in their haste on one another's heels.[350] And now they began to bring white hairs, and scatter[351] them over the head of Ernest; they made reverend[352] wrinkles across his forehead, and furrows[353] in his cheeks. He was an aged man. But not in vain had he grown old: more than the white hairs on his head were the sage[354] thoughts in his mind; his wrinkles and furrows were inscriptions that Time had graved,[355] and in which he had written legends of wisdom[356] that had been tested by the tenor

---

349 Lo : 보라, 자!
350 treading in their haste on one another's heels : 서두른 나머지 서로의 뒤꿈치를 밟으며
351 scatter : 흩어 놓다, 흩뿌리다
352 reverend : 귀한, 거룩한
353 furrow : 고랑, 깊은 주름
354 sage : 슬기로운, 현명한, 사려 깊은
355 inscriptions that Time had graved : 시간이 새긴 비명(碑銘)들
356 a legend of wisdom : 지혜가 담긴 제명(題名), 경구(警句)

of a life.[357] And Ernest had ceased to be obscure. Unsought for, undesired, had come the fame which so many seek, and made him known in the great world, beyond the limits of the valley in which he had dwelt so quietly. College professors, and even the active men of cities, came from far to see and converse[358] with Ernest; for the report had gone abroad that this simple husbandman had ideas unlike those of other men, not gained from books, but of a higher tone, — a tranquil and familiar majesty, as if he had been talking with the angels as his daily friends. Whether it were sage, statesman, or philanthropist,[359] Ernest received these visitors with the gentle sincerity[360] that had characterized[361] him from boyhood, and spoke freely with them of whatever came uppermost, or lay deepest in his heart or their own.[362] While they talked together, his face would kindle, unawares, and shine upon them, as with a mild

---

357 tenor of a life : 인생 행로

358 converse : 대화하다, 이야기를 나누다

359 philanthropist : 박애가(박애주의자), 자선가

360 sincerity : 성실, 진심, 순수함, 성의

361 characterize : 특징짓다

362 whatever came uppermost, or lay deepest in his heart or their own : 그의 가슴이나 그들 자신의 가슴속에서 맨 먼저 떠오른 것이나 가장 깊이 자리한 것이나 간에 그 모든 것에 대해

evening light. Pensive with the fulness of such discourse,[363] his guests took leave and went their way; and passing up the valley, paused to look at the Great Stone Face, imagining that they had seen its likeness in a human countenance, but could not remember where.

While Ernest had been growing up and growing old, a bountiful Providence[364] had granted a new poet to this earth. He likewise, was a native of the valley, but had spent the greater part of his life at a distance from that romantic region, pouring out his sweet music amid the bustle and din of cities.[365] Often, however, did the mountains which had been familiar to him in his childhood lift their snowy peaks[366] into the clear atmosphere of his poetry.[367] Neither was the Great Stone Face forgotten, for the poet had celebrated it in an ode,[368] which was grand enough to have been uttered[369]

---

363 Pensive with the fulness of such discourse : 그런 담화의 충만함으로 생각
   에 잠겨
364 bountiful Providence : 너그러운(자비로운) 신의 섭리
365 bustle and din of cities : 도시의 부산스러움과 소음
366 snowy peak : 눈 덮인 봉우리
367 the clear atmosphere of his poetry : 그의 시의 맑은 대기(분위기)
368 ode : (특정한 사람·사물·사건에 부치는) 시, –송(頌)[부(賦)]
369 utter : (입으로 어떤 소리를) 내다, (말을) 하다

by its own majestic lips.[370] This man of genius, we may say, had come down from heaven with wonderful endowments.[371] If he sang of a mountain, the eyes of all mankind beheld a mightier grandeur reposing on its breast, or soaring to its summit,[372] than had before been seen there. If his theme were a lovely lake, a celestial smile had now been thrown over it, to gleam forever on its surface. If it were the vast old sea, even the deep immensity of its dread bosom[373] seemed to swell the higher, as if moved by the emotions of the song. Thus the world assumed another and a better aspect from the hour that the poet blessed it with his happy eyes. The Creator had bestowed him, as the last best touch to his own handiwork.[374] Creation was not finished till the poet came to interpret, and so complete it.

---

370 grand enough to have been uttered by its own majestic lips : 그(큰 바위 얼굴) 자신의 위풍당당한 입술로 읊어도 좋을 만큼 웅장한

371 endowment : (학교 등의 기관에 주는) 기부(금), 타고난 재능이나 자질

372 beheld a mightier grandeur reposing on its breast, or soaring to its summit : 더 커다란 장엄이 그(산) 가슴 부위에 자리 잡거나 정상으로 솟아 오르는 것을 보았다 *현실의 사물이 시(詩)를 통해 더 고양된다는 의미임.

373 the deep immensity of its dread bosom : 그(바다) 두려운 가슴의 깊은 광 대무변함

374 as the last best touch to his own handiwork : 그(창조주) 자신의 예술적 작품의 최후의, 최상의 손질 마무리로서

The effect was no less high and beautiful, when his human brethren were the subject of his verse. The man or woman, sordid[375] with the common dust of life, who crossed his daily path, and the little child who played in it, were glorified[376] if he beheld them in his mood of poetic faith. He showed the golden links of the great chain that intertwined them with an angelic kindred;[377] he brought out the hidden traits[378] of a celestial birth that made them worthy of such kin. Some, indeed, there were, who thought to show the soundness of their judgment by affirming that all the beauty and dignity of the natural world existed only in the poet's fancy.[379] Let such men speak for themselves, who undoubtedly appear to have been spawned[380] forth by Nature with a contemptuous

---

375 sordid: 더러운, 지저분한

376 glorify: (실제보다) 아름답게 보이게 하다, 미화하다, 찬미하다, 칭송하다

377 intertwined them with an angelic kindred: 그들(일상의 보통 사람들)을 천사의 일족과 밀접하게 연관되게 하는

378 hidden traits: 감춰진 특성들

379 who thought to show the soundness of their judgment by affirming that all the beauty and dignity of the natural world existed only in the poet's fancy: 자연 세계의 아름다움과 존엄성은 모두 시인의 상상력에서나 존재하는 것이라고 주장함으로써 자기 판단의 건전함을 보여 주고자 생각한

380 spawn: 알을 낳다, (어떤 못마땅한 결과나 상황을) 낳다

bitterness;[381] she having plastered[382] them up out of her refuse[383] stuff, after all the swine[384] were made. As respects[385] all things else, the poet's ideal was the truest truth.

The songs of this poet found their way to Ernest. He read them after his customary toil,[386] seated on the bench before his cottage-door, where for such a length of time he had filled his repose with thought, by gazing at the Great Stone Face. And now as he read stanzas[387] that caused the soul to thrill within him, he lifted his eyes to the vast countenance beaming on him so benignantly.

"O majestic friend," he murmured, addressing[388] the Great Stone Face, "is not this man worthy to resemble thee?"

The Face seemed to smile, but answered not a word.

Now it happened that the poet, though he dwelt so far

---

381 contemptuous bitterness : 경멸하는 신랄함
382 plaster : (벽 등에) 회반죽을 바르다, (물기가 있거나 끈적한 것을) 바르다
383 refuse : 쓰레기
384 swine : 돼지, 비열한 사람 ＊돼지같이 비열한 인간들을 모두 만들고 난 뒤에 남은 찌꺼기 재료로 반죽해서 만들었다는 의미
385 as respects : ~에 관해서는
386 customary toil : 일상적인(늘상 있는) 노고(수고, 노동)
387 stanza : (시의) 연(聯) ＊보통 4행 이상의 각운이 있는 시구
388 address : ~에게 이야기를(말을) 걸다

away, had not only heard of Ernest, but had meditated much upon his character, until he deemed nothing so desirable as to meet this man,[389] whose untaught wisdom walked hand in hand with the noble simplicity of his life. One summer morning, therefore, he took passage[390] by the railroad, and, in the decline of the afternoon,[391] alighted[392] from the cars at no great distance from Ernest's cottage. The great hotel, which had formerly been the palace of Mr. Gathergold, was close at hand, but the poet, with his carpet-bag[393] on his arm, inquired[394] at once where Ernest dwelt, and was resolved to[395] be accepted as his guest.

Approaching the door, he there found the good old man, holding a volume in his hand, which alternately[396] he read, and then, with a finger between the leaves, looked lovingly at

---

389 he deemed nothing <u>so</u> desirable <u>as</u> to meet this man : 그는 이 사람을 만나는 것만큼 바람직한 일은 없다고 생각했다

390 take passage : 여행하다

391 in the decline of the afternoon : 오후가 저물어 갈 때 ＊decline : 감소, 하락, 기울기

392 alight : 내리다

393 carpet-bag : 여행용 가방

394 inquire : 묻다, 질문하다, 수소문하다

395 be resolved to : ~ 하려고 굳게 결심하다

396 alternately : 번갈아, 교대로, 엇갈리게, 하나씩 걸러

the Great Stone Face.

"Good evening," said the poet. "Can you give a traveller a night's lodging?"[397]

"Willingly,"[398] answered Ernest; and then he added, smiling, "Methinks[399] I never saw the Great Stone Face look so hospitably[400] at a stranger."

The poet sat down on the bench beside him, and he and Ernest talked together. Often had the poet held intercourse with[401] the wittiest and the wisest, but never before with a man like Ernest, whose thoughts and feelings gushed up with such a natural freedom, and who made great truths so familiar by his simple utterance[402] of them. Angels, as had been so often said, seemed to have wrought with him at his labor in the fields; angels seemed to have sat with him by the fireside; and,

---

397 lodging: 임시 숙소, 하숙, 숙박, 묵어 가기 ＊board and lodging: 식사를 제공하는 하숙 ＊dry lodging: 식사 없이 잠만 자는 하숙
398 willingly: 기꺼이요
399 methinks: <고어, 시어> 생각건대 ~이다(it seems to me)
400 hospitably: 대접이 좋게, 환대하여 ＊이 대목은 Ernest와 큰 바위 얼굴 사이에 이제는 거의 한 몸이 된 듯 서로의 정서와 생각을 교감되고 있음을 보여 줌.
401 hold intercourse with: ~와 교류하다, 소통하다
402 utterance: 말함, 발언

dwelling with angels as friend with friends, he had imbibed the sublimity of their ideas, and imbued it with the sweet and lowly charm of household words.[403] So thought the poet. And Ernest, on the other hand, was moved and agitated[404] by the living images which the poet flung out of his mind, and which peopled[405] all the air about the cottage-door with shapes of beauty, both gay[406] and pensive. The sympathies of these two men instructed them with a profounder sense than either could have attained alone. Their minds accorded into one strain, and made delightful music[407] which neither of them could have claimed as all his own, nor distinguished his own share from the other's. They led one another, as it were, into

---

403 imbibed the sublimity of their ideas, and imbued it with the sweet and lowly charm of household words: 그들(천사들)의 이념의 숭고함을 흡수하여 그 숭고함을 평상시 흔히 사용되는 말의 상쾌하고 소박한 매력으로 가득 채웠다 ＊imbibe: 마시다, 흡수하다 ＊imbue: (강한 감정·의견·가치를) 가득 채우다

404 agitate: 주장하다, 뒤흔들다

405 people: 채우다

406 gay: 명랑한, 유쾌한, 화려한, 즐거운

407 accorded into one strain, and made delightful music: 한 가락으로 합쳐져 즐거운 음악을 만들었다 ＊accord: <명사> 합의, <동사> 부여하다, 부합하다 ＊strain: (연주되어 들려오는) 가락 선율

a high pavilion[408] of their thoughts, so remote, and hitherto so dim, that they had never entered it before, and so beautiful that they desired to be there always.

As Ernest listened to the poet, he imagined that the Great Stone Face was bending forward to listen too. He gazed earnestly into the poet's glowing eyes.

"Who are you, my strangely gifted[409] guest?" he said.

The poet laid his finger on the volume that Ernest had been reading.

"You have read these poems," said he. "You know me, then, — for I wrote them."

Again, and still more earnestly than before, Ernest examined the poet's features; then turned towards the Great Stone Face; then back, with an uncertain[410] aspect, to his guest. But his countenance fell;[411] he shook his head, and sighed.

"Wherefore are you sad?" inquired the poet.

"Because," replied Ernest, "all through life I have awaited

---

408 pavilion : (공공 행사 · 전시회) 임시 구조물, 파빌리온(공원 안의 쉼터 · 공연장 등 아름다움을 강조하여 지은 건물), 대형 경기장
409 strangely gifted : 이상하리만큼 재능이 있는
410 uncertain : 확신이 없는, 잘 모르는, 머뭇거리는
411 fall : 안색 따위가 생기를 잃다, 침울해지다, 낙심하다

the fulfilment of a prophecy; and, when I read these poems, I hoped that it might be fulfilled in you."

"You hoped," answered the poet, faintly smiling, "to find in me the likeness of the Great Stone Face. And you are disappointed, as formerly with Mr. Gathergold, and Old Blood-and-Thunder, and Old Stony Phiz. Yes, Ernest, it is my doom. You must add my name to the illustrious three,[412] and record another failure of your hopes. For — in shame and sadness do I speak it, Ernest — I am not worthy to be typified[413] by yonder benign and majestic image."

"And why?" asked Ernest. He pointed to the volume. "Are not those thoughts divine?"[414]

"They have a strain of the Divinity," replied the poet. "You can hear in them the far-off echo of a heavenly song. But my life, dear Ernest, has not corresponded with[415] my thought. I have had grand dreams, but they have been only dreams, because I have lived — and that, too, by my own choice —

---

412 the illustrious three : 그 저명한 세 사람
413 typify : 전형적 · 대표적인 특징을 드러내다
414 divine : 성스러운, 신성한
415 correspond with : ~와 대응하다, 부합하다, 조화하다

among poor and mean[416] realities. Sometimes even — shall I dare[417] to say it? — I lack faith in the grandeur, the beauty, and the goodness, which my own words are said to have made more evident in nature and in human life.[418] Why, then, pure

5 seeker of the good and true, shouldst thou[419] hope to find me, in yonder image of the divine?"

The poet spoke sadly, and his eyes were dim with tears. So, likewise, were those of Ernest.

At the hour of sunset, as had long been his frequent

10 custom,[420] Ernest was to discourse to an assemblage[421] of the neighboring inhabitants in the open air. He and the poet, arm in arm, still talking together as they went along, proceeded to[422] the spot. It was a small nook among the hills, with a gray

---

416 mean: 뒤떨어지는, 비열한, 부끄러운

417 dare: 감히 ~하다, 대담하게(뻔뻔스럽게도) ~하다

418 the grandeur, the beauty, and the goodness, which my own words are said to have made more evident in nature and in human life: 내 자신의 언어[시어(詩語)]가 자연과 인간의 삶을 통해서(그려 냄으로써) 더 자명하게 드러나도록 했다고 언급되는 장엄함, 아름다움, 선함

419 shouldst thou: should you

420 frequent custom: 잦은 습관

421 assemblage: <격식 전문 용어> 집합(체), 모임

422 proceed to: ~으로 나아가다, ~에 이르다, 계속 진행하다

precipice behind, the stern front of which was relieved[423] by the pleasant foliage[424] of many creeping plants that made a tapestry[425] for the naked rock, by hanging their festoons[426] from all its rugged[427] angles. At a small elevation[428] above the ground, set in a rich framework of verdure,[429] there appeared a niche,[430] spacious enough to admit a human figure, with freedom for such gestures as spontaneously accompany earnest thought and genuine emotion.[431] Into this natural pulpit Ernest ascended, and threw a look of familiar kindness around upon his audience. They stood, or sat, or reclined[432] upon the grass, as seemed good to each, with the departing

---

423 relieve: 경감하다, 덜다, 누그러지다

424 foliage: 나뭇잎(한 나무의 나뭇잎이나, 나뭇잎과 줄기를 총칭)

425 tapestry: 태피스트리(여러 가지 색실로 그림을 짜 넣은 직물. 또는 그런 직물을 제작하는 기술)

426 festoon: 꽃줄 장식

427 rugged: 바위투성이의, 기복이 심한

428 elevation: 승진, 승격, 지면보다 높은 곳

429 verdure: <문예체> (특정 장소의) 푸른 초목, 신록

430 niche: 아주 편한(꼭 맞는) 자리(역할·일) 등, 틈새

431 with freedom for such gestures as spontaneously accompany earnest thought and genuine emotion: 진지한 생각과 진정한 감정에 자연스럽게 동반되는 그런 동작을 수용할 여유가 있는

432 recline: 기대다, 의지하다, 눕다

sunshine falling obliquely over them,[433] and mingling its subdued[434] cheerfulness with the solemnity of a grove of ancient trees, beneath and amid the boughs of which the golden rays were constrained[435] to pass. In another direction was seen the Great Stone Face, with the same cheer, combined with the same solemnity, in its benignant aspect.

Ernest began to speak, giving to the people of what was in his heart and mind. His words had power, because they accorded with[436] his thoughts; and his thoughts had reality and depth, because they harmonized with the life which he had always lived. It was not mere breath that this preacher uttered; they were the words of life, because a life of good deeds and holy love was melted into them. Pearls, pure and rich, had been dissolved into[437] this precious draught.[438] The poet, as he listened, felt that the being and character of Ernest were a

---

433 with the departing sunshine falling obliquely over them : 저무는 햇살이 그들 위로 비스듬히 내리비치는 상태에서

434 subdue : 진압하다, 가라앉히다 ＊subdued : (기분이) 가라앉은, 까라진, 좀 우울한, 부드러운, 은은한

435 constrain : ~하게 만들다, 강요하다

436 accord with : ~와 일치하다, 조화하다

437 dissolve into : ~안으로 녹다, 분해하다(되다)

438 draught : =draft. 한 모금 마시기

nobler strain of poetry than he had ever written. His eyes glistening with tears, he gazed reverentially[439] at the venerable man, and said within himself that never was there an aspect so worthy of a prophet and a sage as that mild, sweet, thoughtful countenance, with the glory of white hair diffused[440] about it. At a distance, but distinctly[441] to be seen, high up in the golden light of the setting sun, appeared the Great Stone Face, with hoary mists around it,[442] like the white hairs around the brow of Ernest. Its look of grand beneficence[443] seemed to embrace the world.

At that moment, in sympathy with a thought which he was about to utter, the face of Ernest assumed a grandeur of expression, so imbued with benevolence,[444] that the poet, by an irresistible impulse, threw his arms aloft[445] and shouted,

---

439 reverentially : 겸허하게
440 diffuse : 발산하다, 퍼지다
441 distinctly : 뚜렷하게, 명백하게
442 with hoary mists around it : 백발 같은 허연 안개를 그(얼굴) 주변에 드리운 채
443 beneficence : 선행, 은혜, 자선
444 benevolence : 자비심, 박애, 선행, 자선
445 aloft : 높이

"Behold!^{446} Behold! Ernest is himself the likeness of the Great Stone Face!"

Then all the people looked, and saw that what the deep-sighted poet said was true. The prophecy was fulfilled. But Ernest, having finished what he had to say, took the poet's arm, and walked slowly homeward, still hoping that some wiser and better man than himself would by and by^{447} appear, bearing a resemblance to the GREAT STONE FACE.

---

446 behold : 보다
447 by and by : 얼마 안 있어, 이윽고, 곧

작품 해설

1. '큰 바위 얼굴'이라는 흥미진진한 소재

이 이야기는 산꼭대기에 자리한 자애로운 미소를 띤 인간의 얼굴을 닮은 바위를 바라보며 지혜를 배우는 어느 소박한 뉴잉글랜드 주민의 삶에 초점을 맞추고 있다. 이 소박한 주제 자체가 일반 독자들의 마음을 사로잡지만 재미난 이름의 등장인물들을 통해 스토리를 끌어가는 과정도 한껏 흥미를 더해 준다. 마치 우화나 동화, 혹은 알레고리처럼 Mr. Gathergold('금모아' 씨), Old Blood-and-Thunder['피와 우레' 노(老)장군] ─ 달리 표현하면 '유혈과 폭력' 장군 ─, Old Stony Phiz['늙은 돌 같은(돌처럼 차가운) 용모' 씨], Poet(시인) 등 별명만으로도 짐작 가능한, 경제·군사·정치·문학·예술 분야의 걸출한 유명 인물이 흥미롭게 등장한다.

별명에 걸맞게 각 인물에 대한 형상화도 깔끔한 캐리커처 같은 인상을 준다. Mr. Gathergold는 돈 버는 데 영특한(shrewd) 재주를 지녔으되 존재 자체가 탐욕스럽고 잔인한 갈퀴 같은 누런 발톱(a yellow claw)처럼 되어 버렸다. Old Blood-and-Thunder 장군의 전쟁에 닳고 닳은 얼굴에는 무쇠 같은 의지만 가득할 뿐 온화한 지혜나 깊고 부드러운 공감 따위는 눈꼽만큼도 찾아볼 수 없다. Old Stony Phiz라는 별명의 정치가는 세치 혀를 놀려 진실과 거짓을 뒤섞는 등 세상이 놀랄 만한 재주를 부리지만 아무런 고귀한 목표 없이 인생이 텅 빈 존재이다.

그렇다고 각 인물이 그저 허접하기만 한 것은 아니다. 제각기 그 역할과 위업만큼 세상의 존경을 받으며 작가의 설명을 통해서가 아니면 실제 현실에서는 더욱 위세를 떨칠 인물일 것이며, 심지어 큰 바위 얼굴 예언에 맞춰 볼 만한 면모가 전혀 없다고 할 수는 없다. 물론 최종적으로 이들은 예언상의 인물의 도래를 꿈꿀 정도로 자신들의 현실에 대해 품고 있는 당대인의 희망찬 '자신감'을 실망으로 탈색시키면서 그 기대를 더욱 간절한 것으로 만드는 계기로 작용한다.

결국은 'Ernest'(진지하고 열심히 삶을 살아간다는 의미)가 큰바위 얼굴의 최종 후보자가 된다는 설정도 흥미진진하다. Ernest가 큰 바위 얼굴이냐 아니냐의 문제에 앞서 그가 맡은 역할 중 하나는 기존의 큰 바위 얼굴 후보자들을 향한 이데올로기에 침윤된 세인들의 환호를 뚫고 이들이 '가짜'임을 단박에 알아본다는 점이다. 이들에 대한 Ernest의 반응은 이중의 역할을 수행한다. 우선은 각 인물에 대한 판단의 시금석이 되면서 당대 사회의 일면에 대한 비판을 보여 준다. 예컨대 Mr. Goldgather에 대한 남들의 찬사에도 불구하고 Ernest가 그에게 당혹감을 느끼며 슬프게 돌아서는 것은 해당 인물에 대한 Ernest의 개인적인 반응이기도 하지만 당대 미국 사회의 훼손(defaced)된 삶에 대한 작가 자신의 당혹감과 슬픈 외면이 함께 자리한다.

예언상의 인물이 못 된다는 점에서는 위의 세 인물과 다를 바 없지만 도시에서 활동하면서 큰 바위 얼굴에 대해 송시를 쓴 일도 있을뿐더러 뛰어난 재능을 지니기도 한 Poet는 위 세 인물과는 다른 대접을 받을 만하다. 이 인물은 Ernest에 대한 이야기를 들어 오면서 많은 생각을 기울인 끝에 마침내 그의 오두막을 찾아가 나그네로 묵기를 청한다. Ernest는 Poet의 시집을 읽으며 그를 예언상의 인물로 조금은 떠올려 본다. 반면 Poet는 앞서의 세 인물과는 달리 자신이 그 예언상의 인물로 자처하지 않는 것은 물론 자신이 신념 없는 몽상가(dreamer)에 불과하다는 사실을 토로한다. 그는 오히려 큰 바위 얼굴의 후보로 Ernest를 지목한다. 흰머리가 느는 만큼 마음속에 사려 깊은 생각도 늘고 주름살들은 삶의 시련을 거친 지혜의 비문들인 듯한 Ernest가 점차로 두루 남다른 평가를 받으며 위 세 인물을 중심으로 벌어지던 피상적인 환호와는 달리 공동체의 중심 역할을 한다.

특정 인물 누구 하나를 예언상의 인물로 지목하는 것 못지않게, 아니 그 이상으로 중요한 것이 Ernest와 Poet가 이루는 공감이라고 할 수 있다. 이들은 공감을 통해 둘 중 어느 누구의 것만이랄 수 없는 소중하고도 한층 고귀한 영역을 이뤄 낸다. 이는 누가 큰 바위 얼굴이냐는 문제 풀이에 앞서는 중요한 성취라고 할 수 있다.

2. 열린 결말의 의미

Hawthorne은 여기에서 Ernest에 시선을 못 박지 않고 여기서 한 걸음 더 나아간다. 큰 바위 얼굴 예언의 최종 후보로 보통 사람들의 위대함을 위치시키되 그 마지막 자리에서 Ernest가 기다림을 거두지 않음으로써 이 이야기는 열린 결말이 된다. 즉, 작가는 자연, 원주민의 세계, 백인 이주민 세계, 그리고 다시 또 이 전체를 아우르는 새로운 시공간을 설정함으로써 이 이야기를 광대무변한 시공간을 아우르는 이야기로 도약시킨다. 그런 점에서 이 이야기는 백인들만의 잔치가 아닌 신대륙 전체의 예언, 희망과 닿아 있다.

부연하면, 큰 바위 얼굴 예언이 백인 이주민으로부터 시작된 것이 아니라 이 지역에 원주민들이 살았을 때, 심지어 어쨌든 인간적인 삶이 시작되기 이전부터 계곡의 시냇물과 나무 꼭대기의 바람, 곧 자연의 음성에서 인간의 삶으로 이어진 것이라고 규정함으로써 그 인물은 백인 이주민만의 고귀한 인물을 넘어 이런 신대륙적인 규모의 의미를 지닌 인물이어야 하는 광대한 스케일을 부여받는다.

위와 같이 "The Great Stone Face"는 이주와 더불어 시작된 미국의 꿈과 이상이 물질주의적 축적으로 함몰되고 변질되는 미국 사회의 역사적 과정에 대해 우화적이고 동화적인 패러디를 보여 준다. 또한 신의 뜻을 물질의 축적에 가둔 자본주의적 역사 전개 자체에 대해 비판하면서 동시에 '보통 사람'인 Ernest를 큰 바위 얼굴과 겹쳐 놓음으로써 예언의 실현을 전혀 다른 방향에서 확인케 한다. 이 이야기의 마지막은 Ernest가 여전히 큰 바위 얼굴과 닮은 더 현명하고 나은 인물을 희망하는 것으로 끝나면서 열린 결말을 보여 준다. 이 아름다운 한 편의 동화는 여전히 뒷이야기를 기다리고 있다.

영미 명작 단편선_2

The Tell-Tale Heart

Edgar Allan Poe

Edgar Allan Poe(1809~1849)는 자기 자신의 어둡고 음산한 고딕소설의 주인공처럼 유별나고 불운한 삶을 살았다. 여기에 수록한 "The Tell-Tale Heart"(1843)와 같이 Poe는 고딕소설의 경향이 강한 일련의 빼어난 단편소설과 탐정추리소설을 통해 서구문명의 근저에 자리한 근본적인 문제와 인간의 심층적 이상심리를 깊이 탐구함으로써 미국문학에 중요한 기여를 했다. Poe는 "The Fall of the House of Usher"(1839), "The Murders in the Rue Morgue"(1841), "The Black Cat"(1843), "The Purloined Letter"(1844) 등으로 잘 알려졌다.

The Tell-Tale Heart

➤

TRUE! — nervous — very, very dreadfully[1] nervous I had
been and am; but why will you say that I am mad? The disease
had sharpened my senses — not destroyed — not dulled them.[2]
Above all was the sense of hearing acute.[3] I heard all things in
5 the heaven and in the earth. I heard many things in hell. How,
then, am I mad? Hearken! and observe how healthily — how
calmly[4] I can tell you the whole story.

It is impossible to say how first the idea entered my brain;

---

1 dreadfully : 몹시, 지독하게, 무시무시하게
2 sharpened my senses — not destroyed — not dulled them : 내 감각을 파괴
   하지도 무디게 하지도 않고 오히려 날카롭게(예민하게) 했다
3 acute : 예리한 ＊문장이 도치되었는데 'the sense of hearing was acute'임.
4 Hearken! and observe how healthily — how calmly ... : 귀를 기울여 들어 보
   고 얼마나 말짱하게(건강하게), 얼마나 차분하게 ~인지를 관찰해 보라

but once conceived,[5] it haunted[6] me day and night. Object there was none. Passion there was none.[7] I loved the old man. He had never wronged[8] me. He had never given me insult.[9] For his gold I had no desire. I think it was his eye! yes, it was this! He had the eye of a vulture[10] — a pale blue eye, with a film[11] over it. Whenever it fell upon me, my blood ran cold; and so by degrees[12] — very gradually — I made up my mind[13] to take the life of the old man, and thus rid myself of[14] the eye forever.

Now this is the point. You fancy me mad. Madmen know

---

5   once conceived : 일단 생겨나자 ＊conceive : 생각해 내다, 마음에 품다
6   haunt : 따라다니다, 출몰하다
7   Object there was none. Passion there was none : 어떤 목적이 있었던 것도 아니었고 격정이란 것도 전혀 없었다 ＊화자는 이 일이 뭔가의 목적하에, 아니면 감정상의 문제가 결부되어 벌어진 일이 아니라고 강변하고 있음.
8   wrong : 잘못을 저지르다, 그르치다, 부당하게 취급하다, 모욕하다
9   insult : <명사> 모욕, <동사> 모욕하다
10 vulture : 독수리, 욕심 많은 무자비한 사람, 남을 등쳐 먹는 사람
11 film : 얇은 막
12 by degrees : 차츰, 단계적으로
13 make up one's mind : 결심하다
14 rid oneself of ... : ~에서 벗어나다, ~를 제거하다

nothing.[15] But you should have seen[16] me. You should have seen how wisely I proceeded[17] — with what caution[18] — with what foresight[19] — with what dissimulation[20] I went to work![21] I was never kinder to the old man than during the whole week before I killed him. And every night, about midnight, I turned the latch of his door and opened it — oh so gently! And then, when I had made an opening sufficient for my head,[22] I put in a dark lantern, all closed, closed, that no light shone out,[23] and then I thrust in my head. Oh, you would have laughed[24]

---

15 Madmen know nothing: 미친 사람은 아무것도 모른다 * 화자는 'mad' 의 특징(정의)을 언급하는 한편, 자신은 그런 특징에 해당되지 않으므로 'mad'에는 해당되지 않음을 강변함.

16 should have *p.p.* : ~했어야 했다

17 proceed: 진행하다

18 caution: 주의

19 foresight: 예지, 선견, 통찰

20 dissimulation: 위장

21 how wisely I proceeded — with what caution — with what foresight — with what dissimulation I went to work: 일을 해 나갈 때 얼마나 주의하고 얼마나 예지력을 발휘하고 얼마나 위장(僞裝)하며 내가 얼마나 현명하게 진행했는지

22 sufficient for my head: 내 머리가 들어갈 정도로 충분한

23 a dark lantern, all closed, closed, that no light shone out: 온통 감싸고 감 싸서 어떤 빛도 새어 나오지 않은 (어두운) 각등 * dark lantern: (한 면만 비치게 되고) 가릴 수도 있는 각등(角燈)

24 would have *p.p.* : ~했을 텐데

to see how cunningly I thrust it in! I moved it slowly — very, very slowly, so that I might not disturb[25] the old man's sleep. It took me an hour to place my whole head within the opening so far that[26] I could see him as he lay upon his bed. Ha! would a madman have been so wise as this, And then, when my head was well in the room, I undid[27] the lantern cautiously — oh, so cautiously — cautiously (for the hinges creaked) — I undid it just so much that a single thin ray fell upon the vulture eye. And this I did for seven long nights — every night just at midnight — but I found the eye always closed; and so it was impossible to do the work; for it was not the old man who vexed[28] me, but his Evil Eye. And every morning, when the day broke, I went boldly[29] into the chamber, and spoke courageously to him, calling him by name in a hearty tone,[30] and inquiring how he has passed the night. So you see

---

25 disturb : 방해하다, (평화, 질서, 휴식을) 어지럽히다, 교란하다

26 so far that : ~할 정도로

27 undo : 풀다, 열다, 벗기다

28 vex : 성가시게 하다, 난처하게 하다, 화나게 하다

29 boldly : 대담하게

30 calling him by name in a hearty tone : 쾌활한 어조로 그의 이름을 부르면서 ＊ 'Mr. + 성(姓)'과 같이 경칭을 쓰지 않고 그냥 이름을 불렀다는 의미임.

he would have been a very profound[31] old man, indeed, to suspect that[32] every night, just at twelve, I looked in upon him while he slept.

Upon the eighth night I was more than usually cautious in opening the door. A watch's minute hand[33] moves more quickly than did mine. Never before that night had I felt the extent of my own powers — of my sagacity.[34] I could scarcely contain[35] my feelings of triumph.[36] To think that there I was, opening the door, little by little, and he not even to dream of my secret deeds[37] or thoughts. I fairly[38] chuckled[39] at the idea; and perhaps he heard me; for he moved on the bed suddenly,

---

31 profound : 심오한

32 to suspect that … : ~임을 의심하고 있었다면 ＊밤 동안 벌어진 그런 사실 을 알고서도 아침에 아무렇지도 않게 대한 것을 보면 그 노인이 보통 인간 은 아니라는 의미에서 상식적으로는 의미가 통함. 한편, 화자의 비정상성 을 고려하면 그가 매일 밤 화자가 벌이는 행동을 알아차리는 것 자체를 '아 주 심오하다'라는 증거로 연관 지어 인식한다고 해도 의아스러울 일은 아 님. 다만, 이렇게 볼 때 그 이유가 제시되지 않음.

33 minute hand : 분침

34 sagacity : 현명함

35 contain : 참다

36 triumph : 승리, 위업, 환희

37 secret deeds : 비밀스러운 행동(행위)

38 fairly : 꽤, 어지간히, 상당히

39 chuckle : 낄낄대다

as if startled.[40] Now you may think that I drew back[41] — but no. His room was as black as pitch[42] with the thick darkness, (for the shutters were close fastened, through fear of robbers,) and so I knew that he could not see the opening of the door, and I kept pushing it on steadily, steadily.

I had my head in, and was about to open the lantern, when my thumb slipped upon the tin fastening,[43] and the old man sprang up in bed, crying out — "Who's there?"

I kept quite still and said nothing. For a whole hour I did not move a muscle,[44] and in the meantime[45] I did not hear him lie down. He was still sitting up in the bed listening; — just as I have done, night after night, hearkening to the death watches[46] in the wall.

---

40 as if startled : 마치 깜짝 놀란 듯이

41 draw back : 물러나다

42 as black as pitch : 새카만, 깜깜한 ＊pitch : 송진, 끈적끈적한 검은 물질

43 when my thumb slipped upon the tin fastening : 내 엄지가 양철 잠금쇠 위에서 미끄러졌을 때

44 do not move a muscle : 꿈쩍도 않다, 눈 하나 깜짝 않다 ＊muscle : 근육

45 in the meantime : 그 사이에

46 a death watch : 죽음의 시계 ＊death watch는 우선 벽에 걸린 째깍거리는 시계를 가리킬 수 있으며 시간과 결부된 죽음의 이미지를 담고 있다고 볼 수 있음. 또한 death watch beetle(빗살수염벌레, 나무를 갉아먹을 때 나는 소리가 째깍거리는 시계 소리와 비슷하다고 함)를 의미한다고 볼 수도 있을

Presently[47] I heard a slight groan, and I knew it was the groan of mortal terror.[48] It was not a groan of pain or of grief — oh, no! — it was the low stifled sound that arises from the bottom of the soul when overcharged with awe.[49] I knew the sound well. Many a night, just at midnight, when all the world slept, it has welled up[50] from my own bosom, deepening, with its dreadful echo, the terrors that distracted[51] me.[52] I say I knew it well. I knew what the old man felt, and pitied him, although I chuckled at heart.[53] I knew that he had been lying awake ever since the first slight noise, when he had turned in the bed. His fears had been ever since[54] growing upon him. He had been trying to fancy them causeless,[55] but could not.

듯함. 어떤 경우든 '임박한 죽음의 신호'로 봄 직함.

47 presently: 곧

48 mortal terror: 극심한 공포

49 when overcharged with awe: 경외감으로 과도하게 차(격앙되어) 있을 때

50 well up: 차오르다

51 distract: 주의를 산만하게 하다

52 deepening, with its dreadful echo, the terrors that distracted me: 그 끔찍한 메아리로 나를 산란케 한 공포를 더 깊어지게 하면서 ＊가슴이 마치 깊은 우물의 구조를 띤 듯 묘사하고 있음.

53 at heart: 마음속으로는

54 ever since: 그 이후로 쭉

55 causeless: 이유 없는

He had been saying to himself — "It is nothing but the wind in the chimney — it is only a mouse crossing the floor," or "It is merely a cricket which has made a single chirp."[56] Yes, he had been trying to comfort himself with these suppositions:[57] but he had found all in vain.[58] All in vain; because Death, in approaching him had stalked with his black shadow before him,[59] and enveloped the victim. And it was the mournful influence of the unperceived shadow[60] that caused him to feel — although he neither saw nor heard — to feel the presence of my head within the room.

When I had waited a long time, very patiently,[61] without hearing him lie down, I resolved[62] to open a little — a very, very little crevice[63] in the lantern. So I opened it — you cannot

---

56 a single chirp : 단 한 번의 지저귐

57 supposition : 가정, 추측

58 in vain : 헛된

59 Death, in approaching him had stalked with his black shadow before him :
죽음이 그에게 다가오면서 자신의 검은 그림자를 앞세우고 몰래 다가왔
다 *stalk : 살금살금 접근하다 *stalker : 집요하게 남을 따라다니는 사람

60 the mournful influence of the unperceived shadow : 그 인식되지 않는 (죽
음의) 그림자가 미친 음산한(애처로운) 영향

61 patiently : 참을성 있게

62 resolve : 결심하다

63 crevice : 갈라진 틈, 찢어진 틈

imagine how stealthily,[64] stealthily — until, at length[65] a simple dim ray, like the thread of the spider, shot[66] from out the crevice and fell full upon[67] the vulture eye.

It was open — wide, wide open — and I grew furious[68] as I gazed upon it. I saw it with perfect distinctness[69] — all a dull[70] blue, with a hideous[71] veil over it that chilled[72] the very marrow[73] in my bones; but I could see nothing else of the old man's face or person: for I had directed[74] the ray as if by instinct, precisely upon the damned spot.[75]

And have I not told you that what you mistake for[76] madness

---

64 stealthily : 몰래

65 at length : 마침내

66 shoot : 발사되다, 분출하다

67 fall full upon : 정면으로 비치다

68 furious : 격노한

69 distinctness : 분명함

70 dull : 무딘, 둔감한, 흐릿한(dim), 또렷하지 않은

71 hideous : 끔찍한

72 chill : 서늘하게 하다, 오싹하게 하다

73 marrow : 골수

74 direct : 향하게 하다

75 precisely upon the damned spot : 정확하게 그 저주받은 부위(노인의 눈) 위에

76 mistake A for B : A를 B로 잘못 보다

is but over-acuteness[77] of the sense? — now, I say, there came to my ears a low, dull, quick sound, such as[78] a watch makes when enveloped in cotton. I knew that sound well, too. It was the beating[79] of the old man's heart. It increased my fury, as the beating of a drum stimulates[80] the soldier into courage.

But even yet I refrained[81] and kept still. I scarcely[82] breathed. I held the lantern motionless. I tried how steadily I could maintain[83] the ray upon the eye. Meantime the hellish tattoo[84] of the heart increased. It grew quicker and quicker, and louder and louder every instant.[85] The old man's terror must have been extreme![86] It grew louder, I say, louder every moment! — do you mark me well I have told you that I am nervous: so I am. And now at the dead hour of the night,[87]

---

77 over-acuteness : 극도의 민감함, 과도한 예민함
78 such as : ~와 같은
79 beating : 박동, 고동, 타격, 치는 것
80 stimulate : 자극하다
81 refrain : 삼가다
82 scarcely : 거의 ~ 아니다
83 maintain : 유지하다
84 tattoo : (경고하는) 북소리, 둥둥(톡톡) 치는 소리
85 every instant : 매 순간
86 extreme : 극도의
87 the dead hour of the night : 한밤중

amid the dreadful silence of that old house, so strange a noise
as this excited me to uncontrollable[88] terror. Yet, for some
minutes longer I refrained and stood still. But the beating
grew louder, louder! I thought the heart must burst.[89] And
now a new anxiety[90] seized[91] me — the sound would be heard
by a neighbour! The old man's hour had come![92] With a loud
yell, I threw open the lantern and leaped[93] into the room. He
shrieked once — once only. In an instant[94] I dragged[95] him to
the floor, and pulled the heavy bed over him. I then smiled
gaily, to find the deed so far[96] done. But, for many minutes,
the heart beat on with a muffled[97] sound. This, however, did
not vex me; it would not be heard through the wall. At length
it ceased. The old man was dead. I removed the bed and

---

88 uncontrollable : 통제 불가능한
89 burst : 터지다
90 anxiety : 불안
91 seize : 사로잡다
92 The old man's hour had come : 그 노인의 종말이 다가왔다
93 leap : 뛰다 * leap into : 뛰어 들어가다
94 in an instant : 즉시, 순식간에
95 drag : 끌다, 질질 끌다, 끌어당기다
96 so far : 여태까지
97 muffled : 틀어 막힌

examined the corpse. Yes, he was stone, stone dead.[98] I placed my hand upon the heart and held it there many minutes. There was no pulsation.[99] He was stone dead. His eye would trouble[100] me no more.

If still you think me mad, you will think so no longer when I [5] describe the wise precautions[101] I took for the concealment[102] of the body. The night waned,[103] and I worked hastily, but in silence. First of all I dismembered[104] the corpse. I cut off the head and the arms and the legs.

I then took up three planks[105] from the flooring of the [10] chamber, and deposited[106] all between the scantlings.[107] I then replaced[108] the boards so cleverly, so cunningly,[109] that no

---

98 stone dead : 완전히 죽은
99 pulsation : 맥박
100 trouble : 괴롭히다, 번민하게 만들다
101 precaution : 예방책
102 concealment : 숨기기, 은폐
103 wane : 이지러지다, 약해지다, 줄다
104 dismember : 사체를 훼손하다
105 plank : 널빤지
106 deposit : 두다
107 scantling : 켜 낸 재목
108 replace : 제자리에 놓다, 되돌리다, 대체하다
109 cunningly : 교묘하게

human eye — not even his — could have detected[110] any thing wrong. There was nothing to wash out — no stain of any kind — no blood-spot whatever. I had been too wary for that.[111] A tub had caught all[112] — ha! ha!

When I had made an end of[113] these labors, it was four o'clock — still dark as midnight. As the bell sounded the hour, there came a knocking at the street door. I went down to open it with a light heart, — for what had I now to fear? There entered three men, who introduced themselves, with perfect suavity,[114] as officers of the police. A shriek had been heard by a neighbour during the night; suspicion[115] of foul play[116] had been aroused;[117] information had been lodged[118] at the police

---

110 detect : 발견하다

111 I had been too wary for that : 아주 경계해서 그렇지는(그런 흔적을 남기지는) 않았다

112 A tub had caught all : 통 하나로 다 됐다 ＊catch : (떨어지는 액체 따위를) 받아 내다

113 make an end of : ~를 끝내다

114 suavity : 온화함

115 suspicion : 의심, 의혹

116 foul play : 고약한 짓

117 arouse : 일어나다, 환기시키다, 야기하다

118 lodge : 제출하다

office, and they (the officers) had been deputed[119] to search the premises.[120]

I smiled, — for what had I to fear? I bade the gentlemen welcome.[121] The shriek, I said, was my own in a dream. The old man, I mentioned, was absent in the country. I took my visitors all over the house. I bade them search[122] — search well. I led them, at length, to his chamber. I showed them his treasures, secure,[123] undisturbed.[124] In the enthusiasm[125] of my confidence,[126] I brought chairs into the room, and desired them here to rest from their fatigues,[127] while I myself, in the wild audacity[128] of my perfect triumph, placed my own seat upon the very spot beneath which reposed[129] the corpse of the

---

119 depute : 위임하다
120 premise : 전제, <복수로> (한 사업체가 소유 · 사용하는 건물이 딸린) 부지 (지역), 구내
121 bid ... welcome : ~를 환영하다
122 search : 뒤지다, 찾다, 수색하다
123 secure : 안전한
124 undisturbed : 그 누구도 건드리지 않은
125 enthusiasm : 열정
126 confidence : 자신감
127 fatigue : 피로
128 audacity : 뻔뻔함, 대담함
129 repose : 휴식하다, 잠들다, (특정한 장소에) 있다(보관되다)

victim.

The officers were satisfied. My manner had convinced[130] them. I was singularly[131] at ease.[132] They sat, and while I answered cheerily, they chatted of familiar things. But, ere[133]

5   long, I felt myself getting pale and wished them gone. My head ached, and I fancied a ringing in my ears: but still they sat and still chatted. The ringing became more distinct: — It continued and became more distinct: I talked more freely to get rid of[134] the feeling: but it continued and gained definiteness[135] — until,

10 at length, I found that the noise was not within my ears.

No doubt I now grew very pale; — but I talked more fluently, and with a heightened voice.[136] Yet the sound increased — and what could I do? It was a low, dull, quick sound — much such a sound as a watch makes when enveloped in cotton.

15 I gasped for breath[137] — and yet the officers heard it not. I

---

130 convince : ~에게 납득시키다, ~에게 확신시키다

131 singularly : 아주, 몹시, 특이하게

132 at ease : 마음이 편한

133 ere : ~ 전에 * ere long : 오래지 않아, 머지 않아

134 get rid of : ~를 없애다

135 definiteness : 명확함

136 with a heightened voice : 목소리를 높여

137 gasp for breath : 숨이 가빠서 헐떡거리다

talked more quickly — more vehemently;[138] but the noise
steadily increased. I arose and argued about trifles,[139] in a
high key[140] and with violent gesticulations;[141] but the noise
steadily increased. Why would they not be gone? I paced[142]
the floor to and fro[143] with heavy strides,[144] as if excited to   5
fury by the observations[145] of the men — but the noise steadily
increased. Oh God! what could I do? I foamed[146] — I raved[147]
— I swore![148] I swung[149] the chair upon which I had been
sitting, and grated[150] it upon the boards, but the noise arose
over all and continually increased. It grew louder — louder   10
— louder! And still the men chatted pleasantly, and smiled.

---

138 vehemently : 격렬하게

139 trifle : 하찮은 것

140 in a high key : 높은 음조로

141 gesticulation : 몸동작

142 pace : 서성거리다

143 to and fro : 앞뒤로

144 with heavy strides : 묵직한 발걸음으로

145 observation : 관찰

146 foam : 거품을 물다

147 rave : 열변을 토하다, 헛소리를 하다

148 swore : swear(욕하다)의 과거

149 swung : swing(휘두르다)의 과거, (전후좌우로) 흔들다

150 grate : 갈다, 비비다

Was it possible they heard not? Almighty[151] God! — no, no! They heard! — they suspected! — they knew! — they were making a mockery of[152] my horror! — this I thought, and this I think. But anything was better than this agony! Anything was more tolerable[153] than this derision![154] I could bear[155] those hypocritical[156] smiles no longer! I felt that I must scream or die! and now — again! — hark![157] louder! louder! louder! louder!

"Villains!"[158] I shrieked, "dissemble[159] no more! I admit the deed! — tear up[160] the planks! here, here! — It is the beating of his hideous heart!"

---

151 almighty : 전지전능한

152 make a mockery of : ~을 비웃다 *mockery : 조롱, 비웃음

153 tolerable : 참을 만한

154 derision : 조롱

155 bear : 참다, 견뎌 내다

156 hypocritical : 위선적인

157 hark : 들으시오! 들으라!

158 villain : 악당

159 dissemble : 가식으로 꾸미다

160 tear up : 뜯다

작품 해설

1. 이상심리의 화자

　화자에게는 '무죄'보다 '제정신'을 주장하는 게 더 중요하다. 화자의 주장은 근거가 취약하거나 설득력이 부족하지만 본인만이 확실하다고 집착적으로 전제하고 동의를 구하려고 한다는 점에서 오히려 '제정신'이 아니라는 역증거가 되는 경향이 있다. 예컨대 화자는 하늘과 지상의 모든 소리, 심지어 지옥의 소리를 듣기도 하는 극도로 예민한 청각을 예로 들면서 "그러하건대, 어떻게 내가 미쳤느냐"라고 반문한다. '지옥의 소리'가 무엇이며 그것을 들었다고 하는 게 제정신인 사람이 할 법한 얘기인지, 그런 청각을 지녔다 쳐도 그게 제정신의 증거와 무슨 관계가 있는지 분명치 않거늘 그렇다고 주장하는 게 제정신이기나 한지 등 의문을 증폭시킨다는 것이다.

　화자가 '제정신'을 주장하는 핵심적 근거는 '살인'이 얼마나 정교하게 실행되었는지에 맞춰져 있다. '제정신'의 준거는 체계적인 행동과 정확성인데, 이런 준거 자체는 수긍할 만하지만 화자가 이런 준거에 따라 이성적인 설명을 제시하려는 대상이 '살인'이라는 '비이성적인 행동'이다. 따라서 '제정신'의 논거가 더 탄탄할수록 '살인죄' 역시 더 정확한 근거를 갖추게 된다.

'제정신'과 '살인의 정밀한 실행'을 마치 정교한 톱니바퀴처럼 맞물리게 하여 돌리는 화자의 논리구조는 일상인의 상식적인 범주 바깥에 존재한다. 이런 이유로 '살인'의 과정은 충분히 증명될 수 있겠지만 그의 '정신이상' 역시 확고하게 증명이 되어 정신착란성 방위(insanity defense)라는 명목으로 살인죄에서 벗어나는 측면도 배제할 수 없다.

화자는 전체적이고 종합적인 맥락이 아니라 구획 진 어느 하나에 집착함으로써 그것의 고도의 완성을 꾀하지만 다른 부분과의 관계에서는 다분히 주관적이고 자의적인 논리적 관계성을 구축하며 집착할 때 발생하는 문제를 극단적으로 보여 준다. 이렇게 Poe의 소설에는 각각의 지식들이 일정한 수준에서 완성되어 상식으로 고착되고 이 상식의 논리들이 부딪칠 때 발생하는 현대적인 양상을 미리 예시하는 측면도 있다.

2. 상징들

주요 상징 중 하나는 '눈'(eye)이다. 화자는 희생자의 눈을 '독수리 눈'(vulture eye)으로 묘사한다. 'vulture'에 '남의 불행을 이용해 먹는 이'라는 뜻도 염두에 둘 만한데, 바로 그 눈에 대한 혐오 때문에 화자는 희생자의 존재 자체를 지워 버리고 싶어 한다. 이상심리의 화자가 말하는 이유는 '그 눈이 자신의 피를 싸늘하게 식어 버리게 만든다'라는 것이다. 그 눈이 지닌 이상한 힘은 '감시' 혹은 비밀을 파헤치는 능력 등으로 짐작할 수 있는데, 희생자와 화자의 관계를 아버지와 아들(혹은 딸), 집주인과 세입자, 주인과 하인 등 어떻게 설정하느냐에 따라 그 구체적인 양상들을 추론해 볼 수 있다.

화자가 매우 복합적인 동기와 문제적 모순이 집약되게 마련인 '살해'라는 사건에서 아주 기본적인 사회적(혹은 가족적) 관계의 맥락, 그로부터 기인할 법한 분노나 증오, 또는 탐욕 등의 감정이나 동기를 삭제하려고 하고 전체적인 상황을 극히 단순화하려는 경향이 이 상징을 통해서도 드러난다.

또 다른 중요한 상징으로는 여러 차례 등장하는 시계(watch)를 꼽을 수 있다. 시계는 시간을 재는 도구이자 그것이 계속 작동하는 한, 죽음과 일정한 긴장관계를 갖는다. 시계가 일상적인 상황을 벗어나면 죽음을 재촉하고 기다리는 장치가 되기도 한다. 침대 매트리스에 깔려 죽기 직전의 상황에 놓인 노인의 심장 소리에 대해, "그것은 낮고 둔하고 빠른 소리였고 목화솜에 감싸였을 때 시계가 내는 소리와 매우 흡사했다"라고 한 묘사에서는 시계와 죽음의 이미지를 정교하게 겹쳐 놓는다.

이 작품에서 시계는 여러 면에서 활용된다. '빗살수염벌레'(death watch)라는 풍뎅이의 활용 역시 돋보인다. 이 곤충이 나무를 갉아먹을 때 나는 소리가 시계가 째깍거리는 것과 같거나 수놈이 암컷을 부르는 소리는 죽음의 전조라는 미신 따위는 작품의 맥락에서 의미심장한 의미로 활용된다.

The Celebrated Jumping Frog of Calaveras County

Mark Twain

Mark Twain(1835~1910)을 묘사할 때 동원되는 표현이 다채로운데 그중 중요한 것을 꼽자면, '도금시대'(Gilded Age)의 풍자가, 사실주의의 대가, 미시시피강의 작가, 서부의 풍자 작가 등을 들 수 있다. 상징이나 알레고리 등의 성향이 강한 19세기 중반의 미국 고전작가들과 비교할 때 실생활 속의 구어와 방언을 활용하면서 사실주의적 필치를 통해 미시시피강 연안이나 남서부의 삶을 핍진하게 보여 준다. *Life on the Mississippi*(1883), *The Adventures of Huckleberry Finn*(1884) 등의 대표작이 있다. "The Celebrated Jumping Frog of Calaveras County"(1865)는 Twain이 작가로서 세간의 주목을 받은 첫 번째 성공작으로 여겨진다. 이 작품은 제목을 포함해 여러 차례 개정·출판되었다. 예컨대 도입부의 첫 문단을 'Mr. A. Ward'[1]라는 인물에게 답장 편지를 쓰는 것으로 설정된 장면을 포함해 제목 자체도 "Jim Smiley and His Jumping Frog," "The Celebrated Jumping Frog of Calaveras County," "The Notorious Jumping Frog of Calaveras County" 등으로 다양하지만 작품의 내용이나 독서의 재미에 영향을 주지는 않는다.

---

1 A. Ward: Artemus Ward는 Charles Farrar Browne(1834~1867)이라는 편집자, 저널리스트, 소설가, 여행 순회작가의 예명으로 이 작품은 바로 Browne의 제안에 따른 것이었다.

The Celebrated[2] Jumping Frog of Calaveras County[3]

    In compliance with[4] the request of a friend of mine, who wrote me from the East, I called on[5] good-natured, garrulous[6] old Simon Wheeler, and inquired after[7] my friend's friend, Leonidas W. Smiley, as requested to do, and I hereunto[8] append[9] the result. I have a lurking[10] suspicion that *Leonidas W*. Smiley is a myth;[11] that my friend never knew such a

---

2 celebrated : 유명한, 세상에 알려진

3 county : (미국 행정단위, State 밑의 행정구역) 군(郡)

4 in compliance with : ~에 따라

5 call on : 방문하다

6 garrulous : 수다스러운

7 inquire after : ~의 건강(안부)을 묻다, 문병하다

8 hereunto : 이제부터

9 append : 덧붙이다

10 lurk : 도사리다

11 myth : 신화, 꾸며 낸 이야기, 가공의 인물

personage;[12] and that he only conjectured[13] that, if I asked old Wheeler about him, it would remind him of[14] his infamous *Jim Smiley*, and he would go to work and bore[15] me nearly to death with some infernal[16] reminiscence[17] of him as long and tedious[18] as[19] it should be useless to me. If that was the design,[20] it certainly succeeded.

I found Simon Wheeler dozing[21] comfortably by the bar-room stove of the old, dilapidated[22] tavern[23] in the decayed[24] mining camp[25] of Angel's, and I noticed that he was fat and bald-headed, and had an expression of winning gentleness[26]

---

12 personage : 인물

13 conjecture : 추측하다

14 remind A of B : A에게 B를 상기시키다

15 bore : 지루하게 하다, 싫증 나게 하다

16 infernal : 지긋지긋한, 지옥 같은

17 reminiscence : 추억담, 회상담

18 tedious : 지루한, 싫증 나는, 장황한

19 as A as B : B만큼 A하다

20 design : 계획

21 doze : 꾸벅꾸벅 졸다

22 dilapidated : 황폐한

23 tavern : 선술집

24 decayed : 쇠락한, 부패한, 쓰러져 가는

25 mining camp : 채광소

26 winning gentleness : 마음을 끄는 친절함(관대함, 고상함)

and simplicity[27] upon his tranquil countenance.[28] He roused up[29] and gave me good-day.[30] I told him a friend of mine had commissioned me to[31] make some inquiries about a cherished companion[32] of his boyhood named *Leonidas W. Smiley* — *Rev.*[33] *Leonidas W. Smiley*, a young minister of the Gospel,[34] who he had heard was at one time a resident of Angel's Camp. I added that, if Mr. Wheeler could tell me any thing about this Rev. Leonidas W. Smiley, I would feel under many obligations[35] to him.

Simon Wheeler backed[36] me into a corner and blockaded[37] me there with his chair, and then sat down and reeled off[38]

---

27 simplicity: 단순함, 검소함, 수수함
28 tranquil countenance: 고요한 얼굴
29 rouse up: 깨다, 일어나다
30 give me good-day: 인사를 하다
31 commission A to B: A에게 B하도록 위임하다
32 cherished companion: 소중한 친구(동료)
33 Rev.: reverend(목사)의 약자
34 minister of the Gospel: 목사 *Gospel: 복음
35 obligation: 의무
36 back: 뒤로 가게 하다
37 blockade: 봉쇄하다
38 reel off: ~을 술술 말하다

the monotonous[39] narrative[40] which follows this paragraph.[41] He never smiled, he never frowned,[42] he never changed his voice from the gentle-flowing key[43] to which he tuned[44] the initial sentence,[45] he never betrayed[46] the slightest suspicion of enthusiasm; but all through the interminable[47] narrative ₅ there ran a vein of[48] impressive earnestness[49] and sincerity,[50] which showed me plainly[51] that, so far from his imagining that there was any thing ridiculous[52] or funny about his story, he regarded it as a really important matter, and admired its two heroes as men of transcendent genius in *finesse*.[53] To me, ₁₀

---

39 monotonous : 단조로운

40 narrative : 이야기, 서사

41 which follows this paragraph : 다음 문단에 이어질

42 frown : 찡그리다

43 gentle-flowing key : 부드럽게 흐르는 음조(음색)

44 tune : 가락을 맞추다, (악기를) 조율하다, 조음하다

45 initial sentence : 첫 문장(이야기의 첫마디)

46 betray : 배신하다, 무심코 노출시키다(드러내다)

47 interminable : 끝없이 계속되는

48 a vein of : 기분, 기질, 마음의 상태, 분위기 *vein : 핏줄

49 earnestness : 진지함, 진중함

50 sincerity : 성실, 진실, 진심

51 plainly : 분명히, 명백히, 알기 쉽게, 솔직히

52 ridiculous : 어리석은, 우스꽝스러운

53 men of transcendent genius in *finesse* : 예외적으로 뛰어난 사람

the spectacle of a man drifting[54] serenely[55] along through such a queer[56] yarn[57] without ever smiling, was exquisitely[58] absurd.[59] As I said before, I asked him to tell me what he knew of Rev. Leonidas W. Smiley, and he replied as follows.[60] I let him go on in his own way,[61] and never interrupted him once:

Rev. Leonidas W. H'm, Reverend Le — well, there was a feller[62] here once by the name of Jim Smiley, in the winter of '49 — or may be it was the spring of '50 — I don't recollect exactly, somehow, though what makes me think it was one or the other[63] is because I remember the big flume[64] wasn't finished when he first came to the camp; but any way, he was

---

* transcendent: 초월적인　* finesse: 기교, 솜씨, 술책, 수완
54　drift: (비유적으로) 표류하다, 떠돌다, 대중없이 이야기하다
55　serenely: 고요하게, 잔잔하게, 평온하게
56　queer: 이상한
57　yarn: (특히 과장하거나 지어낸) 긴 이야기
58　exquisitely: 아주 아름답게, 절묘하게
59　absurd: 이상한
60　he replied as follows: 그는 다음과 같이 대답했다
61　in his own way: 그 자신의 방식으로
62　feller: = fellow. 녀석
63　one or the other: 이것이거나 저것이다
64　flume: (목재 운반용의) 용수로, 수로(水路), (물레방아의) 방수구

the curiosest[65] man about always betting on[66] any thing that turned up you ever see,[67] if he could get any body to bet on the other side; and if he couldn't, he'd change sides. Any way that suited[68] the other man would suit *him* — any way just so's he got a bet, *he* was satisfied. But still he was lucky, uncommon lucky; he most always come out[69] winner. He was always ready and laying for a chance;[70] there couldn't be no solit'ry thing mentioned but that feller'd offer to bet on it,[71] and take any side you please, as I was just telling you. If there was a horse-race, you'd find him flush,[72] or you'd find him busted[73] at the end of it;[74] if there was a dog-fight, he'd bet on it; if there was a cat-fight, he'd bet on it; if there was a chicken-fight,

---

65 curiosest : most curious. 아주 진기한, 호기심을 끄는, 별난

66 bet on : ~에 내기를 걸다, 내기하다

67 see : saw 대신에 과거시제로 종종 사용됨.

68 suit : ~에게 좋다, 맞다, 괜찮다

69 come out : 결국 ~가 되다

70 lay for a chance : 확률(기회, 찬스)에 베팅하다 ＊lay : bet과 비슷한 의미

71 there couldn't be no solit'ry thing mentioned but that feller'd offer to bet on it : 그 사내가 내기를 제안하지 않을 것은 단 한 가지도 (언급될 수 있는 게) 없었다 ＊solit'ry : = solitary. 단 하나의

72 flush : 돈을 많이 가진, 아낌없이 쓰는

73 busted : 파산의, 무일푼의

74 at the end of it : 결국에, 종국에는

he'd bet on it; why, if there was two birds setting on a fence, he would bet you which one would fly first; or if there was a camp-meeting, he would be there reg'lar,[75] to bet on Parson Walker, which he judged to be the best exhorter[76] about

5 here, and so he was, too, and a good man. If he even seen a straddle-bug[77] start to go anywheres, he would bet you how long it would take him to get to — to wherever he was going to, and if you took him up,[78] he would foller[79] that straddle-bug to Mexico but what[80] he would find out where he was

10 bound for[81] and how long he was on the road. Lots of the boys here has seen that Smiley, and can tell you about him. Why, it never made no difference[82] to him — he would bet on *any*

---

75 reg'lar : = regular(ly). 반드시, 고정적으로 다니는 ＊a regular customer : 고정(단골) 손님

76 exhorter : 권고자, 평신도 설교자

77 straddle-bug : 풍뎅이의 일종

78 take one up : ~에게 가담하다, 함께 따라가다

79 foller : = follow

80 but what : ~이 아니면, ~할 때까지

81 bound for : ~로 향하다

82 make difference : 차이가 나다

thing — the dangdest[83] feller. Parson Walker's wife laid[84] very sick once, for a good while,[85] and it seemed as if they warn't going to save[86] her; but one morning he come in, and Smiley asked how she was, and he said she was considerable[87] better — thank the Lord for his inf'nit[88] mercy — and coming on[89] so 5 smart[90] that, with the blessing of Prov'dence,[91] she'd get well yet; and Smiley, before he thought, says, "Well, I'll resk[92] two-and-a-half she don't, any way."

Thish-yer[93] Smiley had a mare[94] — the boys called her the

---

83 dangdest: = dandiest(dandy: 멋진, 멋부리는), = darnedest(=damnedest) ※도박꾼 Jim Smiley가 어떤 작자인지 표현하기 위한 욕설에 가까운 말로 이해할 수 있으며 dang을 damn의 '부드러운' 표현으로 볼 수 있음.
84 laid: = lied. 눕다
85 for a good while: 꽤 오래
86 save: (목숨을) 구하다
87 considerable: = considerably. 상당히
88 inf'nit: = infinite. 무한한
89 come on: 진전되다, 호전되다, 발전되다, 차차 ~하게 되다
90 smart: 활발한, 기민한
91 Prov'dence: = providence. 신의 섭리
92 resk: risk(~를 무릅쓰다)의 과거
93 thish-yer: this here의 준말, 방언
94 mare: 암말

fifteen-minute nag,[95] but that was only in fun,[96] you know, because, of course, she was faster than that — and he used to win money on that horse, for all she was so slow and always had the asthma,[97] or the distemper,[98] or the consumption,[99] or something of that kind. They used to give her two or three hundred yards' start,[100] and then pass her under way;[101] but always at the fag-end[102] of the race she'd get excited and desperate like, and come cavorting[103] and straddling[104] up, and scattering[105] her legs around *limber,*[106] sometimes in the air, and sometimes out to one side amongst the fences, and

---

95 the fifteen-minute nag: 늙어빠진 15분 경주마 * 경주 트랙을 한 바퀴 도는 데 15분 걸릴 정도로 아예 기다시피 하는 말이라는 의미로 보임.

96 only in fun: 그저 재미로

97 asthma: 천식

98 distemper: <병> 디스템퍼(특히 개와 고양이가 잘 걸리는 전염병)

99 consumption: 폐결핵

100 give her two or three hundred yards' start: 그 말이 200~300야드 먼저 출발하도록 하다 cf. head start: (남보다 일찍 시작해서 갖게 되는) 유리함.

101 pass her under way: 진행 중에(중간에) 그 말을 추월하다

102 fag-end: ~의 끝부분

103 cavort: 신이 나서 뛰어다니다

104 straddle: 가로지르다

105 scatter: 흩뜨려 놓다, 산개하다

106 limber: 유연한, 흐느적흐느적

kicking up m-o-r-e dust, and raising m-o-r-e racket[107] with her coughing and sneezing and blowing her nose[108] — and always fetch up[109] at the stand just about a neck ahead, as near as you could cipher it down.[110]

And he had a little small bull pup,[111] that to look at him you'd think he warn't worth a cent, but to set around and look ornery,[112] and lay for a chance to steal something. But as soon as money was up on him, he was a different dog; his under-jaw'd[113] begin to stick out like the fo'castle[114] of a steamboat,[115] and his teeth would uncover,[116] and shine like the furnaces. And a dog might tackle[117] him, and bully-rag[118] him, and bite

---

107 racket : 소음
108 blow one's nose : 코를 풀다
109 fetch up : 도착하다
110 cipher down : 생각해 내다, 계산하다
111 bull pup : = bullpup. 불도그의 새끼 * pup : 강아지
112 ornery : 성질 더러운 * 맥락을 고려하여 ornery를 ordinary로 볼 수도 있음.
113 under-jaw : 아래턱
114 fo'castle : = forecastle. (배 앞부분의) 선원 선실, 앞 갑판, 상갑판
115 steamboat : 증기선
116 uncover : 드러나다, 벗겨지다
117 tackle : 씨름하다, 맞붙다
118 bully-rag : 으르다, 곯리다(bully)

him, and throw him over his shoulder two or three times, and Andrew Jackson — which was the name of the pup — Andrew Jackson would never let on but what *he* was satisfied, and hadn't expected nothing else[119] — and the bets being doubled and doubled on the other side all the time, till the money was all up; and then all of a sudden[120] he would grab[121] that other dog jest[122] by the j'int[123] of his hind leg[124] and freeze to[125] it — not chaw,[126] you understand, but only jest grip[127] and hang on[128] till they throwed up the sponge,[129] if it was a year.[130] Smiley always come out winner on that pup, till he

---

119 would never let on but what *he* was satisfied, and hadn't expected nothing else : 자기 주제에 이만하면 됐지 그 밖에 달리 뭘 기대하지도 않았다는 듯한 태도 외에는 (다른 비밀은) 전혀 드러내지 않고는 했다(시치미를 떼고는 했다)

120 all of a sudden : 갑자기

121 grab : 잡다, 움켜쥐다

122 jest : = just

123 j'int : = joint. 관절

124 hind leg : 뒷다리

125 freeze to : ~에 꼭 달라붙다, 붙들고 늘어지다

126 chaw : = chew. 씹다

127 grip : 꽉 쥐다, 움켜쥐다

128 hang on : 물고 늘어지다, 버티다

129 throw up the sponge : 시합을 포기하다, 패배를 인정하다

130 if it was a year : 일 년이라도 되듯, 세월아 네월아 하며

harnessed[131] a dog once that didn't have no hind legs, because they'd been sawed off[132] by a circular saw,[133] and when the thing had gone along far enough, and the money was all up, and he come to make a snatch[134] for his pet holt,[135] he saw in a minute how he'd been imposed on,[136] and how the other dog had him in the door,[137] so to speak,[138] and he 'peered[139] surprised, and then he looked sorter[140] discouraged-like, and didn't try no more to win the fight, and so he got shucked out[141] bad. He give Smiley a look, as much as to say[142] his heart was broke, and it was *his* fault, for putting up a dog that hadn't

---

131 harness : <명사> 굴레, <동사> 굴레를 씌우다, ~를 끌어들이다

132 saw off : 톱질하여 잘라 내다

133 circular saw : 둥근 톱(buzz saw)

134 snatch : 낚아챔

135 pet holt : favorite hold. 좋아하는 홀드(레슬링 같은 스포츠에서 특정한 방식으로 잡는 것)

136 impose on : 함정에 빠뜨리다

137 had him in the door : 그를 문틈에 끼워 놓은 셈이 되었다, 궁지에 몰아넣었다

138 so to speak : 소위 말하자면

139 'peer : = appear. 나타나다, ~처럼 보이다

140 sorter : = sort of. 일종의

141 shucked out : = beaten, defeated ＊shuck : 껍질을 벗기다, 껍데기를 까다

142 as much as to say : ~라고 말하려는 듯

The Celebrated Jumping Frog of Calaveras County **105**

no hind legs for him to take holt of,[143] which was his main dependence[144] in a fight, and then he limped off[145] a piece[146] and laid down and died. It was a good pup, was that Andrew Jackson, and would have made a name for[147] hisself[148] if he'd lived, for the stuff[149] was in him, and he had genius — I know it, because he hadn't had no opportunities to speak of, and it don't stand to reason[150] that a dog could make such a fight as he could under them circumstances, if he hadn't no talent. It always makes me feel sorry when I think of that last fight of his'n,[151] and the way it turned out.[152]

Well, thish-yer Smiley had rat-tarriers,[153] and chicken

---

143 take holt of: = take hold of. 잡다, 쥐다

144 dependence: 의존

145 limp off: 절름거리며 떠나다

146 a piece: 조금

147 make a name for: 이름을 알리다

148 hisself: himself

149 the stuff: 특성, 소질, 재능

150 stand to reason: 당연하다, 이치에 맞다, 이해가 가다

151 his'n: = his own

152 turn out: 밝혀지다, ~한 상태가 되다

153 rat-tarrier: rat terrier. *특히 쥐를 잡도록 개량된 테리어의 종류. 이 맥락에서는 그냥 'rat'을 가리킬 가능성도 있음.

cocks,[154] and tomcats,[155] and all of them kind of things, till you couldn't rest,[156] and you couldn't fetch[157] nothing for him to bet on but he'd match[158] you. He ketched[159] a frog one day, and took him home, and said he cal'klated[160] to edercate[161] him; and so he never done nothing for three months but set in his back yard and learn[162] that frog to jump. And you bet you he *did* learn him, too. He'd give him a little punch[163] behind, and the next minute you'd see that frog whirling[164] in the air like a doughnut — see him turn one summerset,[165] or may be a couple, if he got a good start, and come down flat-footed[166] and all right, like a cat. He got him

---

154 chicken cock : 투계

155 tomcat : 수고양이

156 till you couldn't rest : 가만히 있을 수 없을 때까지

157 fetch : (가서) 가져오다, 데려오다

158 match : 상대하다

159 ketch : = catch

160 cal'klate : = calculate. 계산하다, 계획하다

161 edercate : = educate. 교육하다

162 learn : <고어 · 속어 · 우스개> 가르치다

163 punch : 타격, 때리기, 펀치

164 whirl : 빙글 돌다

165 summerset : =somersault. 공중제비

166 flat-footed : 단호히, 편평하게, 반듯하게

up so in the matter of catching flies, and kept him in practice so constant,[167] that[168] he'd nail[169] a fly every time as far as he could see him. Smiley said all a frog wanted was education, and he could do most any thing — and I believe him. Why, I've seen him set Dan'l Webster down here on this floor — Dan'l Webster was the name of the frog — and sing out, "Flies, Dan'l, flies!" and quicker'n[170] you could wink, he'd spring straight[171] up, and snake[172] a fly off'n the counter there, and flop[173] down on the floor again as solid[174] as a gob[175] of mud, and fall to scratching[176] the side of his head with his hind foot as indifferent[177] as if he hadn't no idea he'd been doin' any more'n any frog might do. You never see a frog so modest and

---

167 constant : 꾸준한, 계속적인
168 so A that B : 너무 A해서 B하다
169 nail : 잡다
170 quicker'n : = quicker than
171 straight : 곧장
172 snake : = sneak. 뒤통수치다
173 flop : 털썩 주저앉다
174 solid : 견고한, 확실한
175 gob : (걸쭉한 것의) 조금
176 fall to scratching : 긁기 시작하다
177 indifferent : 냉담한, 무관심한

straightforward[178] as he was, for all he was so gifted.[179] And when it come to fair and square jumping on a dead level,[180] he could get over more ground at one straddle[181] than any animal of his breed[182] you ever see. Jumping on a dead level was his strong suit,[183] you understand; and when it come to[184] that, 5 Smiley would ante up[185] money on him as long as he had a red.[186] Smiley was monstrous[187] proud of his frog, and well he might be, for fellers that had traveled and been everywheres, all said he laid over[188] any frog that ever *they* see.

---

178 straightforward : 간단한, 솔직한

179 for all he was so gifted : 그렇게나 재능이 있음에도 불구하고

180 fair and square jumping on a dead level : 평지에서 다짜고짜 도약하기
　　 ＊fair and square : 공명정대하게, 대놓고, 정확히

181 get over more ground at one straddle : 한 번 도약으로 더 높은 지면을 넘다 ＊straddle : 두 다리를 벌려 걸치고 올라앉기

182 of one's breed : ~와 같은 종류의

183 strong suit : (비유적) 장점, 장기(카드놀이에서 높은 끗수의 패를 가리킴.)

184 when it comes to : ~에 대해 말하자면, ~에 관한 한

185 ante up : (분담금을) 내다, 치르다

186 have a red : 푼돈이 있다 ＊종종 한 푼도 없다(not have a red)는 부정형으로 쓰임. ＊a red : a red cent(a penny의 속어)

187 monstrous : 괴물 같은, 끔찍한 ＊본문에서는 monstrously라는 부사형을 대신하여 사용됨.

188 lay over : ~를 누르다, ~보다 더 낫다, 능가하다

Well, Smiley kept the beast in a little lattice[189] box, and he used to fetch him down town sometimes and lay for[190] a bet. One day a feller — a stranger in the camp, he was — come across[191] him with his box, and says:

"What might it be that you've got in the box?"

And Smiley says, sorter indifferent like, "It might be a parrot, or it might be a canary,[192] may be, but it ain't[193] — it's only just a frog."

And the feller took it, and looked at it careful,[194] and turned it round this way and that,[195] and says, "H'm — so 'tis.[196] Well, what's he good for?"[197]

"Well," Smiley says, easy and careless,[198] "He's good enough

---

189 lattice : 격자 모양의
190 lay for : 매복하여 기다리다, ~할 틈만 노리다
191 come across : 마주치다
192 canary : 카나리아
193 ain't : = isn't
194 careful : = carefully. 조심스럽게, 신중하게, 주의 깊게
195 this way and that : 이곳저곳으로, 이 방향 저 방향으로
196 'tis : = it is의 준말
197 good for : ~에 소용이 있다
198 careless : 부주의한, 경솔한, 무관심한

for *one* thing, I should judge[199] — he can outjump[200] any frog in Calaveras county."

The feller took the box again, and took another long, particular[201] look, and give it back to Smiley, and says, very deliberate,[202] "Well, I don't see no p'ints[203] about that frog that's any better'n any other frog."

"May be you don't," Smiley says. "May be you understand frogs, and may be you don't understand 'em; may be you've had experience, and may be you an't only a amature,[204] as it were. Anyways, I've got *my* opinion, and I'll risk forty dollars that he can outjump any frog in Calaveras county."

And the feller studied[205] a minute, and then says, kinder[206] sad like, "Well, I'm only a stranger here, and I an't got no frog; but if I had a frog, I'd bet you."

And then Smiley says, "That's all right — that's all right — if

---

199 judge : = think. 판단하다, 생각하다

200 outjump : ~보다 더 높이(멀리) 점프하다

201 particular : 특정한, 특유의, 꼼꼼한, 세심한

202 deliberate : = deliberately. 의도적으로, 신중하게, 침착하게

203 p'ints : = points. 요점, 요지, 논지

204 amature : = amateur. 아마추어

205 study : 고민하다, 숙고하다, 검토하다, 살피다

206 kinder : = kind of (= sort of. 일종의)

you'll hold my box a minute, I'll go and get you a frog." And
so the feller took the box, and put up[207] his forty dollars along
with Smiley's, and set down to wait.

So he set there a good while thinking and thinking to hisself,
and then he got the frog out and prized[208] his mouth open and
took a teaspoon and filled him full of quail shot[209] — filled him
pretty near up to his chin — and set him on the floor. Smiley
he went to the swamp[210] and slopped[211] around in the mud for
a long time, and finally he ketched[212] a frog, and fetched him
in, and give him to this feller, and says:

"Now, if you're ready, set him alongside of[213] Dan'l, with his
fore-paws[214] just even[215] with Dan'l, and I'll give the word."[216]
Then he says, "One — two — three — *git!*"[217] and him and the

---

207 put up : 내놓다

208 prize : 비집어 열다, 지레로 들어 올리다, 억지로 열다

209 quail shot : 납탄 (메추라기를 잡는 데 사용하는) * quail : 메추라기

210 swamp : 늪

211 slop : 찰랑거리다

212 ketch : = catch. 잡다

213 alongside of : ~와 나란히

214 fore-paw : 앞발

215 even : 가지런히, 나란히

216 give the word : 신호를 하다, 명령을 하다

217 git : = get. 시작, 출발

feller touched up the frogs from behind, and the new frog hopped[218] off lively,[219] but Dan'l give a heave,[220] and hysted[221] up his shoulders — so — like a Frenchman,[222] but it wan's no use[223] — he couldn't budge;[224] he was planted[225] as solid as a church,[226] and he couldn't no more stir[227] than if he was anchored out.[228] Smiley was a good deal[229] surprised, and he was disgusted too, but he didn't have no idea what the matter was, of course.

The feller took the money and started away;[230] and when he

---

218 hop : 뛰어오르다, 도약하다

219 lively : 생기 있게

220 heave : 힘주어 들어 올리다, 허덕이다, (한숨을) 쉬다

221 hyst : = hoist. 들어 올리다

222 like a Frenchman : 프랑스인처럼 ＊당시 미국인들이 즐거워했을 유럽인에 대한 악의 없는 풍자적인 묘사로 볼 수 있음.

223 no use : 소용없는

224 budge : 약간 움직이다

225 plant : 놓다, 좌정하다, 앉다

226 as solid as a church : 반석 위에 굳게 선 교회처럼 ＊『신약성서』에 나온 표현임.

227 stir : 약간 움직이다

228 anchor out : 정박하다, 닻을 내리다

229 a good deal : 꽤나, 많이

230 start away : 길을 떠나다

was going out at the door, he sorter jerked[231] his thumb over his shoulders this way at Dan'l, and says again, very deliberate, "Well," he says, "I don't see no p'ints about that frog that's any better'n any other frog."

Smiley he stood scratching his head and looking down at Dan'l a long time, and at last he says, "I do wonder[232] what in the nation[233] that frog throw'd off[234] for — I wonder if there an't something the matter with him — he 'pears to look mighty baggy,[235] somehow." And he ketched Dan'l by the nap[236] of the neck, and *hefted*[237] him up and says, "Why, blame my cats,[238] if he don't weigh five pound!" and turned him upside down,[239] and he belched[240] out a double handful of shot. And then he see how it was, and he was the maddest man — he set

---

231 jerk : 홱 움직이다

232 wonder : 궁금해하다, 의아하게 여기다, 의심하다

233 what in the nation : 도대체 어째서

234 throw off : 내팽개치다, 일부러 지다

235 baggy : 헐렁한, 축 늘어진, 처진

236 nap : = nape. 목의 뒷덜미

237 heft : 들어 올리다, 들어서 무게를 달다

238 blame my cats : 내 고양이들을 저주해도 좋아 * Smiley 특유의 비유적인 표현 중 하나임.

239 upside down : 거꾸로

240 belch : 내뿜다, 뿜어져 나오다

the frog down and took out after[241] that feller, but he never ketchd him. And —

[Here Simon Wheeler heard his name called from the front yard, and got up to see what was wanted.] And turning to me as he moved away, he said: "Just set where you are, stranger, and rest easy I ain't going to be gone a second."[242]

But, by your leave,[243] I did not think that a continuation[244] of the history of the enterprising[245] vagabond[246] *Jim Smiley* would be likely to afford[247] me much information concerning[248] the Rev. *Leonidas W. Smiley*, and so I started away.

At the door I met the sociable[249] Wheeler returning, and he

---

241 take out after : 뒤쫓다
242 a second : 잠시라도
243 by your leave : 실례지만, 미안하지만
244 continuation : 지속, 계속함
245 enterprising : 진취적인, 모험적인
246 vagabond : 방랑자, 무뢰한
247 afford : 주다, 제공하다
248 concerning : ~와 관련된
249 sociable : 사교적인

button-holed[250] me and recommenced:[251]

"Well, thish-yer Smiley had a yeller[252] one-eyed cow that didn't have no tail, only jest a short stump[253] like a bannanner,[254] and — "

However, lacking[255] both time and inclination,[256] I did not wait to hear about the afflicted[257] cow, but took my leave.[258] [259]

---

250 button-hole: 멱살을 잡다, (특히 듣고 싶어 하지 않는 사람에게) 잠자코 말을 듣게 만들다

251 recommence: 다시 시작하다

252 yeller: = yellow

253 stump: 그루터기, 잘린 부분

254 bannanner: = banana

255 lack: 결핍하다, 모자라다

256 inclination: 좋아함, 경향, 기분, 의향

257 afflicted: 괴로워하는

258 take one's leave: (작별 인사를 하고) 떠나가다

259 However, lacking ... took my leave.: 이 책에서 기준으로 삼은 1875년 출간된 판본의 결말임. 1865년 초판본이 발표되었을 때는 아래와 같은 결말이었음.

"Oh! hang Smiley and his afflicted cow!"

I muttered, good-naturedly, and bidding the old gentleman good-day, I departed.

작품 해설

1. 이야기 속의 이야기(frame story)

캘리포니아 Angels Camp의 Angels Hotel 바텐더 Simon Wheeler에게 들은 도박꾼 Jim Smiley에 대한 이야기를 다시 화자가 독자에게 전해 주는 형식을 띤다. 즉, 화자 '나'의 이야기 안에 Simon Wheeler의 이야기가 들어 있는 액자구조 형식이다. 동부의 친구에게 부탁을 받은 '나'는 서부에서 Simon Wheeler를 만나 Leonidas W. Smiley에 대한 안부를 묻는다. Wheeler는 Leonidas W. Smiley 대신 엉뚱하게 Jim Smiley에 대한 이야기를 해 주며 '나'는 꼼짝없이 붙잡혀 그 이야기를 다 듣게 된다.

'나'의 이야기 속 주인공 Simon Wheeler가 다시 화자가 되어 전하는 액자구조 안에 든 이야기의 주인공은 Jim Smiley이다. Smiley는 세상의 모든 것을 도박의 대상으로 삼는다. 그는 경마, 투계, 투견처럼 내놓고 도박을 벌이는 곳에서는 말할 것도 없고 일상에서 흔히 볼 수 있는 담장에 앉은 새 두 마리, 심지어 중병을 앓는 목사님 부인의 수명마저도 내기의 주제로 삼는다. 세상 전체를 도박대 위에 올려놓고 자신의 운을 시험하는 이 모습 자체가 구세계 유럽과 대조되는 신대륙 전체의 운명이지만, 신대륙 안에서도 법과 규칙의 점진적인 적용을 기반으로 완성도를 더해 가며 견고해지는 동부와는 달리 변동성이 커다란 당시 서부의 시대상을 암시하는 측면도 있다. 어쩌면 Jim Smiley는 내기에서의 승패 못지않게 내기의 목전에서 감지되는 운명적 변화의 가능성 앞에서 더 전율했을 듯도 하다. Jim Smiley의 인생 자체를 진정 새로운 삶의 가능성 탐색과 연결 짓기는 어렵겠지만 이 인물을 둘러싼 서부의 꽤나 허풍스러운 이야기에서, 이를테면 신대륙에 열렸다가 점점 닫혀 가는 어떤 새로운 삶의 가능성에 대한 헛헛한 갈급을 멀게나마 짐작할 수 있는 것은 아닐까.

2. 액자구조와 이야기꾼의 중요성

액자구조의 안팎에 동부와 서부, 문명과 반(비)문명, 세련미와 투박함, 중심과 변경, 표준어와 사투리 등의 대립항이 촘촘히 맞닿아 있다.

고딕소설에서와 같이 터무니없고도 황당한 사건과 인물의 이야기를 완충해서 전달하는 '액자구조' 이야기는 팽창하는 나라에서 뚜렷하게 대립되는 지역과 인물의 차이, 예컨대 동부의 세련되고 교양 있는 인물과 서부 변경의 투박한 인물 사이의 차이를 담아내는 틀로서 작용한다. 동부인 '나'의 이야기 스타일과 서부인 Wheeler의 이야기 스타일의 차이 역시 이 틀 안에 위치한다.

쇠락한 광산촌 호텔의 술집에서 졸고 있던 Simon Wheeler는 뚱뚱하고 대머리이며 부드럽고 소박한 표정을 지닌 인물로 다소는 게으른 인상을 풍긴다. 이야기를 장황하게 늘어놓고 싶어 하는 수다스러운 인물인데, 그런 욕구와는 달리 말재주가 있다고 보기는 힘들다. 교양, 말주변, 세련미가 부족한 인물로 보인다.

바로 이렇게 투박한 서부의 이야기꾼을 내세웠다는 것 자체가 작가의 모험일 수 있다. 실제로 조금 더 꼼꼼히 살펴보면, 이 투박한 이야기꾼이 그렇게 단순한 인물인지는 쉽게 답할 수 없다. Wheeler의 단순한 모습은 그저 마스크일 뿐 실은 서부인의 단순성을 미리 전제한 외부자 '나'의 선입견을 충족시켜 주는 척하면서 오히려 '나'를 속여 넘기는 것은 아닌지 하는 인상도 받기 때문이다.

Wheeler가 '나'를 도망치지 못하게 구석에 몰아넣고 풀어내는 단조로운 이야기이자 '나'에게는 '쓸모도 없을뿐더러 거의 죽을 지경으로 길고 지루한 지긋지긋한 회상담'이 딱히 자신의 목적에 부합하지도 않으며 듣고 있을 시간과 마음도 없어 빈틈이라도 생기면 빠져나갈 궁리를 하는 '나'와 형성하는 묘한 긴장관계는 작가와 독자 사이에 형성되는 관계의 한 단면을 잘 보여 준다. 우선, 작가는 독자의 다소 완강한 방어벽을 뚫고 비집고 들어가 자신의 이야기를 듣도록 만들어야 하며 독자의 주의를 일시적인 것을 넘어 일정 시간 이상 지속해서 끌어야 하며 이마저도 때가 되면 가차 없이 거두고 돌아서야 하는 것이다.

다소 엉뚱하고도 황당한 이야기를, 그 못지않게 엉뚱한 상황에 처한 화자가 전하는 꽤나 재미있는 이 이야기는 사실 작가의 굉장한 문학적 모험이자 자신감을 보여 준다고 할 수 있다.

영미 명작 단편선_4

Désirée's Baby

Kate Chopin

Kate Chopin(1850~1904)은 미주리주 세인트루이스(St. Louis)에서 아일랜드계의 아버지(Thomas O'Flaherty)와 프랑스계 캐나다인의 자손인 어머니(Eliza Faris) 사이에서 태어났다. Chopin 소설의 주요 무대는 남부 크리올(creole, 미국 남부에 정착한 프랑스인·스페인인의 후예나 그들의 언어와 문화 전반을 일컬음)이며 여성과 인종 문제를 다루었다. Chopin은 단편소설 "The Story of an Hour"(1894), "The Storm"(1898), 그리고 장편소설 *The Awakening*(1899) 등에서와 같이 여성의 욕망을 거침없이 그려낸다. 여기에 수록한 "Désirée's Baby"(1893)는 남북전쟁 이전 시기 루이지애나의 크리올 사회를 배경으로 인종 문제를 다루며 반전의 결말을 통해 사회적 통념과 전제들에 통렬히 문제를 제기한다.

Désirée's Baby

>>~

As the day was pleasant, Madame Valmonde drove over to L'Abri[1] to see Désirée[2] and the baby.

It made her laugh to think of Désirée with a baby. Why, it seemed but[3] yesterday that Désirée was little more than[4] a baby herself; when Monsieur[5] in riding through the gateway[6] of Valmonde had found her lying asleep in the shadow of the big stone pillar.[7]

The little one awoke in his arms and began to cry for "Dada."[8] That was as much as[9] she could do or say. Some people

---

1 L'Abri : shelter라는 뜻을 지닌 지명

2 Désirée : much desired의 뜻을 지닌 이름

3 but : 다름 아니고, 단지

4 little more than : ~에 지나지 않는

5 monsieur : <프랑스어> ~ 씨, ~ 님

6 gateway : 입구, 출입구, 문

7 pillar : 기둥

8 dada : <구어> (어린이들의 표현) 아버지, 아빠

9 as much as : ~ 하는 게 다(전부)

thought she might have strayed[10] there of her own accord,[11] for she was of the toddling[12] age. The prevailing[13] belief was that she had been purposely[14] left by a party of[15] Texans,[16] whose canvas-covered[17] wagon, late in the day, had crossed[18] the ferry that Coton Mais kept, just below the plantation. In time[19] Madame Valmonde abandoned[20] every speculation[21] but[22] the one that Désirée had been sent to her by a beneficent[23] Providence[24] to be the child of her affection,[25] seeing that she was without child of the flesh.[26] For the girl

---

10 stray: 길을 잃다
11 of one's own accord: 자진해서, 저절로
12 toddle: 아장아장 걷다
13 prevailing: 널리 퍼진, 유력한
14 purposely: 일부러, 고의로, 특별히
15 a party of: 한 무리의
16 Texan: 텍사스인
17 canvas-covered: 캔버스 천으로 덮인
18 cross: 건너다, 마주치다
19 in time: 머지않아, 조만간
20 abandon: 버리다
21 speculation: 심사숙고, 추론, 사색
22 but: = except. ~을 제외하고
23 beneficent: 자비심 많은, 인정 많은
24 Providence: 신의 섭리
25 child of her affection: 그녀가 애정을 쏟을 아이
26 child of the flesh: 육신으로 낳은 아이

grew to be beautiful and gentle, affectionate[27] and sincere, —
the idol[28] of Valmonde.

It was no wonder,[29] when she stood one day against the
stone pillar in whose shadow she had lain asleep, eighteen
years before, that Armand Aubigny riding by and seeing her
there, had fallen in love with her. That was the way all the
Aubignys fell in love, as if struck by a pistol shot.[30] The wonder
was that he had not loved her before; for he had known her
since his father brought him home from Paris, a boy of eight,
after his mother died there. The passion that awoke in him
that day, when he saw her at the gate, swept[31] along like an
avalanche,[32] or like a prairie fire,[33] or like anything that drives
headlong over all obstacles.[34]

Monsieur Valmonde grew practical and wanted things

---

27 affectionate : 애정이 넘치는

28 idol : 우상

29 wonder : 놀랄 만한 일

30 as if struck by a pistol shot : 마치 권총에 맞은 것처럼

31 sweep : 휩쓸다

32 avalanche : 눈(산)사태

33 prairie fire : 요원의 불, 들불

34 like anything that drives headlong over all obstacles : 모든 장애물을 넘어
    저돌적으로 밀고 나아가는 무엇처럼

well considered:[35] that is, the girl's obscure origin.[36] Armand looked into her eyes and did not care. He was reminded[37] that she was nameless. What did it matter[38] about a name when he could give her one of the oldest and proudest in Louisiana? He ordered the *corbeille*[39] from Paris, and contained himself[40] with what patience he could[41] until it arrived; then they were married.

Madame Valmonde had not seen Désirée and the baby for four weeks. When she reached L'Abri she shuddered at the first sight of it,[42] as she always did. It was a sad looking place, which for many years had not known the gentle presence of a mistress,[43] old Monsieur Aubigny having married and buried his wife in France, and she having loved her own land too well ever to leave it. The roof came down steep and

---

35 wanted things well considered : 상황이 잘 심사숙고되기를 원했다

36 obscure origin : 애매한(불분명한) 출신(태생)

37 remind : 상기시키다

38 matter : 상관 있다, 중요하다

39 corbeille : 꽃바구니 장식, 남편의 결혼 선물

40 contain oneself : 자제하다

41 with what patience he could : 할 수 있는 온갖 참을성을 가지고

42 shuddered at the first sight of it : 그곳이 처음 눈에 띄자 몸서리를 쳤다

43 gentle presence of a mistress : 안주인의 온화한 존재(감)

black like a cowl,[44] reaching out[45] beyond the wide galleries[46] that encircled[47] the yellow stuccoed[48] house. Big, solemn[49] oaks grew close to it, and their thick-leaved,[50] far-reaching[51] branches shadowed it like a pall.[52] Young Aubigny's rule[53] was a strict[54] one, too, and under it his negroes had forgotten how to be gay,[55] as they had been during the old master's easy-going[56] and indulgent[57] lifetime.[58]

The young mother was recovering slowly, and lay full length,[59] in her soft white muslins and laces, upon a couch.

---

44 cowl : (수도승들이 머리에 쓰는) 고깔
45 reach out : (뻗어 나가서) ~에 이르다
46 gallery : 회랑
47 encircle : 둘러싸다
48 stuccoed : 치장 벽토를 바른
49 solemn : 엄숙한, 장엄한, 무게 있는
50 thick-leaved : 잎이 무성한
51 far-reaching : 멀리까지 뻗어 있는
52 pall : 관, 장막
53 rule : 규칙, 다스림, 지도
54 strict : 엄격한, 엄한
55 gay : 즐거운
56 easy-going : 태평한, 안이한
57 indulgent : 관대한, 너그럽게 봐 주는
58 lifetime : 생애
59 lay full length : 큰대자로 쭉 누워 있었다

The baby was beside her, upon her arm, where he had fallen asleep, at her breast. The yellow[60] nurse[61] woman sat beside a window fanning[62] herself.

Madame Valmonde bent her portly[63] figure[64] over Désirée and kissed her, holding her an instant[65] tenderly in her arms. Then she turned to the child.

"This is not the baby!" she exclaimed, in startled tones.[66] French was the language spoken at Valmonde in those days.

"I knew you would be astonished," laughed Désirée, "at the way he has grown. The little *cochon de lait!*[67] Look at his legs, mamma, and his hands and fingernails, — real fingernails. Zandrine had to cut them this morning. Isn't it true, Zandrine?"

---

60 yellow : =high yellow. 황갈색 피부의 흑인 ＊여기의 'yellow'가 '황인종'을
    지칭하며 '모욕적인' 표현인가 하는 의문과 관련해 Kate Chopin이 활동하
    던 시기와 지역에서는 '옅은 피부의 흑인'을 가리키는 단순 묘사적 표현에
    가깝다고 보는 경우가 많음.
61 nurse : 유모
62 fan : 부채질하다
63 portly : 살찐, 약간 뚱뚱한, 당당한
64 figure : 인물, 모양, 체형
65 instant : 순간
66 in startled tones : 깜짝 놀란 어조로
67 *cochon de lait* : 젖먹이 돼지, 유아를 애정 어리게 부르는 말(a suckling pig)

The woman bowed her turbaned[68] head majestically,[69] "Mais si,[70] Madame."

"And the way he cries," went on Désirée, "is deafening.[71] Armand heard him the other day as far away as La Blanche's cabin."

Madame Valmonde had never removed[72] her eyes from the child. She lifted it and walked with it over to the window that was lightest. She scanned[73] the baby narrowly,[74] then looked as searchingly[75] at Zandrine, whose face was turned to gaze[76] across the fields.

"Yes, the child has grown, has changed," said Madame Valmonde, slowly, as she replaced[77] it beside its mother. "What does Armand say?"

---

68 turbaned : 터번을 쓴

69 majestically : 당당하게, 장엄하게

70 mais si : but, yes

71 deafening : 귀청이 터질 것 같은

72 remove : 제거하다, 떼다

73 scan : 죽 훑어보다, 자세히 살피다

74 narrowly : 주의 깊게

75 searchingly : 면밀하게

76 gaze : 응시하다

77 replace : 돌려놓다

Désirée's face became suffused[78] with a glow[79] that was happiness itself.

"Oh, Armand is the proudest father in the parish, I believe, chiefly because it is a boy, to bear[80] his name; though he says not, — that he would have loved[81] a girl as well. But I know it isn't true. I know he says that to please me. And mamma," she added, drawing[82] Madame Valmonde's head down to her, and speaking in a whisper, "he hasn't punished one of them — not one of them — since baby is born. Even Negrillon, who pretended to have burnt his leg[83] that he might rest from work[84] — he only laughed, and said Negrillon was a great scamp.[85] oh, mamma, I'm so happy; it frightens[86] me."

What Désirée said was true. Marriage, and later the birth

---

78 suffuse : 가득 차게 하다, 뒤덮다

79 glow : 빛, 광채

80 bear : 짊어지다, (이름, 칭호 등을) 지니다

81 would have *p.p.* : ~했을 텐데

82 draw : 잡아 끌다

83 pretended to have burnt his leg : 다리를 덴 척했다

84 rest from work : 일을 쉬다

85 scamp : 건달, 장난꾸러기

86 frighten : 겁나게 하다

of his son had softened[87] Armand Aubigny's imperious[88] and exacting[89] nature greatly. This was what made the gentle Désirée so happy, for she loved him desperately.[90] When he frowned, she trembled, but loved him. When he smiled, she asked no greater blessing of God. But Armand's dark, handsome face had not often been disfigured by frowns[91] since the day he fell in love with her.

When the baby was about three months old, Désirée awoke one day to the conviction[92] that there was something in the air menacing[93] her peace. It was at first too subtle to grasp.[94] It had only been a disquieting suggestion;[95] an air of mystery[96]

---

87 soften : 부드럽게 하다

88 imperious : 오만한, 고압적인

89 exacting : 엄격한, 혹독한

90 desperately : 필사적으로, 지독하게

91 disfigured by frowns : 찡그려서 일그러진

92 awoke one day to the conviction : 어느 날 깨닫고는 확신하게 되었다, 어느 날 정신을 차려 보니 ~라는 확신이 들었다

93 menace : 위협하다

94 too subtle to grasp : 너무나 미묘해서 파악할 수 없는

95 a disquieting suggestion : 불안하게 하는 암시

96 an air of mystery : 미스터리(수수께끼) 같은 분위기

among the blacks; unexpected[97] visits from far-off[98] neighbors who could hardly account for[99] their coming. Then a strange, an awful change in her husband's manner, which she dared[100] not ask him to explain. When he spoke to her, it was with averted[101] eyes, from which the old love-light seemed to have gone out. He absented himself from[102] home; and when there, avoided her presence[103] and that of her child, without excuse.[104] And the very spirit of Satan seemed suddenly to take hold of[105] him in his dealings[106] with the slaves. Désirée was miserable enough to die.

She sat in her room, one hot afternoon, in her *peignoir,*[107]

---

97   unexpected : 예상치 못한

98   far-off : 멀리 떨어진

99   account for : ~를 해명하다, ~을 설명해 주다

100 dare : 감히 ~하다, 위험을 무릅쓰고 ~하다

101 avert : ~을 돌리다, 비키다

102 absent oneself from : 결석하다, 자리를 비우다

103 avoided her presence : 그녀가 있는 곳을 피했다, 그녀와 함께 있는 것을 피했다

104 without excuse : 아무런 변명도 없이, 이유를 대지 않고

105 take hold of : 꽉 쥐다, 붙들다

106 dealing : 다룸, 대처, 대우

107 peignoir : 화장옷, 실내복

listlessly[108] drawing through her fingers the strands[109] of her long, silky[110] brown hair that hung about[111] her shoulders. The baby, half naked, lay asleep upon her own great mahogany bed, that was like a sumptuous[112] throne, with its satin-lined[113] half-canopy.[114] One of La Blanche's little quadroon[115] boys — half naked too — stood fanning the child slowly with a fan of peacock feathers. Désirée's eyes had been fixed absently[116] and sadly upon[117] the baby, while she was striving[118] to penetrate[119] the threatening mist that she felt closing about her.[120] She looked from her child to the boy who stood beside

---

108 listlessly : 생기 없게

109 strand : 가닥

110 silky : 부드러운

111 hang about : 늘어지다, 드리우다

112 sumptuous : 사치스러운

113 satin-lined : 수자직(공단)으로 안감을 댄

114 canopy : 닫집, 천개, 캐노피(침대 위의 망)

115 quadroon : 흑인의 피가 4분의 1 섞인 흑백 혼혈아

116 absently : 멍하니, 방심하여

117 fix upon : ~에 고정하다

118 strive : 애쓰다

119 penetrate : 관통하다

120 the threatening mist that she felt closing about her : 자기 주위에 조여들어 오고 있다고 느낀 위협적인 분위기

him, and back again; over and over.[121] "Ah!" It was a cry that she could not help;[122] which she was not conscious of having uttered.[123] The blood turned like ice in her veins, and a clammy[124] moisture[125] gathered[126] upon her face.

She tried to speak to the little quadroon boy; but no sound 5 would come, at first. When he heard his name uttered, he looked up, and his mistress was pointing to the door. He laid aside[127] the great, soft fan, and obediently[128] stole away,[129] over the polished[130] floor, on his bare tiptoes.

She stayed motionless, with gaze riveted[131] upon her child, 10

---

121 over and over : 계속해서, 연달아서, 자꾸만
122 cannot help : ~할 수밖에 없다 ＊이 대목에서 Désirée가 탄성을 지른 이유를 단정하기는 어렵지만, La Blanche의 아이와 자신의 아이가 닮았음을 자각하면서 La Blanche와 남편이 오랜 기간 성관계를 유지해 왔음을 알게되었기 때문이 아닌가 생각해 볼 수 있음.
123 utter : 말하다, (입 밖에) 내다
124 clammy : 진득거리고 차가운
125 moisture : 습기, 땀
126 gather : 모이다
127 lay aside : 옆에 내려 놓다
128 obediently : 고분고분하게, 공손하게
129 steal away : 몰래 가 버리다
130 polished : 광택이 나는
131 rivet : 못, 못을 박다, 고정시키다

and her face the picture[132] of fright.[133]

Presently[134] her husband entered the room, and without noticing[135] her, went to a table and began to search among some papers which covered it.

5 "Armand," she called to him, in a voice which must have stabbed[136] him, if he was human.[137] But he did not notice. "Armand," she said again. Then she rose and tottered[138] towards him. "Armand," she panted[139] once more, clutching[140] his arm, "look at our child. What does it mean? tell 10 me."

He coldly but gently loosened her fingers from about his arm and thrust[141] the hand away from him. "Tell me what it

---

132 the picture: 꼭 닮은 것, 화신 * the picture of … : 극도로(완전히)~인 것

133 fright: 공포

134 presently: 이내, 곧, 현재

135 notice: 발견하다, 주목하다, 인지하다

136 stab: 찌르다

137 human: 인간의, 인간적인, 인간미가 있는, 인간이기에 갖게 되는 (약점 등)

138 totter: 비틀거리다

139 pant: 헐떡이다

140 clutch: 움켜쥐다

141 thrust: 밀치다

means!" she cried despairingly.[142]

"It means," he answered lightly,[143] "that the child is not white; it means that you are not white."

A quick conception[144] of all that this accusation[145] meant for her nerved[146] her with unwonted[147] courage to deny it. "It is a lie; it is not true, I am white! Look at my hair, it is brown; and my eyes are gray, Armand, you know they are gray. And my skin is fair,"[148] seizing[149] his wrist. "Look at my hand; whiter than yours, Armand," she laughed hysterically.[150]

"As white as La Blanche's," he returned[151] cruelly;[152] and went away leaving her alone with their child.

When she could hold a pen in her hand, she sent a

---

142 despairingly : 절망하여, 자포자기하여
143 lightly : 가볍게, 태연하게, 경솔하게
144 conception : 개념, 파악, 이해
145 accusation : 비난
146 nerve : 용기를 주다
147 unwonted : 드문, 평소에 없는
148 fair : (피부 · 머리카락이) 흰
149 seize : 붙잡다
150 hysterically : 히스테릭하게, 발작적으로
151 return : 되돌려 주다, 대꾸하다
152 cruelly : 잔인하게

despairing[153] letter to Madame Valmonde.

"My mother, they tell me I am not white. Armand has told me I am not white. For God's sake[154] tell them it is not true. You must know it is not true. I shall die. I must die. I cannot
5 be so unhappy, and live."

The answer that came was brief:[155]

"My own Désirée: Come home to Valmonde; back to your mother who loves you. Come with your child."

When the letter reached Désirée she went with it to her
10 husband's study,[156] and laid it open upon the desk before which he sat. She was like a stone image: silent, white, motionless after she placed it there.

In silence he ran his cold eyes over the written words.

He said nothing. "Shall I go, Armand?" she asked in tones
15 sharp with agonized[157] suspense.[158]

"Yes, go."

"Do you want me to go?"

---

153 despairing : 자포자기의, 절망적인

154 for God's sake : 제발, 부디, 도대체

155 brief : 간략한

156 study : 서재

157 agonized : 고뇌하는, 괴로워하는

158 suspense : 불안, 지속적 긴장감, 걱정

"Yes, I want you to go."

He thought Almighty[159] God had dealt cruelly and unjustly[160] with him; and felt, somehow,[161] that he was paying Him back[162] in kind[163] when he stabbed[164] thus into his wife's soul. Moreover he no longer loved her, because of the unconscious injury she had brought upon his home and his name.[165]

She turned away like one stunned by a blow,[166] and walked slowly towards the door, hoping he would call her back.

"Good-by, Armand," she moaned.

He did not answer her. That was his last blow at fate.[167]

Désirée went in search of[168] her child. Zandrine was

---

159 almighty : 전지전능한

160 unjustly : 불공평하게

161 somehow : 여하튼, 어쨌든, 아무래도

162 pay back : 되갚다, 앙갚음하다

163 in kind : 같은 방법으로

164 stab : 찌르다

165 the unconscious injury she had brought upon his home and his name : 그녀가 그의 가문과 이름에 초래한 무의식적인(모른 채 저지른) 해악

166 like one stunned by a blow : 강타당하여 망연해진 사람처럼 * stun : 어리벙벙하게 하다, 실신시키다

167 his last blow at fate : 그가 운명에 가한 마지막 일격

168 in search of : ~를 찾아

pacing[169] the sombre[170] gallery with it. She took the little one from the nurse's arms with no word of explanation, and descending the steps, walked away, under the live-oak[171] branches.

It was an October afternoon; the sun was just sinking. Out in the still[172] fields the negroes were picking cotton.

Désirée had not changed the thin white garment[173] nor the slippers which she wore. Her hair was uncovered[174] and the sun's rays brought a golden gleam from its brown meshes.[175]

She did not take the broad, beaten[176] road which led to the far-off plantation of Valmonde. She walked across a deserted[177] field, where the stubble[178] bruised[179] her tender feet, so

---

169 pace: 서성거리다, 속도(리듬)를 유지하다

170 sombre: = somber. 어두컴컴한

171 live-oak: 떡갈나무의 일종(미국 남부산)

172 still: 고요한

173 garment: 의복, 옷차림

174 uncovered: 아무것도 덮여 있지 않은, 아무것도 쓰지 않은

175 the sun's rays brought a golden gleam from its brown meshes: 햇살들이 그(그녀 머리칼의) 갈색 망들에 부딪혀 황금빛으로 빛났다

176 beaten: 다져진, 발길이 많이 닿은

177 deserted: 버려진

178 stubble: 그루터기

179 bruise: 멍들게 하다

delicately shod,[180] and tore her thin gown to shreds.[181]

She disappeared among the reeds and willows that grew thick along the banks of the deep, sluggish[182] bayou;[183] and she did not come back again.

Some weeks later there was a curious scene enacted[184] at L'Abri. In the centre of the smoothly[185] swept back yard was a great bonfire.[186] Armand Aubigny sat in the wide hallway[187] that commanded a view of the spectacle;[188] and it was he who dealt out[189] to a half dozen negroes the material which kept this fire ablaze.[190]

A graceful cradle of willow, with all its dainty[191]

---

180 her tender feet, so delicately shod : 섬세한 신발이 신겨진 그녀의 연한 발

181 tore her thin gown to shreds : 그녀의 얇은 가운을 발기발기 찢었다
    ＊ shred : 가늘고 작은 조각, 갈기갈기 자르다, 채를 썰다

182 sluggish : 완만한, 굼뜬

183 bayou : (미국 남부 지역의) 늪처럼 된 강의 내포(지류)

184 enact : 상연하다, 연기하다

185 smoothly : 부드럽게

186 bonfire : 모닥불

187 hallway : 복도, 현관, 통로

188 that commanded a view of the spectacle : 그 광경이 바라다보이는

189 deal out : 분배하다, 나누어 주다

190 ablaze : 타는

191 dainty : 우아한, 화사한

furbishings,[192] was laid upon the pyre,[193] which had already been fed with the richness of a priceless[194] layette.[195] Then there were silk gowns, and velvet and satin ones added to these; laces, too, and embroideries;[196] bonnets[197] and gloves; for the corbeille[198] had been of rare quality.[199]

The last thing to go was a tiny bundle of letters; innocent little scribblings[200] that Désirée had sent to him during the days of their espousal.[201] There was the remnant[202] of one back in the drawer[203] from which he took them. But it was not Désirée's; it was part of an old letter from his mother to his father. He read it. She was thanking God for the blessing of her husband's love: —

---

192 furbishing : 비치 가구, 비품, 세간, 장신구 * furbish : 닦다, 윤내다
193 pyre : 장작더미
194 priceless : 아주 귀중한, 돈으로 살 수 없는
195 layette : 신생아 용품 일습(배내옷, 침구 따위)
196 embroidery : 자수
197 bonnet : 보닛(턱밑에서 끈을 매는 여자·어린이용의 챙 없는 모자)
198 corbeille : 꽃바구니 장식
199 of rare quality : 드문 품질의
200 scribble : 낙서하다
201 espousal : 약혼, 결혼
202 remnant : 남은 것
203 drawer : 서랍

"But above all," she wrote, "night and day, I thank the good God for having so arranged[204] our lives that our dear Armand will never know that his mother, who adores[205] him, belongs to[206] the race that is cursed with the brand of slavery."[207]

---

204 arrange : 마련하다, 일을 처리하다
205 adore : 흠모하다, 아주 좋아하다
206 belong to : ~에 속하다, 소속되다
207 cursed with the brand of slavery : 노예(제)의 낙인이 찍혀 저주받은
     * brand : 낙인

작품 해설

1. 비극적인 결말

　작가의 여주인공들이 왕왕 맞닥뜨리는 비극적인 결말이나 '갈 길 없음'의 막연한 상태는 당대 여성이 처한 내적·외적 현실의 제반 양태를 총체적으로 생각해 볼 기회를 제공한다. 이런 비극성은 작가의 글쓰기 스타일을 통해 효과적으로 전달된다. 예컨대 Armand이 Désirée와 사랑에 빠져드는 장면을 보자. "정문에서 그녀를 본 그날 그 안에서 깨어난 열정은 산사태처럼, 혹은 프레리의 불길처럼, 모든 장애물을 넘어 저돌적으로 질주하는 무엇처럼 휩쓸고 지나갔다"라는 대목에서 보듯, 작가는 작중인물의 감정을 강렬한 비유를 통해 전달하기 때문에 결말의 비극적 효과가 더욱 배가된다. 그 어떤 장애물도 파괴하고 넘어갈 듯한, Armand의 Désirée에 대한 열정은 피부색(인종주의)이라는 장벽 앞에서 속절없이 무너져 버린다. 아니, 그냥 무너져 버리는 게 아니라 더욱 기세등등하게 되돌아서서 그때까지 소중하게 여겨 온 것들을 향해 걷잡을 수 없이 가혹한 파괴력을 행사한다.

　그렇지만 작가의 문체 자체는 매우 담담하여 거의 메마른 느낌마저 들 정도로 감상성이 배제되어 있다. 즉, 남녀 도덕을 기준으로 한 훈계, 여성의 억압적 처지에 대한 영탄조 등 기타 감상성을 걷어 내고 주요 사실 제시를 중심으로 비극을 그려 낸다.

이것은 분명 주인공들의 비극적인 결말을 망설임 없이 간명하게 드러내 주지만, 자살이라는 결말 외에 다른 삶의 가능성을 찾기 어려운 삶에 직면한 여주인공이 아이를 데리고 가며 행하는 최종적 선택은 독자로 하여금 많은 생각을 하게 한다. Désirée와 아이의 비극적 파국을 좀 더 지연시키며 재고하는 과정에서 궁리해 낼 수도 있을 만한 대안적 삶의 가능성은 없었을까. 혹시 '길 없음'을 너무 일찍 단정해 버린 나머지 모든 대안적 가능성이 한꺼번에 망실된 것은 아닐까 하는 느낌이 없지 않다. 달리 말해 작가가 그려 보이는 결말은 비타협적인 만큼 당대의 (남성 중심) 이데올로기에 대해 비판적이지만 너무나 단호해 미래의 시간이 통째로 날아간 느낌을 준다. 예컨대 "The Storm"처럼 더러 잠시 숨을 돌리듯 일상의 단조로움과 억압에서 놓여나 자유를 호흡하는 순간이 있기는 하나, 이 순간은 그 앞과 뒤의 현실의 시간과는 닿아 있지 않은 고립된 섬 같은 시간으로 남아 있다.

2. 남겨진 이의 시련과 시험

"그는 아이가 태어난 이후로는 그들(노예들) 중 한 명도 처벌하지 않았다"라는 대목은 본래 흑인들에게 가혹하게 굴며 체벌까지도 서슴지 않았던 Armand에게 Désirée와의 관계가 어떻게 구원의 가능성이 될 수 있을지를 암시한다. 그의 급하고 격한 성미는 Désirée와 아이로 인해 순화된 측면이 있다. 하지만 Armand은 아이의 피부색을 Désirée 탓으로 돌리면서 아내, 아이와의 관계를 저버리고 난 뒤 원래의 모습으로, 어찌 보면 더 심각해진 모습으로 돌아간다. "노예들을 다루는 것을 보면, 다름 아닌 사탄의 정신이 갑자기 그를 사로잡은 듯했다"라는 대목에서는 결과적으로 그가 Désirée와 아이를 통해 자신에게 내려진 구원의 가능성을 어떻게 스스로 내팽개쳐 버렸는가를 잘 설명해 준다.

작품의 마지막에 그간의 사태를 밝혀 주면서 독자의 관심을 새롭게 확 끄는 부분은 과연 Armand이 어떻게 살아갈 것인가 하는 점이다. 게다가 Armand은 Désirée와 아이를 죽음으로 몰아낸 장본인이 아니던가. Désirée와 아이를 내팽개친 이유는 Armand이 자신의 가문이 루이지애나에서 가장 오래되고 가장 자부심이 강한 가문 중 하나라고 생각하기 때문이고 알고 보면 인종적 편견 위에 견고하게 자리한 그의 사랑과 결혼의 핵심인 Désirée와 아이가 이 명성에 해악을 끼쳤다고 생각하기 때문일 것이다. 그렇다면 아이의 피부색이 모친의 피에 섞인 흑인 피, 즉, 다름 아닌 바로 자신 안에 흐르는 흑인 피 때문임을 알게 된 Armand은 어떻게 될 것인가? 자신의 잘못을 깨닫고 Désirée와 아이를 찾아 나설 것인가? 자신의 잘못으로 그들을 잃었다는 자괴감으로 비참한 인생을 살게 될 것인가? 아니면, 어찌됐든 아내와 아이의 문제는 안중에도 없고 오로지 자기 몸에 지금껏 그렇게나 경멸해 오던 흑인의 피가 섞인 것을 견디지 못해 자살하고 말 것인가? 흑인들과의 관계는 어떻게 될 것인가? 그들과 좀 더 부드러운 관계를 형성하게 될까? 아니면, 자신의 신원을 숨기는 동시에 마치 자신의 신원을 들키기라도 할까 봐두려워하며 훨씬 더 가혹하게 굴 것인가? 남겨진 Armand의 앞날에는 여러 물음표가 붙는다.

어떤 경우든 간에 인종주의에 갇혀 그 바깥으로 나오지 못하는 한, Armand이 마주한 날들은 지옥의 시간이 될 것이다. 어쩌면 Armand

의 운명은 인종주의에 갇혀 서로를 대해야 하는 미국 전체의 운명이 될 수도 있다. 본연적으로 깊은 관계를 맺고자 하지만, 막상 깊은 관계로 들어가서 후세를 통해 상대방의 몸속에 흐르는 피의 성분이 확연히 드러나고 나면 그 진실을 감당할 수 없기 때문에 진정한 인간관계 형성에서 장애를 겪을 수 있다.

이렇듯 이 작품에서 인종주의는 '사랑'으로도 넘어설 수 없는 거대한 벽으로 설정되어 있다. 어떤 종교나 이념을 통해 옹호될지는 몰라도 인종주의는 인종적 타자로 간주된 인물의 삶을 벼랑 끝으로 밀어 버릴 뿐만 아니라 갱생의 기회를 얻어 가해자의 위치에서 벗어날 수 있을지도 모를 Armand 같은 인물까지도 악마의 손아귀에 들어가게 한다.

영미 명작 단편선_5

The Gift of the Magi

O. Henry

O. Henry(1862~1910)는 William Sydney Porter의 필명이다. 노스캐롤라이나에서 태어난 그는 세 살 때 모친이 결핵으로 사망한 뒤 아버지와 함께 할머니집으로 이주하여 살았다. 약사 자격증을 취득해 일하는 한편, 그림 등의 예술적 재능을 발휘했다. 건강상의 이유로 텍사스로 이주하여 건축 제도사, 은행원, 저널리스트 등의 일을 했는데 은행에서의 횡령 혐의로 복역을 했다. 1901년 복역을 마치고 출소한 뒤, 왕성한 저작과 출판을 위해 뉴욕으로 이주하여 1년 이상 1주일에 1편의 이야기를 썼다. 뉴욕 체재 시 381편이나 집필했고 일생에 걸쳐 전체 거의 600편에 이르는 단편소설을 남겼다. 과도한 음주로 건강이 악화되어 일찍 생을 마감했다. 대부분의 이야기는 작가 당대인 20세기 초의 뉴욕 시를 배경으로 하며 은행원, 경찰관, 웨이트리스 등 보통 사람들의 삶을 다룬다. 위트, 말장난, 예기치 않은 결말 등으로 잘 알려졌으며 모파상에 비견되기도 하는데 작가의 이런 특징을 잘 보여 주는 작품이 널리 알려진 "The Gift of the Magi"(1905)이다. 흥미로운 소재를 다루지만 의외로 원문 읽기가 만만치 않은 이 단편소설은, 가난하지만 서로에게 최상의 선물을 해 주고 싶어 하는 젊은 부부의 크리스마스이브 에피소드를 다룬다.

The Gift of the Magi

One dollar and eighty-seven cents. That was all. And sixty
cents of it was in pennies. Pennies saved[1] one and two at a
time by bulldozing[2] the grocer and the vegetable man and the
butcher until one's cheeks burned with the silent imputation

5 of parsimony that such close dealing implied.[3] Three times
Della counted it. One dollar and eighty-seven cents. And the
next day would be Christmas.

There was clearly nothing to do but flop down[4] on the

---

1 pennies saved : 저축한 푼돈 *penny : <미국> 1센트 동전

2 bulldoze : 강행하다, 막무가내로 밀어붙이다

3 burned with the silent imputation of parsimony that such close dealing
   implied : 그런 악착스러운 거래가 은연중에 풍기게 되는 노랑이짓(돈에 인
   색함)에 대한 말없는 타박으로 낯이 뜨거워졌다 *burn : 화끈해지다, 타는
   듯이 느끼다, (붉게) 타오르다 *imputation : (책임) 전가, 돌리기, 지우기
   *parsimony : 절약, 인색 *imply : 암시하다

4 flop down : 털썩 주저앉다

shabby[5] little couch and howl.[6] So Della did it. Which instigates the moral reflection[7] that life is made up of[8] sobs, sniffles,[9] and smiles, with sniffles predominating.[10]

While the mistress of the home is gradually subsiding[11] from the first stage to the second, take a look at the home.[12] A furnished flat[13] at $8 per week. It did not exactly beggar description,[14] but it certainly had that word on the lookout for the mendicancy squad.[15]

---

5 shabby : 초라한

6 howl : 울부짖다

7 Which instigates the moral reflection : 이것(앞의 행동)이 ~라는 교훈적인 성찰을 부추기는 법이다 *instigate : 부추기다. '앞의 행동을 하다 보면 ~ 라는 교훈적인 성찰이 부쩍 들게 마련이다'는 의미임.

8 be made up of : ~로 만들어진(구성된)

9 sniffle : 훌쩍임, 코를 킁킁거림

10 predominate : 우세하다, 주되다

11 subside : 가라앉다

12 take a look at the home : 집 안을 둘러보시오 *마치 연극이 벌어지는 장 면을 앞에 두고 내레이터가 관중에게 '주인공이 이러는 사이, 자, 우리는 ~ 합시다'식으로 말을 거는 형식을 취하고 있음.

13 a furnished flat : 가구가 갖추어진 아파트

14 beggar description : 필설로 다할 수 없다 *beggar : (표현, 비교를) 무력 (빈약)하게 하다

15 that word on the lookout for the mendicancy squad : 거지(혹은 노숙자) 단속반이 들이닥칠까 봐 망 보고 있는 그 단어(beggar) *mendicancy : 구 걸, 탁발, 거지 신세 cf. vagrancy squad : 부랑자 단속반. 이 대목은 작가가

In the vestibule below was a letter-box into which no letter would go, and an electric button from which no mortal finger could coax a ring.[16] Also appertaining[17] thereunto was a card bearing the name "Mr. James Dillingham Young."

The "Dillingham" had been flung to the breeze[18] during a former period of prosperity when its possessor was being paid $30 per week. Now, when the income was shrunk to

---

'beggar'라는 낱말을 가지고 말재간을 부리고 있는 것으로 볼 수 있음. 앞 문장의 'beggar description'에서 'beggar'는 동사로 쓰여 '묘사하기가 어렵다'라는 의미가 되었는데, 지금 이 문장에서 'that word'는 명사 'beggar', 즉 '거지'의 의미로 쓰였다고 볼 수 있음. 즉, 주인공이 세 든 집안 꼴이 너무 보잘것없어 거지 단속반이 들이닥칠까 봐 망을 보고 있는 거지가 기겁할 법할 정도임을 묘사한다고 할 수 있음.

16 an electric button from which no mortal finger could coax a ring : 어떤 인간의 손가락도 벨 소리가 나도록 구슬릴 수 없는 전기 버튼 ＊고장이 나서 울리지 않는 초인종을 이렇게 표현하고 있음. 바로 앞에 '어떤 편지도 들어가지 않을 우편함'이라는 표현도 우편함이 제대로 활용되기보다는 대충 우편물들을 쌓아 놓으면 각각 알아서 찾아가는 이 아파트의 영락한 이미지를 잘 전달하고 있음.

17 appertain : 속하다, 부속되다, 관계하다

18 The "Dillingham" had been flung to the breeze : "Dillingham"이라는 이름이 산들바람에 내맡겨져 나부꼈다 ＊flung : fling(내던지다)의 과거분사. 상대적으로 수입이 좋을 때는 이름 역시 바람에 나부끼며 쫙 펴져서 철자가 모두 제대로 다 보였지만, 바로 다음의 대목처럼 수입이 줄고 나니 이름 역시 쪼그라들어 'D'만 남았다며 비유와 말재주를 보이고 있음.

$20, though, they were thinking seriously of contracting[19] to a modest and unassuming[20] D. But whenever Mr. James Dillingham Young came home and reached his flat above he was called "Jim" and greatly hugged by Mrs. James Dillingham Young, already introduced to you as Della. Which is all very good.

Della finished her cry and attended to[21] her cheeks with the powder rag. She stood by the window and looked out dully[22] at a gray cat walking a gray fence in a gray backyard. Tomorrow would be Christmas Day, and she had only $1.87 with which to buy Jim a present. She had been saving every penny she could for months, with this result. Twenty dollars a week doesn't go far.[23] Expenses had been greater than she had calculated.[24] They always are. Only $1.87 to buy a present for Jim. Her Jim. Many a happy hour she had spent planning for something nice for him. Something fine and rare and

---

19 contract : 줄어들다, 줄이다, 축소하다
20 unassuming : 주제넘지 않는
21 attend to : 처리하다, 돌보다
22 dully : 멍하니
23 go far : 성공하다, 충분하다, 쓸 품이 있다
24 calculate : 계산하다

sterling[25]—something just a little bit near to being worthy of the honor of being owned by Jim.[26]

There was a pier-glass[27] between the windows of the room. Perhaps you have seen a pier-glass in an $8 flat. A very thin and very agile person may, by observing his reflection in a rapid sequence of longitudinal strips, obtain a fairly accurate conception of his looks.[28] Della, being slender,[29] had mastered[30] the art.[31]

---

25 sterling : 순은, 진짜의

26 being worthy of the honor of being owned by Jim : 짐에 의해 소유될 영광을 누릴 가치가 있음 ＊worthy of : ~할 가치가 있는

27 pier-glass : 큰 거울, 체경(體鏡)

28 A very thin and very agile person may, by observing his reflection in a rapid sequence of longitudinal strips, obtain a fairly accurate conception of his looks : 아주 가냘프고 그러면서도 아주 민첩한 사람이라면 빠르게 연속되는 세로로 길쭉한 조각들에 자신이 비친 모습을 관찰함으로써 자신의 외모를 상당히 정확하게 파악할 수 있을지 모른다 ＊sequence : 연속 ＊longitudinal : 세로의, 경도(經度)의 ＊strip : (햇살 등의) 길쭉한 조각 ＊conception : 개념, 파악, 이해. 좁은 셋집 내부의 창문들 사이, 폭이 아주 좁은 벽에 세로로 길쭉한 거울이 걸려 있는데 그 폭이 좁다 보니 한 번에 온몸을 비춰 볼 수 없기 때문에 빠르게 좌우로 움직여 거기에 비친 신체의 모습들을 연속해서 이어 붙여 조합해야 온몸을 알 수 있음을 다소 코믹하게 전달하고 있음.

29 slender : 호리호리한

30 master : ~에 숙달하다, 정통하다, 길들이다, ~의 주인이 되다

31 art : 기술, 기교

Suddenly she whirled[32] from the window and stood before the glass. Her eyes were shining brilliantly, but her face had lost its color within twenty seconds. Rapidly she pulled down her hair and let it fall to its full length.[33]

Now, there were two possessions[34] of the James Dillingham Youngs in which they both took a mighty[35] pride. One was Jim's gold watch that had been his father's and his grandfather's. The other was Della's hair. Had the queen of Sheba[36] lived in the flat across the airshaft,[37] Della would have let her hair hang out[38] the window some day to dry just to depreciate[39] Her Majesty's[40] jewels and gifts. Had King

---

32 whirl: 회전하다, 빙그르르 돌다
33 to its full length: 최대한도의 길이로
34 possession: 소유물
35 mighty: 강력한, 대단한
36 the queen of Sheba: 고대 왕국 Sheba의 여왕이었다는 전설상의 인물(솔로몬 왕과 관계된, 성서에 나오는 인물)
37 airshaft: 환기통
38 hang out: 밖으로 내다 걸다, 밖에서 말리다
39 depreciate: 가치를 떨어뜨리다 ＊ 'just to depreciate'는 부정사의 결과적 용법으로 해석하여 'Della가 머리를 말리려고 창밖으로 머리 타래를 늘어뜨렸더라면 오직(정말) Sheba의 보석과 재능 들의 가치를 뚝 떨어뜨렸을 것이다'라는 의미로 파악할 수 있음.
40 Her Majesty: 여왕 폐하

Solomon[41] been the janitor, with all his treasures piled up[42] in the basement, Jim would have pulled out[43] his watch every time he passed, just to see him pluck at his beard from envy.[44]

So now Della's beautiful hair fell about her rippling[45] and shining like a cascade[46] of brown waters. It reached below her knee and made itself almost a garment for her. And then she did it up[47] again nervously and quickly. Once she faltered[48] for a minute and stood still while a tear or two splashed[49] on the worn[50] red carpet.

On went her old brown jacket; on went her old brown hat. With a whirl of skirts and with the brilliant sparkle[51] still in

---

41 King Solomon : 성서에 나오는 솔로몬 왕(다윗 왕의 아들이자 고대 이스라엘 왕국의 강력한 왕)

42 pile up : 쌓다

43 pull out : ~을 빼내다, 뽑아내다

44 pluck at his beard from envy : 부러워서 수염을 잡아 뜯다

45 ripple : 잔물결을 일으키다

46 cascade : 작은 폭포

47 do up : 손질하다

48 falter : 비틀거리다

49 splash : 튀기다, 텀벙하다

50 worn : 닳은

51 sparkle : 번쩍임

her eyes, she fluttered[52] out the door and down the stairs to the street.

Where she stopped the sign read: "Mme. Sofronie. Hair Goods[53] of All Kinds." One flight[54] up Della ran, and collected herself,[55] panting.[56] Madame, large, too white, chilly, hardly looked the "Sofronie."

"Will you buy my hair?" asked Della.

"I buy hair," said Madame. "Take yer[57] hat off and let's have a sight at[58] the looks of it."

Down rippled the brown cascade.

"Twenty dollars," said Madame, lifting the mass[59] with a practised hand.[60]

"Give it to me quick," said Della.

---

52 flutter: 파닥이다, 동요하다, 훨훨 날아가다
53 goods: 상품, 품목
54 flight: 층
55 collect oneself: 진정시키다
56 pant: 헐떡이다
57 yer: your
58 have a sigh at: ~를 한 번 보다
59 mass: 덩어리
60 with a practised hand: 익숙한 솜씨로

Oh, and the next two hours tripped[61] by on rosy wings.[62] Forget the hashed[63] metaphor.[64] She was ransacking[65] the stores for Jim's present.

She found it at last. It surely had been made for Jim and no one else. There was no other like it in any of the stores, and she had turned all of them inside out.[66] It was a platinum[67] fob chain[68] simple and chaste[69] in design, properly proclaiming its value by substance alone and not by meretricious ornamentation[70] — as all good things should do. It was even worthy of The Watch. As soon as she saw it she knew that it must be Jim's. It was like him. Quietness and value — the

---

61 trip : 경쾌하게 걷다
62 on wings : (마음이 들떠서) 가벼운 발걸음으로
63 hash : 아무렇게나 뒤섞다
64 metaphor : 비유, 은유
65 ransack : 샅샅이 뒤지다
66 turn inside out : (안팎을) 뒤집다
67 platinum : 백금
68 fob chain : 시곗줄
69 chaste : 순결한, 품위 있는
70 properly proclaiming its value by substance alone and not by meretricious ornamentation : 겉만 번지르르한 장식이 아니라 재질만으로도 그 가치를 제대로 증명하는(분명히 나타내는) * meretricious : 겉치레만의, 저속한

description applied to both.[71] Twenty-one dollars they took from her for it, and she hurried home with the 87 cents. With that chain on his watch Jim might be properly anxious about the time in any company.[72] Grand as the watch was, he sometimes looked at it on the sly[73] on account of[74] the old 5 leather strap that he used in place of[75] a chain.

When Della reached home her intoxication[76] gave way a little to[77] prudence[78] and reason. She got out her curling irons[79] and lighted the gas and went to work repairing the ravages made by generosity added to love.[80] Which is always a 10

---

71 applied to both : 둘 다(시계와 Jim)에 적용되었다

72 Jim might be properly anxious about the time in any company : Jim은 어떤 사람들과 있어도 시간에 대해 예의 바르게(정정당당하게) 알고 싶어 할 것이다 ＊어떤 사람들과 함께 있을지라도 현재 시각이 얼마일지 꽤 궁금할 때, 시곗줄이 부끄러워 몰래 볼 필요 없이 '제대로(당당하게)' 시계를 보게 될 것이라는 말임.

73 on the sly : 살그머니, 남모르게

74 on account of : ~ 때문에

75 in place of : ~의 자리에(대신하여)

76 intoxication : 흥분, 도취

77 give way to : ~에 자리를(길을, 위치를) 내주다

78 prudence : 신중함

79 curling iron : 머리에 컬을 넣는 기구

80 went to work repairing the ravages made by generosity added to love : 사랑에 너그러움이 더해져 일어난 참화(머리칼을 확 자른 일)를 회복시키는

tremendous[81] task,[82] dear friends — a mammoth[83] task.

Within forty minutes her head was covered with tiny, close-lying curls that made her look wonderfully like a truant schoolboy.[84] She looked at her reflection in the mirror long, carefully, and critically.

"If Jim doesn't kill me," she said to herself, "before he takes a second look at me, he'll say I look like a Coney Island[85] chorus girl. But what could I do — oh! what could I do with a dollar and eighty-seven cents?"

At 7 o'clock the coffee was made and the frying-pan was on the back of the stove hot and ready to cook the chops.[86]

Jim was never late. Della doubled[87] the fob chain in her hand and sat on the corner of the table near the door that he always entered. Then she heard his step on the stair away down on

---

일을 시작했다 ＊go to work : 일을 시작하다, 착수하다 ＊ravage : 손해, 파괴, 약탈

81 tremendous : 엄청난
82 task : 일, 과업
83 mammoth : 거대한
84 a truant schoolboy : 무단결석한 학생
85 Coney Island : 뉴욕 시 롱아일랜드에 있는 해안 유원지
86 chop : 두꺼운 토막 고기
87 double : 두 겹이 되게 하다, 둘로 접다

the first flight,[88] and she turned white for just a moment. She had a habit for saying little silent prayer about the simplest everyday things, and now she whispered: "Please God, make him think I am still pretty."

The door opened and Jim stepped in and closed it. He looked thin and very serious. Poor fellow, he was only twenty-two — and to be burdened[89] with a family! He needed a new overcoat and he was without gloves.

Jim stopped inside the door, as immovable[90] as a setter at the scent of quail.[91] His eyes were fixed upon[92] Della, and there was an expression in them that she could not read, and it terrified[93] her. It was not anger, nor surprise, nor

---

88 on the stair away down on the first flight : 계단 저 아래 첫 번째 층계에
     ＊건물의 층과 층 사이의 계단 전체를 'stairs'라고 하고, 한 개 층을 올라갈
     때 대개 중간에 꺾어 도는 지점이 있는데 이를 층계참(landing)이라고 하며
     층계참을 사이에 둔 나머지 경사 계단들을 'flight'라고 함.
89 burden : 짐을 지우다
90 immovable : 움직일 수 없는, 움직이지 않는
91 as a setter at the scent of quail : 메추라기의 냄새를 맡은 사냥개처럼
     ＊setter : 사냥감의 위치를 알려 주는 사냥개
92 be fixed upon : ~에 고정되어 있다
93 terrify : 겁에 질리게 하다

disapproval,[94] nor horror, nor any of the sentiments[95] that she had been prepared for.[96] He simply stared at her fixedly[97] with that peculiar expression on his face.

Della wriggled[98] off the table and went for him.

5 "Jim, darling," she cried, "don't look at me that way. I had my hair cut off and sold because I couldn't have lived through[99] Christmas without giving you a present. It'll grow out[100] again — you won't mind, will you? I just had to do it. My hair grows awfully fast. Say 'Merry Christmas!' Jim, and

10 let's be happy. You don't know what a nice — what a beautiful, nice gift I've got for you."

"You've cut off your hair?" asked Jim, laboriously,[101] as if he had not arrived at that patent fact[102] yet even after the hardest mental labor.[103]

---

94 disapproval : 불만, 비난, 불찬성
95 sentiment : 감정
96 been prepared for : 대비하다, 각오하다
97 fixedly : 꼼짝 않고, 고정된 채로
98 wriggle : 몸을 비틀며(꿈틀대며) 나아가다, 꿈틀거리다
99 live through : ~을 헤쳐 나가다, 버텨 내다
100 grow out : 다시 자라다
101 laboriously : 힘들게, 수고스럽게
102 a patent fact : 명백한 사실
103 even after the hardest mental labor : 아무리 힘들게 정신적인 산고를 거

"Cut it off and sold it," said Della. "Don't you like me just as well,[104] anyhow? I'm me without my hair, ain't[105] I?"

Jim looked about the room curiously.[106]

"You say your hair is gone?" he said, with an air almost of idiocy.[107]

"You needn't look for it," said Della. "It's sold, I tell you — sold and gone, too. It's Christmas Eve, boy. Be good to me, for it went for you. Maybe the hairs of my head were numbered,"[108] she went on with sudden serious sweetness, "but nobody could ever count my love for you. Shall I put the chops on, Jim?"

Out of his trance[109] Jim seemed quickly to wake. He enfolded[110] his Della. For ten seconds let us regard with discreet scrutiny some inconsequential object in the other

---

치고 난 뒤에도 ＊labor : 고역, 산고, 진통
104 just as well : 꼭 마찬가지로
105 ain't : am not의 줄임말
106 curiously : 호기심에 찬 눈길로, 의아하게
107 idiocy : 멍청함
108 number : 헤아리다
109 trance : 홀린 상태, 비몽사몽
110 enfold : 껴안다

direction.[111] Eight dollars a week or a million a year — what is the difference? A mathematician or a wit[112] would give you the wrong answer. The magi[113] brought valuable gifts, but that was not among them. This dark assertion[114] will be illuminated[115] later on.[116]

Jim drew a package from his overcoat pocket and threw it upon the table.

"Don't make any mistake, Dell," he said, "about me. I don't think there's anything in the way of a haircut or a shave or a shampoo that could make me like my girl any less. But if you'll unwrap[117] that package you may see why you had me going a while at first."[118]

---

111 regard with discreet scrutiny some inconsequential object in the other direction : 어떤 사소한 대상을 신중한 조사를 통해 다른 방향에서 주목해서 보다 *discreet : 신중한, 조심스러운 *scrutiny : 정밀한 조사, 감시

112 wit : 기지가 풍부한 사람

113 the magi : 동방 박사

114 assertion : 주장, 단언, 자기주장

115 illuminate : 밝히다, (문제 따위를) 해명(설명)하다, 계몽하다

116 later on : 추후에

117 unwrap : ~의 포장을 풀다, (꾸러미 따위를) 끄르다, 열다

118 why you had me going a while at first : 왜 당신이 처음에 잠깐 동안 나를 멍하게 했는지 *going : 흥분되는, 두려운, 걱정되는

White fingers and nimble[119] tore at the string and paper. And then an ecstatic scream of joy;[120] and then, alas![121] a quick feminine change to hysterical tears and wails,[122] necessitating the immediate employment of all the comforting powers of the lord of the flat.[123]

For there lay The Combs — the set of combs, side and back, that Della had worshipped long in a Broadway window. Beautiful combs, pure tortoise shell,[124] with jewelled rims[125] — just the shade to wear in the beautiful vanished hair.[126] They were expensive combs, she knew, and her heart had simply

---

119 White fingers and nimble : = White and nimble fingers. 희고 재빠른 손
    가락들
120 an ecstatic scream of joy : 무아지경의 기쁨의 환호성
121 alas : 아아, 슬프도다, 불쌍한지고
122 hysterical tears and wails : 히스테릭한 눈물과 울부짖음
123 necessitating the immediate employment of all the comforting powers
    of the lord of the flat : 아파트 주인(Jim)이 지닌 모든 위로의 능력을 즉각
    적으로 동원할 필요가 있는 *necessitate : 필요로 하다 *employment :
    동원, 사용, 사역
124 tortoise shell : 거북딱지(껍질)
125 with jewelled rims : 보석으로 테를 두른
126 just the shade to wear in the beautiful vanished hair : 사라진 아름다운 머
    리칼에 꽂으면 어울릴 딱 그런 색깔 *shade : 색조, 기미, 그늘, 음영

craved[127] and yearned[128] over them without the least hope of possession. And now, they were hers, but the tresses that should have adorned the coveted adornments[129] were gone.

But she hugged them to her bosom, and at length she was able to look up with dim eyes and a smile and say: "My hair grows so fast, Jim!"

And them Della leaped up[130] like a little singed[131] cat and cried, "Oh, oh!"

Jim had not yet seen his beautiful present. She held it out to him eagerly upon her open palm. The dull precious metal seemed to flash[132] with a reflection of her bright and ardent[133] spirit.

"Isn't it a dandy,[134] Jim? I hunted[135] all over town to find it.

---

127 crave : 열망하다, 간청하다, 필요로 하다
128 yearn : 동경하다, 그리워하다
129 the tresses that should have adorned the coveted adornments : 그 탐
     나는 장식품을 장식해 주어야 할 머리 타래 *tress : 삼단 같은 머리털
     *adorn : 꾸미다, 돋보이게 하다 *covet : 탐내다
130 leap up : 뛰어오르다
131 singe : 그슬리다, 태우다
132 flash : 번쩍이다
133 ardent : 열렬한, 격렬한, 불타는 듯한
134 dandy : 멋있는 것, 굉장히 좋은 것
135 hunt : 찾아 헤매다, 뒤지다

You'll have to look at the time[136] a hundred times a day now.
Give me your watch. I want to see how it looks on it."

Instead of obeying, Jim tumbled[137] down on the couch and
put his hands under the back of his head and smiled.

"Dell," said he, "let's put our Christmas presents away and 5
keep 'em a while. They're too nice to use just at present. I sold
the watch to get the money to buy your combs. And now
suppose[138] you put the chops on."

"The magi, as you know, were wise men — wonderfully
wise men — who brought gifts to the Babe in the manger.[139] 10
They invented the art of giving Christmas presents. Being
wise, their gifts were no doubt wise ones, possibly bearing
the privilege of exchange in case of duplication.[140] And here I
have lamely[141] related[142] to you the uneventful[143] chronicle[144]

---

136 look at the time : 시간을 확인하다
137 tumble : 비틀거리다
138 suppose : ~해야만 하다, 예정이다, 추정하다, 생각하다
139 the Babe in the manger : 말 구유에서 태어난 아기 예수
140 possibly bearing the privilege of exchange in case of duplication : 어쩌면
      중복될 경우 교환할 수 있을 특권을 지니는 * duplication : 겹침, 중복
141 lamely : 불충분하게, 변변찮게
142 relate : 이야기하다
143 uneventful : 무사 평온한, 평범한
144 chronicle : 연대기, 이야기, 역사

of two foolish children in a flat who most unwisely sacrificed for each other the greatest treasures of their house. But in a last word to the wise of these days let it be said that of all who give gifts these two were the wisest. Of all who give and receive gifts, such as they are wisest. Everywhere they are wisest. They are the magi.

작품 해설

1. 반전(twist)을 지닌 결말(ending)

이 이야기의 총체적이고 핵심적인 효과는 결말의 '반전'에서 나온다. 반전의 양상을 두 가지 차원에서 살펴볼 수 있다. 우선, 표층적인 차원에서 보면, 빈궁한 처지의 부부가 상대방에게 좋은 선물을 사 줄 돈을 마련하기 위해 자신의 가장 소중한 것을 팔아 상대방의 가장 소중한 물건에 어울리는 선물을 산다. 하지만 이미 상대방의 소중한 그것이 처분되었기 때문에 선물 자체도 당장은 쓸모가 없어졌다는 다소 어처구니 없는 상황이 발생한다. 즉, 상대방에게 최상의 선물을 마련하는 과정이 자기 최상의 소유물을 처분하는 과정과 정확히 일치한다. 생각을 거듭해 나온 각자의 묘수는 한 지점에서 만나 이제는 사라지고 없는 것, 그 부재에 대한 강력한 기표가 된다. 선물의 극적 효과를 높이기 위한 깜짝 선물이 정작 상대방을 고려하지 않은 자기 멋대로의 결정과 행동이 되어 그야말로 '깜짝스럽기만 한' 것이 될 우려를 잘 보여 준다.

이 어처구니없는 엇갈림을 어리석은 행동이라고 쉽게 비판하지 못하는 부분은 이 두 부부의 서로에 대한 뜨거운 감정일 것이다. 상대방을 위해 생각하고 공들인 선물이 아니었다면 이와 같은 극단적 반전은 불가능했을 것이다. 이들의 선물이 당장의 '실패'와 '낭패'에 이르는 것은 바로 상대방에 대한 '배려'에서 나온다.

이들의 '실패'는 아이러니하게도 그 어떤 선물의 '성공'보다도 상대방의 가슴을 깊이 사로잡는 효과를 지닌다는 의미에서, 그 어떤 특정한 선물이 물질적 차원에서 거둘 수 있는 것 이상의 비물질적인 '성공'을 거둔다. 이런 점에서 보면, 이 두 남녀는 선물을 통해 추구되는 최종적 효과를 극적으로 달성한 셈이다.

다만 이들이 얻은 비물질적인 차원의 교감과 성취는 상대방에 대한 성숙한 존중과 앞날에 대한 설계에 따라 깊이 있게 기획되고 실천되었다고 보기는 어렵다. 아직은 성숙하지 못한 관계, 아직은 깊이를 얻지 못한 관계에서 상대방을 위해 자신의 감정을 '물질적으로' 표하려던 노력이 어쩌다 보니 궁핍의 밑그림에 다소 자학의 정서를 여백으로 하여 얼마간 괜찮은 습작 같은 것이었을 수 있다.

2. 반전의 의미에 대하여

한편, 가난하지만 서로 사랑하는 젊은 부부가 상대방을 위해 자신으로서는 상당히 큰 희생을 감수하면서 비밀스럽게 준비한 크리스마스 선물이 실제로는 상대방의 생각과 행동의 범주에서 완전히 벗어난 일이 되고 말았다는 역설을 어떻게 이해해야 할 것인가? 상대방을 사랑한다고 암묵적으로 내세운 정도와 상대방을 둘러싼 제반 상황에 대한 이해와 예측 사이의 차이마저도 소위 '사랑'의 강도를 더해 주는 비극적인 재료가 되는 것인가?

결말의 반전은 감상성을 고조시키려는 다소 과장되고 억지스러운 반전은 아닐까. (자기 생각에 따라) 상대방을 '위한답시고' (제멋대로) 해

준 일이 애초에 의도한 결과로부터 한껏 비극적인 차이를 만들며 비켜 갈 때 발생하는 주된 정서가 자학적이고 카타르시스적인 쾌감 쪽에 가깝지 진정한 사랑과는 관계가 없는 게 아니냐고 까칠하고 비판적으로 바라볼 여지는 없을까. 하지만 이렇게 자기만의 생각과 판단에 따른 행위들이 일상적으로, 또 중요한 계기마다 반복된다면 모를까, 이번 한 번의 에피소드를 가지고 그렇게 침소봉대할 필요도 없을 듯하다. 다시 생각해 보면, 이 부부의 크리스마스 선물 교환 행위에서 어떤 정신적인 면은 살아날지 모르지만 엇갈린 물건 자체는 '실패'가 아니냐고 꼭 단정 지을 필요는 없을지 모른다. Della 말대로 그녀의 머리는 '빨리' 자랄 것이며, 그때까지 남편이 선물한 머리빗은 자신의 아름다운 외양에 더해 두 사람 사이의 소중한 시간과 의미를 안으로 새기며 더 특별한 머리빗이 되어 갈 것이다.

그렇다면 할아버지에서 아버지를 거쳐 물려받은 금시계가 없어진 상황에서 Jim이 선물 받은 시곗줄은 어떤 가치를 지닐까. 지금 당장은 무용지물일 것이고 또 언제 실제로 쓰이게 될지 기약할 수 없을지는 모르나 자신들의 삶 전체를 업그레이드시키고 그 줄에 걸맞은 새로운 시계를 마련하려는 노력을 자극하고 격려하는 역할에서 이 시곗줄만큼 커다란 역할을 할 수 있는 증표를 찾기는 힘들 것이다. 이들의 엇갈린 선물을 아직은 어린 젊은 부부가 자신들의 불투명한 앞날에 서로에 대한 소중한 생각을 담아 던져놓은, 웃음과 눈물을 동시에 머금은 약속으로 여겨 주는 게 어떨까.

영미 명작 단편선_6

The Curious Case of Benjamin Button

Francis Scott Fitzgerald

Francis Scott Fitzgerald(1896~1940)는 미네소타주 세인트 폴(Saint Paul)의 명문가에서 태어났다. 그는 프린스턴 대학 재학 중 제1차 세계대전이 발발하자 남부에서 군 복무를 했는데 이 때의 경험이 작품의 주요한 모티프가 되기도 했다. *The Great Gatsby*(1925)는 출간된 이래 오늘날까지 미국인뿐만 아니라 전 세계적으로 널리 읽혀 온 작품으로 이후 Fitzgerald는 1920년 대를 대표하는 작가로 군림하게 되었다. Fitzgerald의 삶과 소 설은 소위 '재즈 시대'(Jazz Age)로 명명되는 1920년대의 문화— 돈과 성공과 쾌락 추구를 삶의 목표로 삼는 젊은 세대의 사치스 러운 문화—를 여실하게 반영하고 있다. "The Curious Case of Benjamin Button"(1922)의 주인공 Button은 70세의 언어와 사 고 능력, 그리고 육체를 지닌 채 태어난다. 이 작품은 남들의 정 상적인 성장 과정과는 정반대로 세월이 갈수록 점차 어려지다가 마침내 태어나기 전의 상태로 회귀하는 주인공의 '특이하고 기 이한' 사례에 대한 코믹하고 풍자적이며 비극적인 탐구이다.

The Curious Case of Benjamin Button

Chapter I

As long ago as 1860 it was the proper thing to be born at home. At present, so I am told, the high gods of medicine[1] have decreed that the first cries of the young shall be uttered upon the anaesthetic[2] air of a hospital, preferably[3] a fashionable[4] one. So young Mr. and Mrs. Roger Button were fifty years ahead of[5] style when they decided, one day in the summer of 1860, that their first baby should be born in a

5

---

1 the high gods of medicine: (오늘날의) 지고한 신과 같으신 의학계의 권위자들
2 anaesthetic: 마취제의
3 preferably: 되도록
4 fashionable: 사교계의, 상류사회의, 유행의
5 ahead of: 시대를 앞선

hospital. Whether this anachronism[6] had any bearing upon[7] the astonishing history I am about to set down[8] will never be known.

I shall tell you what occurred, and let you judge for yourself. The Roger Buttons held an enviable[9] position, both social and financial, in ante-bellum[10] Baltimore. They were related to the This Family and the That Family, which, as every Southerner knew, entitled them to membership[11] in that enormous peerage[12] which largely populated[13] the Confederacy.[14] This was their first experience with the charming old custom of having babies — Mr. Button was naturally nervous. He hoped it would be a boy so that he could be sent to Yale College in Connecticut, at which institution[15] Mr. Button himself had been known for four years by the somewhat obvious

---

6 anachronism : 시대착오적인 것

7 have any bearing upon : 어떤 관계를 지니다

8 set down : 적어 두다

9 enviable : 부러운, 샘 나는

10 ante-bellum : (미국 남북)전쟁 전의

11 entitled them to membership : 그들에게 멤버의 자격을 부여했다

12 peerage : 귀족적 지위

13 populate : 살다, ~에 사람을 거주케 하다

14 confederacy : 미국 남부 연합국

15 institution : 기관

nickname of "Cuff."[16]

On the September morning consecrated to the enormous event[17] he arose nervously at six o'clock dressed himself, adjusted an impeccable[18] stock,[19] and hurried forth[20] through the streets of Baltimore to the hospital, to determine whether the darkness of the night had borne in new life upon its bosom.

When he was approximately[21] a hundred yards from the Maryland Private Hospital for Ladies and Gentlemen he saw Doctor Keene, the family physician,[22] descending the front steps, rubbing his hands together with a washing movement — as all doctors are required to do by the unwritten ethics of their profession.[23]

---

16 cuff : 장식용 소매 끝동 * cuff button : 커프스 버튼

17 On the September morning consecrated to the enormous event : 그 엄청난 사건에 봉헌된 그 9월 아침에 * 작가는 과장과 풍자가 섞인 톤을 계속 유지해 가고 있음.

18 impeccable : 나무랄 데 없는

19 stock : = a broad scarf. 칼라와 넥타이를 겸용한 폭넓은 스카프

20 hurry forth : (앞으로) 달려 나가다, 쇄도해 나가다

21 approximately : 대략

22 family physician : = family doctor. 가정의 주치의, 가족 의사

23 by the unwritten ethics of their profession : 그들 직업(의사)의 불문 윤리에 의거해

Mr. Roger Button, the president of Roger Button & Co., Wholesale Hardware,[24] began to run toward Doctor Keene with much less dignity than was expected from a Southern gentleman of that picturesque period.[25] "Doctor Keene!" he called. "Oh, Doctor Keene!"

The doctor heard him, faced around,[26] and stood waiting, a curious expression settling on his harsh, medicinal face as Mr. Button drew near.

"What happened?" demanded[27] Mr. Button, as he came up in a gasping rush.[28] "What was it? How is she? A boy? Who is it? What —"

"Talk sense!"[29] said Doctor Keene sharply, He appeared somewhat irritated.[30]

"Is the child born?" begged Mr. Button.

---

24 wholesale hardware: 도매 철물
25 with much less dignity than was expected from a Southern gentleman of that picturesque period: 그 그림 같은(고풍스러운) 시대의 남부 신사로부터 기대되는 것에서 한참 모자라는 위엄으로
26 face around: 방향을 돌리다
27 demand: 묻다, 힐문하다, 말하라고 다그치다
28 in a gasping rush: 숨을 헐떡대며 돌진하여
29 talk sense: 맞는 말을 하다, 이치에 닿는 말을 하다
30 irritated: 안달 난, 화난, 속이 탄

Doctor Keene frowned.[31] "Why, yes, I suppose so — after a fashion."[32] Again he threw a curious glance[33] at Mr. Button.

"Is my wife all right?"

"Yes."

"Is it a boy or a girl?"

"Here now!" cried Doctor Keene in a perfect passion of irritation," I'll ask you to go and see for yourself. Outrageous!"[34] He snapped the last word out[35] in almost one syllable,[36] then he turned away muttering:[37] "Do you imagine a case like this will help my professional reputation? One more would ruin me — ruin anybody."

"What's the matter?" demanded Mr. Button appalled.[38] "Triplets?"[39]

"No, not triplets!" answered the doctor cuttingly.[40] "What's

---

31 frown : 찌푸리다

32 after a fashion : 이럭저럭, 얼마간, 어떤 의미에서는

33 threw a curious glance : 호기심 어린 시선을 던졌다

34 outrageous : 무도한, 괘씸한, 정의롭지 않은

35 snap ... out : 딱딱거리며 내뱉다

36 syllable : 음절

37 mutter : 중얼거리다

38 appall : 오싹하게 하다, 질겁하게 하다

39 triplet : 세쌍둥이

40 cuttingly : 매섭게

more, you can go and see for yourself. And get another doctor. I brought you into the world, young man, and I've been physician to your family for forty years, but I'm through with[41] you! I don't want to see you or any of your relatives ever again! Good-bye!"

Then he turned sharply, and without another word climbed[42] into his phaeton,[43] which was waiting at the curbstone,[44] and drove severely[45] away.

Mr. Button stood there upon the sidewalk, stupefied and trembling[46] from head to foot. What horrible mishap[47] had occurred? He had suddenly lost all desire to go into the Maryland Private Hospital for Ladies and Gentlemen — it was with the greatest difficulty that, a moment later, he forced himself to mount[48] the steps and enter the front door.

---

41 be through with : 끝내다, 절교하다
42 climb : (기어) 오르다, 올라타다
43 phaeton : 4륜 쌍두마차
44 curbstone : 보도의 가장자리 연석
45 severely : 엄하게, 심하게, 격렬하게
46 stupefied and trembling : 넋이 나간 채 떨며
47 horrible mishap : 끔찍한 불행
48 forced himself to mount : 억지로 올라갔다

A nurse was sitting behind a desk in the opaque[49] gloom[50] of the hall. Swallowing his shame,[51] Mr. Button approached her.

"Good-morning," she remarked, looking up at him pleasantly.

5 "Good-morning. I — I am Mr. Button."

At this a look of utter terror[52] spread itself over, girl's face. She rose to her feet and seemed about to fly from the hall, restraining[53] herself only with the most apparent[54] difficulty.

"I want to see my child," said Mr. Button.

10 The nurse gave a little scream. "Oh — of course!" she cried hysterically.[55] "Upstairs. Right upstairs. Go — *up*!"

She pointed the direction, and Mr. Button, bathed[56] in cool perspiration,[57] turned falteringly,[58] and began to mount to the

---

49 opaque : 불투명한

50 gloom : 어둠, 어둑어둑함, 암영, 검은 그림자

51 swallowing his shame : 자신의 수치심을 억누르며

52 a look of utter terror : 완전한(극심한) 공포의 표정

53 restrain : 억제하다, 누르다

54 apparent : 명백한, (눈에) 보이는, 또렷한

55 hysterically : 병적으로 흥분하여, 히스테릭하게

56 bathe : 목욕시키다, 욕조에 넣다, 흠뻑 젖게 하다

57 perspiration : 땀

58 falteringly : 비틀거리며, 말을 더듬으며

second floor. In the upper hall he addressed[59] another nurse who approached him, basin in hand. "I'm Mr. Button," he managed to[60] articulate.[61] "I want to see my —"

Clank![62] The basin clattered[63] to the floor and rolled in the direction of the stairs. Clank! Clank! It began a methodical[64] descent[65] as if sharing in the general terror which this gentleman provoked.[66]

"I want to see my child!" Mr. Button almost shrieked. He was on the verge of collapse.[67]

Clank! The basin reached the first floor. The nurse regained control of herself, and threw Mr. Button a look of hearty contempt.[68]

---

59 address : ~에게 말을 걸다, 부르다
60 manage to : 간신히 ~하다, ~해내다
61 articulate : 똑똑히 말하다, (음을) 형성하다
62 clank : 탕! 소리 나다
63 clatter : 덜거덕하는 소리를 내다
64 methodical : 조직적인, 꼼꼼한, 정연한
65 descent : 하강, 내려감
66 provoke : 성나게 하다, 유발하다
67 on the verge of collapse : 쓰러지기 직전의 ＊on the verge of : 막 ~하려는, ~ 하기 직전의 ＊collapse : <동사> 무너지다, 넘어지다, <명사> 붕괴
68 a look of hearty contempt : 마음속으로부터 우러나오는 경멸

"All *right*, Mr. Button," she agreed in a hushed[69] voice. "Very *well*! But if you knew what a state[70] it's put us all in this morning! It's perfectly outrageous! The hospital will never have a ghost of[71] a reputation after — "

5   "Hurry!" he cried hoarsely. "I can't stand[72] this!"

"Come this way, then, Mr. Button."

He dragged[73] himself after her. At the end of a long hall they reached a room from which proceeded a variety of howls — indeed, a room which, in later parlance,[74] would have been 10 known as the "crying-room."[75] They entered. Ranged around the walls were half a dozen white-enameled rolling cribs, each with a tag tid at the head.

"Well," gasped[76] Mr. Button, "which is mine?"

"There!" said the nurse.

15 Mr. Button's eyes followed her pointing finger, and this is

---

69 hushed: 가라앉은, 조용한, 비밀의

70 state: 상태

71 a ghost of: 극히 적은 가능성, 조금도

72 stand: 견디다, 참다

73 drag: 힘들게 움직이다

74 parlance: 용어, 말투

75 crying-room: <미국 속어> 울음 방(크게 좌절했다든지 할 때 들어가 우는 가상적인 방)

76 gasp: 헐떡이며 말하다

what he saw. Wrapped[77] in a voluminous[78] white blanket, and partly crammed[79] into one of the cribs,[80] there sat an old man apparently about seventy years of age. His sparse[81] hair was almost white, and from his chin dripped[82] a long smoke-coloured beard, which waved absurdly[83] back and forth,[84] fanned[85] by the breeze coming in at the window. He looked up at Mr. Button with dim, faded[86] eyes in which lurked a puzzled question.[87]

"Am I mad?" thundered[88] Mr. Button, his terror resolving into[89] rage. "Is this some ghastly[90] hospital joke?

---

77 wrap : 감싸다

78 voluminous : 방대한, 넓고 넓은

79 cram : (좁은 공간 속으로 억지로) 밀어(쑤셔) 넣다

80 crib : 요람

81 sparse : 숱이 적은

82 drip : 똑똑 떨어지다, 넘칠 정도이다 ＊긴 잿빛 수염이 수북하게 나 있다는
    의미임.

83 absurdly : 터무니없이

84 back and forth : 앞뒤로

85 fan : (물건, 생물이) 펄럭펄럭 흔들리다, 부채로 부치다

86 faded : 색이 바랜, 시든

87 lurked a puzzled question : 곤혹스러운 질문이 숨어 있었다 ＊문장 도치됨.

88 thunder : 크게 소리치다

89 resolve into : ~로 바뀌다

90 ghastly : 무시무시한, 지독한, 터무니없는

"It doesn't seem like a joke to us," replied the nurse severely. "And I don't know whether you're mad or not — but that is most certainly your child."

The cool perspiration redoubled[91] on Mr. Button's forehead. He closed his eyes, and then, opening them, looked again. There was no mistake — he was gazing at[92] a man of threescore[93] and ten — a *baby* of threescore and ten, a baby whose feet hung over the sides of the crib in which it was reposing.[94]

The old man looked placidly[95] from one to the other for a moment, and then suddenly spoke in a cracked and ancient voice.[96] "Are you my father?" he demanded.

Mr. Button and the nurse started[97] violently.[98]

"Because if you are," went on the old man querulously,[99] "I

---

91 redouble : 다시 배가하다, 강화하다
92 gaze at : 응시하다, 노려보다
93 threescore : 60 (*cf.* score=20)
94 repose : 눕다, 쉬다, 엎혀 있다
95 placidly : 조용하게, 차분하게
96 in a cracked and ancient voice : 마치 금이 간 듯 목이 잔뜩 쉬고 아주 나이가 많이 든 듯한 목소리로
97 start : 움찔하다, 놀라다
98 violently : 격렬히
99 querulously : 불만을 늘어놓으며, 투덜거리며, 성을 내며

wish you'd get me out of this place — or, at least, get them to put a comfortable rocker[100] in here,"

"Where in God's name[101] did you come from? Who are you?" burst out[102] Mr. Button frantically.[103]

"I can't tell you *exactly* who I am," replied the querulous whine,[104] "because I've only been born a few hours — but my last name is certainly Button."

"You lie! You're an impostor!"[105]

The old man turned wearily[106] to the nurse. "Nice way to welcome a new-born child," he complained in a weak voice. "Tell him he's wrong, why don't you?"

"You're wrong. Mr. Button," said the nurse severely. "This is your child, and you'll have to make the best of[107] it. We're going to ask you to take him home with you as soon as

---

100 rocker : 흔들의자

101 in God's name : 신의 이름을 걸고, 제발, 도대체

102 burst out : 갑자기 큰소리로 ~하다

103 frantically : 미친 듯이

104 whine : <명사> 낑낑대는 소리, 우는소리, <동사> 징징거리다, 우는소리
　　　를 하다, 투덜대다

105 impostor : 사기꾼, 협잡꾼

106 wearily : 지친 듯, 피곤하여

107 make the best of : ~를 가장 잘 이용하다, 어떻게든 극복하다, 최대한 이용
　　　하다

possible — some time to-day."

"Home?" repeated Mr. Button incredulously.[108]

"Yes, we can't have him here. We really can't, you know?"

"I'm right glad of it," whined the old man. "This is a fine

5 place to keep a youngster of quiet tastes.[109] With all this yelling

and howling, I haven't been able to get a wink[110] of sleep. I

asked for something to eat" — here his voice rose to a shrill

note of protest[111] — "and they brought me a bottle of milk!"

Mr. Button, sank down[112] upon a chair near his son

10 and concealed[113] his face in his hands. "My heavens!" he

murmured, in an ecstasy of horror.[114] "What will people say?

What must I do?"

"You'll have to take him home," insisted the nurse —

"immediately!"

---

108 incredulously : 의심하듯, 수상쩍게, 믿을 수 없다는 듯

109 a youngster of quiet tastes : 조용한 취향의 젊은이

110 wink : 아주 잠깐

111 a shrill note of protest : 항의의 날카로운 음

112 sink down : 맥없이 주저앉다

113 conceal : 감추다

114 in an ecstasy of horror : 공포감에 어쩔 줄 몰라 하며 *ecstasy : 의식 혼탁
상태, 정신 혼미

A grotesque[115] picture formed[116] itself with dreadful[117] clarity[118] before the eyes of the tortured[119] man — a picture of himself walking through the crowded streets of the city with this appalling[120] apparition[121] stalking[122] by his side.

"I can't. I can't," he moaned.

People would stop to speak to him, and what was he going to say? He would have to introduce this — this septuagenarian:[123] "This is my son, born early this morning." And then the old man would gather his blanket around him and they would plod[124] on, past the bustling[125] stores, the slave market — for a dark instant Mr. Button wished passionately that his son was black — past the luxurious[126] houses of the residential

---

115 grotesque : 기괴한
116 form : 형태를 갖추다
117 dreadful : 끔찍한
118 clarity : 분명함
119 torture : 고문하다
120 appalling : 섬뜩하게 하는, 질색인
121 apparition : 유령
122 stalk : 살그머니 접근하다, 활보하다
123 septuagenarian : 70세의 (사람), 70대의 (사람)
124 plod : 터벅터벅 걷다
125 bustling : 분주히 움직이는, 떠들썩한
126 luxurious : 화려한, 사치스러운

district,[127] past the home for the aged....

"Come! Pull yourself together,"[128] commanded the nurse.

"See here," the old man announced suddenly, "if you think I'm going to walk home in this blanket, you're entirely mistaken."

"Babies always have blankets."

With a malicious[129] crackle[130] the old man held up a small white swaddling garment.[131] "Look!" he quavered.[132] "*This* is what they had ready for me."

"Babies always wear those," said the nurse primly.[133]

"Well," said the old man, "this baby's not going to wear anything in about two minutes. This blanket itches.[134] They might at least have given me a sheet."

"Keep it on! Keep it on!" said Mr. Button hurriedly.[135] He

---

127 residential district : 주거 구역
128 pull oneself together : 원기를 되찾다, 회복되다, 자제심을 되찾다
129 malicious : 악의 있는, 심술궂은
130 crackle : 탁탁 소리
131 swaddling garment : 배내옷
132 quaver : 떨리는 목소리로 말하다
133 primly : 단단히, 견고하게
134 itch : 가렵다
135 hurriedly : 서둘러, 다급하게, 허둥지둥

turned to the nurse. "What'll I do?"

"Go down town and buy your son some clothes."

Mr. Button's son's voice followed him down into the hall: "And a cane, father. I want to have a cane."

Mr. Button banged[136] the outer door savagely....[137]   5

Chapter II

"Good-morning," Mr. Button said nervously, to the clerk in the Chesapeake Dry Goods[138] Company. "I want to buy some clothes for my child."

"How old is your child, sir?"

"About six *hours*," answered Mr. Button, without due   10 consideration.[139]

"Babies' supply department in the rear."[140]

"Why, I don't think — I'm not sure that's what I want. It's

---

136 bang : 쾅 닫다

137 savagely : 사납게

138 dry goods : <미국 속어> 의복, 드레스, 코트 *a dry goods store : <미국> 포목상

139 without due consideration : 제대로 생각해 보지도 않고

140 Babies' supply department in the rear : 유아용품부는 뒤쪽에 있어요

— he's an unusually large-size[141] child. Exceptionally — ah large."

"They have the largest child's sizes."

"Where is the boys' department?" inquired Mr. Button, shifting his ground desperately.[142] He felt that the clerk must surely scent[143] his shameful secret.

"Right here."

"Well — " He hesitated. The notion of dressing his son in men's clothes was repugnant[144] to him. If, say,[145] he could only find a *very* large boy's suit, he might cut off that long and awful beard, dye[146] the white hair brown, and thus manage to conceal the worst, and to retain[147] something of his own self-respect — not to mention[148] his position in Baltimore society.

---

141 unusually large-size : 별나게 대형인

142 shifting his ground desperately : 필사적으로(생각다 못해) 입장(의견)을 바꾸며

143 scent : 냄새 맡다

144 repugnant : 싫은, 불쾌한

145 say : 예를 들어, 이를테면

146 dye : 염색하다

147 retain : 유지하다, 보유하다, 간직하다

148 not to mention : ~는 말할 필요도 없이

But a frantic[149] inspection[150] of the boys' department revealed no suits to fit[151] the new-born Button. He blamed[152] the store, of course — in such cases it is the thing to blame the store.

"How old did you say that boy of yours was?" demanded the clerk curiously.

"He's — sixteen."

"Oh, I beg your pardon. I thought you said six hours. You'll find the youths' department in the next aisle."[153]

Mr. Button turned miserably[154] away. Then he stopped, brightened,[155] and pointed his finger toward a dressed dummy[156] in the window display.[157] "There!" he exclaimed. "I'll take that suit, out there on the dummy."

The clerk stared. "Why," he protested,[158] "that's not a child's

---

149 frantic : 굉장한, 당황하여 허둥대는
150 inspection : 면밀한 조사, 시찰
151 fit : 어울리다, 맞다
152 blame : 탓하다, 비난하다
153 aisle : 복도, 통로
154 miserably : 비참하게
155 brighten : 밝아지다
156 dummy : 마네킹
157 display : 전시
158 protest : 항의하다

suit. At least it is, but it's for fancy dress.[159] You could wear it yourself!"

"Wrap it up," insisted his customer nervously. "That's what I want."

5　The astonished clerk obeyed.

Back at the hospital Mr. Button entered the nursery[160] and almost threw the package at his son. "Here's your clothes," he snapped out.[161]

The old man untied the package and viewed the contents[162] with a quizzical[163] eye.

10　"They look sort of funny to me," he complained, "I don't want to be made a monkey of —"[164]

"You've made a monkey of me!" retorted[165] Mr. Button fiercely.[166] "Never you mind how funny you look. Put them

---

159　fancy dress : 가장복, 기발한 의상, 가장무도회용 의상
160　nursery : 육아실, 아이들의 방
161　snap out : 딱딱거리며 말하다, 고함치다
162　content : 내용물
163　quizzical : 기묘한, 미심쩍어하는
164　make a monkey of : 장난치다, 우스갯거리로 만들다
165　retort : 반박하다, 대꾸하다
166　fiercely : 맹렬히, 사납게

on — or I'll — or I'll *spank*[167] you." He swallowed uneasily at the penultimate word,[168] feeling nevertheless that it was the proper thing to say.

"All right, father" — this with a grotesque simulation[169] of filial[170] respect — "you've lived longer; you know best. Just as you say."

As before, the sound of the word "father" caused Mr. Button to start violently.

"And hurry."

"I'm hurrying, father."

When his son was dressed Mr. Button regarded[171] him with depression. The costume consisted of[172] dotted[173] socks, pink pants, and a belted[174] blouse with a wide white collar. Over the

---

167 spank: 엉덩이를 때리다
168 swallowed uneasily at the penultimate word: 뒤에서 두 번째의 말을 할 때 불편하며 꿀꺽 침을 삼켰다 ＊ 'spank'라는 말을 할 때, 아무래도 어울리지 않는 듯해서 그 말이 잘 안 나왔다는 의미임.
169 simulation: 가장하기, 흉내 내기
170 filial: 자식의, 자식다운
171 regard: 보다, 주의를 기울이다
172 consist of: ~로 구성되다
173 dotted: 점박이가 있는
174 belted: 띠를 두른, 줄무늬가 있는

latter waved the long whitish beard, drooping[175] almost to the waist. The effect was not good.

"Wait!"

Mr. Button seized[176] a hospital shears and with three quick
snaps amputated[177] a large section of the beard. But even with this improvement[178] the ensemble[179] fell far short of[180] perfection. The remaining brush[181] of scraggly[182] hair, the watery[183] eyes, the ancient teeth, seemed oddly out of tone with[184] the gaiety[185] of the costume. Mr. Button, however, was
obdurate[186] — he held out his hand. "Come along!" he said sternly.[187]

---

175 droop : 축 처지다, 수그러지다, 숙이다
176 seize : 잡다
177 amputate : 절단하다
178 improvement : 향상
179 ensemble : 전체적 조화, 총체, 종합적 효과, 한 벌의 여성복
180 fall short of : 부족하다, 미치지 못하다
181 brush : <미국 속어> 수염
182 scraggly : 불규칙적인, 헝클어진, 단정치 못한
183 watery : 물기를 머금은
184 out of tone with : ~와 곡조(조화)가 맞지 않는
185 gaiety : 유쾌함
186 obdurate : 완고한, 고집이 센
187 sternly : 완고하게

His son took the hand trustingly.[188] "What are you going to call me, dad?" he quavered[189] as they walked from the nursery — "just 'baby' for a while? till you think of a better name?"

Mr. Button grunted.[190] "I don't know," he answered harshly.[191] "I think we'll call you Methuselah."[192]

Chapter III

Even after the new addition to the Button family had had his hair cut short and then dyed to a sparse[193] unnatural black, had had his face shaved so close that it glistened,[194] and had been attired[195] in small-boy clothes made to order[196] by a

---

188 trustingly : 안심하여, 신용하여

189 quaver : (목소리가) 떨(리)다, 떠는 소리로 말하다

190 grunt : 투덜대다, 불평하다

191 harshly : 난폭하게, 거칠게, 사납게

192 Methuselah : 고령자(Methuselah는 「창세기」에 나오는 노아의 홍수 이전에 969년을 살았다는 유대의 족장)

193 sparse : 성긴, 드문드문한, 숱이 적은

194 glisten : 반짝반짝 빛나다

195 attire : 차려입히다, 성장시키다

196 made to order : 맞춤 제작된

flabbergasted[197] tailor, it was impossible for Button to ignore the fact that his son was a poor excuse for a first family baby. Despite his aged stoop,[198] Benjamin Button — for it was by this name they called him instead of by the appropriate but invidious[199] Methuselah — was five feet eight inches tall. His clothes did not conceal this, nor did the clipping[200] and dyeing of his eyebrows disguise the fact that the eyes underneath were faded[201] and watery and tired. In fact, the baby-nurse who had been engaged[202] in advance[203] left the house after one look, in a state of[204] considerable[205] indignation.[206]

But Mr. Button persisted[207] in his unwavering[208] purpose. Benjamin was a baby, and a baby he should remain. At first

---

197 flabbergasted : 놀란, 당황한

198 stoop : <동사> 몸을 굽히다, 구부정하다, <명사> 구부정한 자세

199 invidious : 비위에 거슬리는

200 clip : 깎다, 다듬다, 자르다

201 faded : 흐릿한, 시든, 빛깔이 바랜

202 engaged : 고용된

203 in advance : 미리, 사전에

204 in a state of~ : ~한 상태에서(상태로)

205 considerable : 상당한

206 indignation : 분노

207 persist : 고집하다, 계속하다

208 unwavering : 동요하지 않는, 확고한

he declared that if Benjamin didn't like warm milk he could go without[209] food altogether, but he was finally prevailed[210] upon to allow his son bread and butter, and even oatmeal by way of a compromise.[211] One day he brought home a rattle and, giving it to Benjamin, insisted[212] in no uncertain terms[213] that he should "play with it," whereupon[214] the old man took it with a weary expression and could be heard jingling[215] it obediently[216] at intervals[217] throughout the day.

There can be no doubt, though, that the rattle bored him, and that he found other and more soothing[218] amusements[219] when he was left alone. For instance, Mr. Button discovered one day that during the preceding[220] week he had smoked

---

209 go without : ~을 갖지 않다, ~ 없이 때우다(지내다)
210 prevail : 우세하다, 이기다, 설득하다, 설복하다
211 by way of a compromise : 협상(타협)으로, 협상을 통해
212 insist : 주장하다, 고집하다, 강요하다, 요구하다
213 in no uncertain terms : 확실하게, 분명히
214 whereupon : = whereon. 그래서, 그 후로, 그 결과
215 jingle : 딸랑딸랑 소리를 내다
216 obediently : 고분고분하게
217 at intervals : 간격을 두고, 사이를 띄워
218 soothing : 위로가 되는
219 amusement : 오락
220 preceding : 앞선

more cigars than ever before — a phenomenon,[221] which was explained a few days later when, entering the nursery unexpectedly, he found the room full of faint blue haze[222] and Benjamin, with a guilty expression on his face, trying to conceal the butt of a dark Havana.[223] This, of course, called for[224] a severe spanking, but Mr. Button found that he could not bring himself to administer it.[225] He merely warned his son that he would "stunt[226] his growth."

Nevertheless he persisted in his attitude. He brought home lead[227] soldiers, he brought toy trains, he brought large pleasant animals made of cotton, and, to perfect[228] the illusion which he was creating — for himself at least — he passionately demanded of the clerk in the toy-store whether "the paint would come off the pink duck if the baby put it in his mouth."

---

221 phenomenon : 현상
222 haze : 아지랑이
223 Havana : (쿠바산) 아바나 담배
224 call for : 요구하다, 불러내다
225 bring himself to administer it : 간신히 그것(엉덩이 매질)을 집행(적용)하다 * bring oneself to : (간신히) ~을 하다
226 stunt : 발육을 가로막다
227 lead : 납으로 된
228 perfect : 완벽하게 만들다

But, despite all his father's efforts, Benjamin refused to be interested. He would steal[229] down the back stairs and return to the nursery with a volume of the Encyclopedia Britannica,[230] over which he would pore[231] through an afternoon, while his cotton cows and his Noah's ark[232] were 5 left neglected on the floor. Against such a stubbornness[233] Mr. Button's efforts were of little avail.[234]

The sensation[235] created in Baltimore was, at first, prodigious.[236] What the mishap[237] would have cost[238] the Buttons and their kinsfolk[239] socially cannot be determined, 10 for the outbreak of the Civil War[240] drew the city's attention

---

229 steal : 몰래 숨어 들어가다, 몰래 가다
230 Encyclopedia Britannica : 브리태니커 백과사전
231 pore over : 세세히 읽어 보다, 응시하다, 열심히 독서(연구) 하다
232 ark : 방주 * Noah's ark : 「창세기」에 나오는 대홍수 이야기에 등장하는 노아의 방주
233 stubbornness : 완고함, 완강함
234 be of little avail : 전혀(거의) 쓸모가 없다, 무익하다
235 sensation : 센세이션(큰 이야깃거리, 대소동)
236 prodigious : 거대한, 막대한
237 mishap : 불운한 일, 재난
238 cost : (귀중한 것을) 희생시키다, 잃게 하다, ~의 비용이 들다
239 kinsfolk : 친척, 일가
240 the Civil War : 미국 남북전쟁

to other things. A few people who were unfailingly[241] polite racked[242] their brains for compliments to give to the parents — and finally hit upon the ingenious[243] device[244] of declaring that the baby resembled his grandfather, a fact which, due to

5 the standard state of decay common to all men of seventy, could not be denied.[245] Mr. and Mrs. Roger Button were not pleased, and Benjamin's grandfather was furiously[246] insulted.

Benjamin, once he left the hospital, took life as he found it. Several small boys were brought to see him, and he spent

10 a stiff-jointed[247] afternoon trying to work up an interest in tops and marbles[248] — he even managed, quite accidentally,

---

241 unfailingly : 틀림없이, 충실히

242 rack : 샅샅이 뒤지다 ＊rack one's brains : 머리를 짜서 생각하다, 생각해 내려고 애쓰다, 골머리 앓다

243 ingenious : 정교한, 독창적인, 교묘한, 머리가 좋은

244 device : 고안, 계획, 계책, 지혜

245 due to the standard state of decay common to all men of seventy, could not be denied : 70세의 모든 사람에게 공통적인 표준 상태의 쇠락 때문에 부인될 수 없었다 ＊아무리 칭찬거리를 찾아봐도 못 찾다가 겨우 찾은 것이 'Benjamin이 할아버지를 닮았다'라는 것인데, 이 말이 이목구비 등 구체적인 특징을 두고 한 언급이라기보다는 둘 다 '늙었다'라는 것이므로 틀린 말은 아니라는 의미임.

246 furiously : 맹렬히, 미쳐 날뛰며, 격노하여

247 stiff-jointed : 뻣뻣한 관절의

248 trying to work up an interest in tops and marbles : 팽이와 구슬에 대한

to break a kitchen window with a stone from a sling shot,[249] a feat which secretly delighted his father.[250]

Thereafter Benjamin contrived[251] to break something every day, but he did these things only because they were expected of him, and because he was by nature[252] obliging.[253]

When his grandfather's initial antagonism[254] wore off,[255] Benjamin and that gentleman took enormous pleasure in one another's company.[256] They would sit for hours, these two, so far apart[257] in age and experience, and, like old cronies,[258] discuss with tireless monotony[259] the slow events of the day. Benjamin felt more at ease in his grandfather's presence[260]

관심을 불러일으키려고 애쓰면서　＊work up : 부추기다, 자극하다

249　sling shot : 새총
250　a feat which secretly delighted his father : 남몰래 그의 아버지를 기쁘게 한 위업
251　contrive : 꾸며 내다, 고안해 내다, 궁리하다
252　by nature : 천성적으로
253　obliging : 남을 기꺼이 돌보는, 친절한, 기대에 부응하는
254　antagonism : 적의
255　wear off : 닳다
256　company : 교제, 친구
257　far apart : 멀리 떨어진
258　crony : 옛 친구, 한 패
259　monotony : 단조로움
260　presence : 존재, (사람이) 있는 자리, 면전

than in his parents' — they seemed always somewhat in awe[261] of him and, despite the dictatorial[262] authority[263] they exercised over him, frequently addressed him as "Mr."

He was as puzzled as any one else at the apparently advanced age of his mind and body at birth. He read up on it in the medical journal, but found that no such case had been previously recorded. At his father's urging[264] he made an honest attempt to play with other boys, and frequently he joined in the milder[265] games — football shook him up too much, and he feared that in case of a fracture[266] his ancient bones would refuse to knit.[267]

When he was five he was sent to kindergarten, where he initiated into[268] the art of pasting[269] green paper on orange

---

261 awe: 외경, 두려움, 외경심
262 dictatorial: 독재적인
263 authority: 권위
264 urge: 재촉하다
265 mild: 온순한, 부드러운, 자극성이 없는, 가벼운
266 fracture: 골절
267 knit: 접합하다
268 initiate into: 시작하다, 개시하다, 입문하다
269 paste: 풀로 붙이다

paper, of weaving[270] coloured maps and manufacturing[271] eternal[272] cardboard necklaces.[273] He was inclined to[274] drowse off to sleep[275] in the middle of these tasks, a habit which both irritated[276] and frightened his young teacher. To his relief[277] she complained to his parents, and he was removed[278] from the school. The Roger Buttons told their friends that they felt he was too young.

By the time he was twelve years old his parents had grown used to[279] him. Indeed, so strong is the force of custom that they no longer felt that he was different from any other child — except when some curious[280] anomaly[281] reminded them

---

270   weave : 짜다, 엮다, 만들어 내다

271   manufacture : 제조하다

272   eternal : 영원한

273   manufacturing eternal cardboard necklaces : 지겹게(끝도 없는) 카드보드 목걸이를 만듦

274   be inclined to : ~하는 경향이 있다

275   drowse off to sleep : 꾸벅꾸벅 졸다가 잠에 빠지다

276   irritate : 초조하게 하다, 노하게 하다, 짜증나게 하다

277   to one's relief : 한시름 놓게(도), 안도의 숨을 쉰 것은

278   remove : 내쫓다, 해직하다, 제거하다, 이동시키다

279   grow used to : ~에 익숙해지다

280   curious : 기묘한, 진기한, 별난

281   anomaly : 예외, 파격

of the fact. But one day a few weeks after his twelfth birthday, while looking in the mirror, Benjamin made, or thought he made, an astonishing discovery. Did his eyes deceive him, or had his hair turned in the dozen years of his life from white to iron-gray under its concealing dye? Was the network of wrinkles[282] on his face becoming less pronounced?[283] Was his skin healthier and firmer, with even a touch[284] of ruddy[285] winter colour? He could not tell.[286] He knew that he no longer stooped, and that his physical condition had improved since the early days of his life.

"Can it be — ?" he thought to himself, or, rather, scarcely[287] dared[288] to think.

He went to his father. "I am grown," he announced determinedly.[289] "I want to put on long trousers."

His father hesitated. "Well," he said finally, "I don't know.

---

282 network of wrinkles : 그물처럼 얽혀 있는 주름
283 pronounced : 뚜렷한
284 touch : 기미, 기운, ~하는 기(機)
285 ruddy : 붉그레한, 혈색 좋은
286 tell : 확인하다, 알아보다, 분간하다
287 scarcely : 거의 ~가 아니다
288 dare : 감히 ~하다
289 determinedly : 단호히, 완강히

Fourteen is the age for putting on long trousers — and you are only twelve."

"But you'll have to admit," protested[290] Benjamin, "that I'm big for my age."

His father looked at him with illusory[291] speculation.[292] "Oh, I'm not so sure of that," he said. "I was as big as you when I was twelve."

This was not true-it was all part of Roger Button's silent agreement with himself to believe in his son's normality.

Finally a compromise was reached. Benjamin was to continue to dye his hair. He was to make a better attempt to play with boys of his own age. He was not to wear his spectacles[293] or carry a cane in the street. In return for these concessions[294] he was allowed his first suit of long trousers....

---

290 protest : 항의하다, 이의를 제기하다
291 illusory : 실체가 없는
292 speculation : 심사숙고, 추론, 사색
293 spectacles : 안경
294 concession : 양보

Chapter IV

Of the life of Benjamin Button between his twelfth and twenty-first year I intend to say little. Suffice to[295] record that they were years of normal ungrowth.[296] When Benjamin was eighteen he was erect[297] as a man of fifty; he had more hair and it was of a dark gray; his step was firm, his voice had lost its cracked quaver[298] and descended to a healthy baritone. So his father sent him up to Connecticut to take examinations for entrance to Yale College. Benjamin passed his examination and became a member of the freshman class.

On the third day following his matriculation[299] he received a notification[300] from Mr. Hart, the college registrar, to call at[301] his office and arrange[302] his schedule. Benjamin, glancing in

---

295 suffice to : 충분하다

296 ungrowth : 성장의 역전

297 erect : 곧추선

298 quaver : (목소리 등이) 떨리는 소리

299 matriculation : 입학식

300 notification : 통지

301 call at : 들르다

302 arrange : 조정하다

the mirror, decided that his hair needed a new application[303] of its brown dye, but an anxious[304] inspection[305] of his bureau[306] drawer[307] disclosed[308] that the dye bottle was not there. Then he remembered — he had emptied[309] it the day before and thrown it away.

He was in a dilemma. He was due at the registrar's in five minutes. There seemed to be no help for it — he must go as he was. He did.

"Good-morning," said the registrar politely. "You've come to inquire about your son."

"Why, as a matter of fact, my name's Button — " began Benjamin, but Mr. Hart cut him off.[310]

"I'm very glad to meet you, Mr. Button. I'm expecting[311] your son here any minute."

---

303 application : 적용

304 anxious : 걱정하는, 불안한

305 inspection : 검사, 조사, 검열

306 bureau : 침실용 옷장

307 drawer : 서랍

308 disclose : (숨겨진 것을) 나타내다, 드러내다(reveal)

309 empty : 비우다, 끝까지 사용하다

310 cut off : 말을 자르다

311 expect : 기다리다

"That's me!" burst out[312] Benjamin. "I'm a freshman."

"What!"

"I'm a freshman."

"Surely you're joking."

5   "Not at all."

The registrar frowned[313] and glanced at a card before him. "Why, I have Mr. Benjamin Button's age down here as eighteen."

"That's my age," asserted[314] Benjamin, flushing[315] slightly.

10   The registrar eyed him wearily.[316] "Now surely, Mr. Button, you don't expect me to believe that."

Benjamin smiled wearily. "I am eighteen," he repeated.

The registrar pointed sternly to the door. "Get out," he said. "Get out of college and get out of town. You are a dangerous

15   lunatic."[317]

"I am eighteen."

Mr. Hart opened the door. "The idea!" he shouted. "A man

---

312 burst out : 갑자기 소리치다, 폭발하다
313 frown : 눈살을 찌푸리다, 불쾌한 얼굴을 하다, 기분 나쁜 모양을 하다
314 assert : 주장하다, 단언하다
315 flush : 얼굴을 붉히다
316 wearily : 피곤하여, 싫증 나서
317 lunatic : 정신이상자, 미친 사람

of your age trying to enter here as a freshman. Eighteen years old, are you? Well, I'll give you eighteen minutes to get out of town."

Benjamin Button walked with dignity[318] from the room, and half a dozen undergraduates,[319] who were waiting in the hall, followed him curiously with their eyes. When he had gone a little way he turned around, faced the infuriated[320] registrar, who was still standing in the door-way, and repeated in a firm voice: "I am eighteen years old."

To a chorus[321] of titters[322] which went up from the group of undergraduates, Benjamin walked away.

But he was not fated to[323] escape so easily. On his melancholy walk to the railroad station he found that he was being followed by a group, then by a swarm,[324] and finally by a dense mass of[325] undergraduates. The word had gone

---

318 with dignity : 위엄을 갖추어, 점잖을 빼고
319 undergraduate : 학부생
320 infuriated : 격노한
321 chorus : 합창, 일제히 내는 소리, 이구동성
322 titter : 킥킥대다, 그 웃음
323 be fated to : ~할 운명이다
324 swarm : 떼
325 a mass of : (양이) 많은 * dense : 빽빽한, 밀집한

around that a lunatic had passed the entrance examinations for Yale and attempted to palm himself off[326] as a youth of eighteen. A fever of excitement permeated[327] the college. Men ran hatless[328] out of classes, the football team abandoned its practice and joined the mob, professors' wives with bonnets awry and bustles out of position,[329] ran shouting after the procession,[330] from which proceeded a continual succession of remarks aimed at[331] the tender sensibilities of Benjamin Button.

"He must be the wandering Jew!"[332]

"He ought to go to prep school[333] at his age!"

---

326 palm off : 속이다, 속여 팔다

327 permeate : 퍼지다, 스며들다

328 hatless : 모자 없이

329 with bonnets awry and bustles out of position : 보닛은 비뚤어지고 버슬은 제 위치를 벗어난 채 *bustle : 버슬, 허리받이(스커트의 뒤를 부풀게 하려고 허리에 대는)

330 procession : 행렬

331 from which proceeded a continual succession of remarks aimed at : 여기(행렬)에서 ~를 겨냥한 계속 이어지는 언급들이 이어졌다

332 wandering Jew : 방랑하는 유대인

333 prep school : preparatory school의 준말 *preparatory school : 사립 중등학교

"Look at the infant prodigy!"[334] "He thought this was the old men's home."

"Go up to Harvard!"

Benjamin increased his gait,[335] and soon he was running. He would show them! He *would* go to Harvard, and then they would regret these ill-considered[336] taunts![337]

Safely on board[338] the train for Baltimore, he put his head from the window. "You'll regret this!" he shouted.

"Ha-ha!" the undergraduates laughed. "Ha-ha-ha!" It was the biggest mistake that Yale College had ever made....

Chapter V

In 1880 Benjamin Button was twenty years old, and he signalised[339] his birthday by going to work for his father in Roger Button & Co., Wholesale Hardware. It was in that same

---

334 infant prodigy : 신동, 천재 아동

335 increased his gait : 걸음을 빨리했다

336 ill-considered : 분별없는, 부적당한, 현명치 못한

337 taunt : 비웃음, 악담

338 on board : 탑승한

339 signalise : 알리다, 눈에 띄게 하다, 신호하다

year that he began "going out socially"[340] — that is, his father insisted on taking him to several fashionable[341] dances. Roger Button was now fifty, and he and his son were more and more companionable[342] — in fact, since Benjamin had ceased to dye his hair (which was still grayish) they appeared[343] about the same age, and could have passed for[344] brothers.

One night in August they got into the phaeton attired in their full-dress suits and drove out to a dance at the Shevlins' country house, situated[345] just outside of Baltimore. It was a gorgeous[346] evening. A full moon drenched[347] the road to the lustreless[348] colour of platinum, and late-blooming[349] harvest flowers breathed into the motionless air aromas that were like low, half-heard laughter. The open country, carpeted for

---

340 go out socially : 사교 활동을 하다, 사교계로 진출하다
341 fashionable : 사교계의, 상류의, 유행의
342 companionable : 붙임성 있는, 서글서글한, 친구답게 ＊신체적 나이가 비슷해지면서 서로 친구같이 보이게 되었다는 의미임.
343 appear : ~처럼 보이다
344 pass for : 통용되다, 인정되어 있다, (~으로) 통하고 있다
345 situated : 위치해 있는
346 gorgeous : 호화로운, 매우 매력적인
347 drench : 흠뻑 적시다
348 lustreless : = lusterless. 윤기 없는, 활기 없는
349 late-blooming : 늦게 피는, 만숙의, 만성형의

rods around with bright wheat,[350] was translucent[351] as in the day. It was almost impossible not to be affected by the sheer[352] beauty of the sky — almost.

"There's a great future in the dry-goods business," Roger Button was saying. He was not a spiritual man — his aesthetic sense[353] was rudimentary.[354]

"Old fellows like me can't learn new tricks," he observed[355] profoundly. "It's you youngsters with energy and vitality that have the great future before you."

Far up the road the lights of the Shevlins' country house drifted[356] into view, and presently there was a sighing sound that crept persistently toward them — it might have been

---

350 The open country, carpeted for rods around with bright wheat : 밝게 빛나는 밀로 주변에 끝도 없이 덮인 탁 트인 지역(광활한 평야 지대) ＊ 'rod' 가 길이나 면적의 단위임을 감안하여 '끝도 없이'의 의미로 의역해 볼 수 있음.
351 translucent : 반투명한, 투명한
352 sheer : 완전한, 섞은 것이 없는
353 aesthetic sense : 미적인 감각
354 rudimentary : 초보의, 미발달의
355 observe : (발언·논평·의견을) 말하다
356 drift : 표류하다, 흐르다

the fine plaint[357] of violins or the rustle[358] of the silver wheat under the moon.

They pulled up[359] behind a handsome brougham[360] whose passengers were disembarking[361] at the door. A lady got out, then an elderly gentleman, then another young lady, beautiful as sin.[362] Benjamin started;[363] an almost chemical change seemed to dissolve[364] and recompose[365] the very elements of his body. A rigour[366] passed over him, blood rose into his cheeks, his forehead, and there was a steady thumping[367] in his ears. It was first love.

The girl was slender and frail, with hair that was ashen under the moon and honey-coloured under the sputtering[368] gas-

---

357 plaint : 비탄(의 소리)

358 rustle : 바삭거리는 소리

359 pull up : (말, 차 따위를) 멈추다, 세우다

360 brougham : 브루엄 마차(사륜마차)

361 disembark : 내리다

362 beautiful as sin : 참으로 아름다운 *(as) ... as sin : 실로, 참으로

363 start : 움찔하다, 깜짝 놀라다

364 dissolve : 없어지다, 해산하다

365 recompose : 개조하다, 다시 조립되다

366 rigour : = rigor. 오한, (근육의) 경직

367 thump : 쾅쾅 소리

368 sputtering : 탁탁 소리를 내는

lamps of the porch. Over her shoulders was thrown a Spanish mantilla[369] of softest yellow, butterflied[370] in black; her feet were glittering buttons at the hem of her bustled dress.

Roger Button leaned over to his son. "That," he said, "is young Hildegarde Moncrief, the daughter of General Moncrief." [5]

Benjamin nodded coldly. "Pretty little thing," he said indifferently. But when the negro boy had led the buggy[371] away, he added: "Dad, you might introduce me to her."

They approached a group, of which Miss Moncrief was [10] the centre. Reared[372] in the old tradition, she curtsied[373] low before Benjamin. Yes, he might have a dance. He thanked her and walked away — staggered[374] away.

The interval until the time for his turn should arrive dragged[375] itself out interminably.[376] He stood close to the [15]

---

369 mantilla : 머리부터 어깨까지 덮는 큰 베일, 짧은 망토
370 butterfly : 나비 날개 모양을 만들다
371 buggy : 마차
372 rear : 기르다, 양육하다
373 curtsy : 인사하다
374 stagger : 비틀거리다
375 drag : (시간을) 질질 끌다
376 interminably : 그칠 줄 모르게, 무기한

wall, silent, inscrutable,[377] watching with murderous[378] eyes the young bloods[379] of Baltimore as they eddied[380] around Hildegarde Moncrief, passionate admiration in their faces. How obnoxious[381] they seemed to Benjamin; how intolerably rosy![382] Their curling[383] brown whiskers aroused in him a feeling equivalent to indigestion.[384]

But when his own time came, and he drifted[385] with her out upon the changing floor to the music of the latest waltz from Paris, his jealousies and anxieties melted from him like a mantle[386] of snow. Blind with enchantment,[387] he felt that life was just beginning.

"You and your brother got here just as we did, didn't you?" asked Hildegarde, looking up at him with eyes that were like

---

377 inscrutable : (사람 · 표정이) 수수께끼 같은, 불가해한

378 murderous : 잔인한, 죽일 듯한

379 young bloods : 혈기 왕성한 청년들

380 eddy : 소용돌이치다

381 obnoxious : 불쾌한, 욕지기 나는

382 rosy : 장밋빛의, 혈색 좋은

383 curling : 곱슬머리의, 곱슬 진

384 a feeling equivalent to indigestion : 소화불량과 같은 어떤 감정

385 drift : 떠돌다, 헤매다, <미국 속어> 출발하다

386 mantle : 덮개

387 enchantment : 매혹

bright blue enamel.

Benjamin hesitated. If she took him for his father's brother, would it be best to enlighten[388] her? He remembered his experience at Yale, so he decided against it. It would be rude to contradict[389] a lady; it would be criminal to mar[390] this exquisite occasion[391] with the grotesque[392] story of his origin.[393] Later, perhaps. So he nodded, smiled, listened, was happy.

"I like men of your age," Hildegarde told him. "Young boys are so idiotic.[394] They tell me how much champagne they drink at college, and how much money they lose playing cards. Men of your age know how to appreciate women."

Benjamin felt himself on the verge of[395] a proposal[396] — with an effort he choked back[397] the impulse. "You're just

---

388 enlighten : 깨우쳐 주다

389 contradict : 반박하다

390 mar : 약화시키다, 망치다, 손상시키다, 훼손하다

391 occasion : 기회

392 grotesque : 기괴한, 이상한, 우스꽝스러운, 어리석은

393 origin : 기원, 근원

394 idiotic : 멍청한

395 on the verge of : ~의 직전에, ~하기 직전에

396 proposal : 프러포즈

397 choke back : (북받쳐 오르는 감정을) 억누르다

the romantic age," she continued — "fifty. Twenty-five is too wordly-wise;[398] thirty is apt to be pale from overwork;[399] forty is the age of long stories that take a whole cigar to tell;[400] sixty is — oh, sixty is too near seventy; but fifty is the mellow[401] age. I love fifty."

Fifty seemed to Benjamin a glorious age. He longed passionately to be fifty.

"I've always said," went on Hildegarde, "that I'd rather marry a man of fifty and be taken care of than marry a man of thirty and take care of *him*."

For Benjamin the rest[402] of the evening was bathed[403] in a honey-coloured mist. Hildegarde gave him two more dances, and they discovered that they were marvellously in accord[404] on all the questions of the day. She was to go driving with him on the following Sunday, and then they would discuss all these

---

398 wordly-wise : 말만 많은

399 pale from overwork : 과로로 창백해진

400 the age of long stories that take a whole cigar to tell : 입을 열면 시가 한 대를 다 피워야 할 만큼 긴 이야기들을 해 대는 나이

401 mellow : 익은, 향기로운, 단

402 rest : 나머지

403 bathe : (빛, 온기 따위를) 가득 채우다, (온몸을) 감싸다

404 in accord : 부합하는, 일치하는

questions further.

Going home in the phaeton just before the crack of dawn,[405] when the first bees were humming[406] and the fading moon glimmered[407] in the cool dew, Benjamin knew vaguely[408] that his father was discussing wholesale hardware.

".... And what do you think should merit[409] our biggest attention after hammers and nails?" the elder Button was saying.

"Love," replied Benjamin absent-mindedly.[410]

"Lugs?"[411] exclaimed[412] Roger Button, "Why, I've just covered[413] the question of lugs."

Benjamin regarded him with dazed eyes just as the eastern sky was suddenly cracked with light, and an oriole[414]

---

405 crack of dawn : 새벽, 이른 아침
406 hum : 윙윙거리다
407 glimmer : 깜박이다
408 vaguely : 막연히, 어렴풋이, 애매하게
409 merit : ~할 만하다(deserve), 이점
410 absent-mindedly : 정신없이, 넋이 나간 채로
411 lug : (채소 운반용) 나무 상자
412 exclaim : 외치다
413 cover : 다루다
414 oriole : 꾀꼬리

yawned[415] piercingly[416] in the quickening[417] trees...

Chapter VI

When, six months later, the engagement[418] of Miss Hildegarde Moncrief to Mr. Benjamin Button was made known (I say "made known," for General Moncrief declared he would rather fall upon his sword than announce it), the excitement in Baltimore society reached a feverish[419] pitch.[420] The almost forgotten story of Benjamin's birth was remembered and sent out upon the winds of scandal in picaresque[421] and incredible forms. It was said that Benjamin was really the father of Roger Button, that he was his brother who had been in prison for forty years, that he was John

---

415 yawn : 하품하다, (틈·아가리 등이) 크게 벌어지다
416 piercingly : 날카롭게, 새되게
417 quickening : 태동하는, 되살아나는
418 engagement : 약혼
419 feverish : 자제력을 잃은, 대단히 바쁜, 열에 들뜬
420 pitch : 음조
421 picaresque : 악한의, 악한을 주인공으로 한

Wilkes Booth[422] in disguise[423] — and, finally, that he had two small conical horns sprouting from his head.[424]

The Sunday supplements[425] of the New York papers played up[426] the case with fascinating sketches which showed the head of Benjamin Button attached to[427] a fish, to a snake, and, finally, to a body of solid brass. He became known, journalistically,[428] as the Mystery Man of Maryland. But the true story, as is usually the case,[429] had a very small circulation.[430]

However, every one agreed with General Moncrief that it was "criminal" for a lovely girl who could have married any beau[431] in Baltimore to throw herself into the arms of a man

---

422 John Wilkes Booth : 미국의 배우로, 링컨 대통령의 암살자

423 in disguise : 변장을 하고 있는, 변장 중인

424 two small conical horns sprouting from his head : 머리에 돋아난 두 개의 작은 원뿔형의 뿔

425 Sunday supplement : 일요판 부록

426 play up : 선전하다, 분투하다

427 attached to : ~에 덧붙인

428 journalistically : 신문 잡지 같은, 신문 잡지의 용어로

429 as is usually the case : ~에 흔히 있는 일이지만

430 circulation : 유통, 순환, 유포

431 beau : 남자 친구, 멋진 남자

who was assuredly[432] fifty. In vain Mr. Roger Button published his son's birth certificate[433] in large type[434] in the Baltimore *Blaze*. No one believed it. You had only to look at Benjamin and see.

On the part of the two people most concerned[435] there was no wavering.[436] So many of the stories about her fiance were false that Hildegarde refused stubbornly to believe even the true one. In vain General Moncrief pointed out[437] to her the high mortality[438] among men of fifty — or, at least, among men who looked fifty; in vain he told her of the instability[439] of the wholesale hardware business. Hildegarde had chosen to marry for mellowness,[440] and marry she did....

---

432 assuredly : 틀림없이

433 birth certificate : 출생증명서

434 in large type : 큰 활자(글꼴)로

435 concerned : 관계된

436 wavering : 흔들림, 갈팡질팡

437 point out : 지적하다, 짚어 주다

438 mortality : 사망률

439 instability : 불안정성

440 mellowness : 감미로움, (인격의) 원숙함, 원만함

Chapter VII

In one particular,[441] at least, the friends of Hildegarde Moncrief were mistaken. The wholesale hardware business prospered amazingly. In the fifteen years between Benjamin Button's marriage in 1880 and his father's retirement in 1895, the family fortune was doubled[442] — and this was due largely to the younger member of the firm.

Needless to say,[443] Baltimore eventually received the couple to its bosom. Even old General Moncrief became reconciled[444] to his son-in-law when Benjamin gave him the money to bring out[445] his *History of the Civil War* in twenty volumes, which had been refused by nine prominent[446] publishers.

In Benjamin himself fifteen years had wrought[447] many changes. It seemed to him that the blood flowed with new

---

441 in one particular : 어느 한 부분에서는

442 double : (두) 배가 되다

443 needless to say : 말할 필요도 없이

444 reconcile : 화해하다

445 bring out : 출판하다

446 prominent : 눈에 띄는, 중요한, 저명한

447 wrought : work(만들다, 형체를 갖추다)의 과거 · 과거분사형

vigour[448] through his veins.[449] It began to be a pleasure to rise in the morning, to walk with an active step[450] along the busy, sunny street, to work untiringly with his shipments[451] of hammers and his cargoes of nails. It was in 1890 that he executed his famous business coup:[452] he brought up[453] the suggestion that *all nails used in nailing up the boxes in which nails are shipped are the property of the shippee*,[454] a proposal which became a statute,[455] was approved by Chief Justice[456] Fossile, and saved Roger Button and Company, Wholesale Hardware, more than *six hundred nails every year.*

In addition, Benjamin discovered that he was becoming more and more attracted[457] by the gay side of life. It was typical of his growing enthusiasm for pleasure that he was the first man in the city of Baltimore to own and run an

---

448 vigour : = vigor. 생기

449 vein : 핏줄, 정맥

450 active step : 활기찬 발걸음(걸음걸이)

451 shipment : 선적

452 coup : (사업 등의) 대히트, 대성공, 멋진 일격, 쿠데타

453 bring up : (논거, 화제 등을) 내놓다

454 shippee : 배달을 받는 사람

455 statute : 법령

456 Chief Justice : 재판장, 법원장, (최고 법원의) 수석재판관, 연방대법원장

457 attract : 매혹하다

automobile. Meeting him on the street, his contemporaries would stare enviously at the picture he made of health and vitality.[458]

"He seems to grow younger every year," they would remark.[459] And if old Roger Button, now sixty-five years old, had failed at first to give a proper welcome to his son he atoned at last by bestowing on him what amounted to adulation.[460]

And here we come to an unpleasant subject which it will be well to pass over[461] as quickly as possible. There was only one thing that worried Benjamin Button; his wife had ceased to attract him.

At that time Hildegarde was a woman of thirty-five, with a son, Roscoe, fourteen years old. In the early days of their

---

458 the picture he made of health and vitality : 그가 보여 준 건강과 활력의
증표 ＊picture of health : 건강 그 자체

459 remark : (소견을) 말하다

460 he atoned at last by bestowing on him what amounted to adulation : 그
(아버지)는 마침내 그(Benjamin)에게 알랑거림(지나친 찬사)이라고 할 만
한 것을 부여함으로써 마침내 (태어날 때 제대로 환영하지 못한 것에 대
해) 보상했다 ＊atone : 보상하다, 속죄하다 ＊amount to : ~에 이르다, ~
와 마찬가지이다

461 pass over : 지나치다, (건드리지 않고) 넘기다

marriage Benjamin had worshipped her. But, as the years passed, her honey-coloured hair became an unexciting brown, the blue enamel of her eyes assumed the aspect of cheap crockery[462] — moreover, and, most of all, she had become too settled in her ways, too placid, too content, too anaemic in her excitements, and too sober in her taste.[463] As a bride it been she who had "dragged"[464] Benjamin to dances and dinners — now conditions were reversed.[465] She went out socially with him, but without enthusiasm, devoured[466] already by that eternal[467] inertia[468] which comes to live with each of us one day and stays with us to the end.

---

462 the blue enamel of her eyes assumed the aspect of cheap crockery: 파란
색 에나멜 같은 그녀의 눈은 싸구려 도자기의 모양을 띠었다 *crockery:
도자기, 오지그릇

463 too settled in her ways, too placid, too content, too anaemic in her
excitements, and too sober: 행동 방식이 너무 변화가 없이 안정적이고,
신나는 일을 찾는 데 있어서도 너무 얌전하고 너무 자족적이며 너무 매가
리가 없으며 취향도 너무 절제된

464 drag: <구어> 힘들게(억지로) 끌고 다니다

465 reverse: 거꾸로 하다, 뒤집다

466 devour: 게걸스레 먹다, 파멸시키다

467 eternal: 끝없는, 영원한, 불멸의

468 inertia: 타성, 활발하지 못함

Benjamin's discontent[469] waxed[470] stronger. At the outbreak[471] of the Spanish-American War[472] in 1898 his home had for him so little charm that he decided to join the army. With his business influence he obtained[473] a commission[474] as captain, and proved so adaptable[475] to the work that he was made a major, and finally a lieutenant-colonel[476] just in time to participate in the celebrated[477] charge[478] up San Juan Hill.[479] He was slightly wounded, and received a medal.

Benjamin had become so attached to the activity and excitement of array[480] life that he regretted to give it up, but his business required attention, so he resigned his commission

---

469 discontent : 불만족

470 wax : 커지다, 증대하다

471 outbreak : (소동, 전쟁, 유행병 따위의) 발발, 돌발, 창궐

472 Spanish-American War : 미서(美西) 전쟁(쿠바섬의 이해관계를 둘러싸고 미국과 스페인 사이에 일어났던 전쟁)

473 obtain : 얻다

474 commission : 위임, 임무

475 adaptable : 융통성 있는, 적응력 있는

476 lieutenant-colonel : 중령

477 celebrated : 저명한

478 charge : 돌격

479 San Juan Hill : 산후안 언덕(쿠바의 지명)

480 array : 배열, 진열 ＊array로 되어 있는 경우가 많은데 army의 뜻으로 보임. 이 부분은 '군대 생활'에 대해 언급하는 대목임.

and came home. He was met at the station by a brass band[481] and escorted to his house.

Chapter VIII

Hildegarde, waving a large silk flag, greeted him on the porch, and even as he kissed her he felt with a sinking of the heart[482] that these three years had taken their toll.[483] She was a woman of forty now, with a faint skirmish line[484] of gray hairs in her head. The sight depressed him.

Up in his room he saw his reflection in the familiar mirror — he went closer and examined his own face with anxiety,[485] comparing it after a moment with a photograph of himself in

---

481 brass band: 취주악대, 브라스 밴드

482 with a sinking of the heart: 가슴이 철렁 가라앉으며

483 take their toll: 큰 타격을 입다 * 좋았던 군대 시절이 종말을 고했다는 의미로 볼 수 있음.

484 skirmish line: <군사> 산병선(散兵線), 전초전, 작은 접전, 소전투 * 40 대에 들어선 아내의 머리에서 아직 두드러지지는 않았지만 흰머리가 나는 것을 보면서 아직 마치 검은 머리와 흰머리가 접전을 벌이는 전쟁터인 양 비유적으로 표현하는 것으로 이해할 수도 있음.

485 with anxiety: 걱정하며

uniform taken just before the war.[486]

"Good Lord!" he said aloud. The process was continuing. There was no doubt of it — he looked now like a man of thirty. Instead of being delighted, he was uneasy — he was growing younger. He had hitherto hoped that once he reached a bodily age equivalent[487] to his age in years, the grotesque[488] phenomenon which had marked[489] his birth would cease to function. He shuddered. His destiny seemed to him awful, incredible.

When he came downstairs Hildegarde was waiting for him. She appeared annoyed, and he wondered if she had at last discovered that there was something amiss.[490] It was with an effort to relieve the tension between them that he broached[491] the matter at dinner in what he considered a delicate way.

"Well," he remarked lightly, "everybody says I look younger than ever."

---

486 a photograph of himself in uniform taken just before the war : 전쟁 직전 에 찍은 제복을 입은 자신의 사진
487 equivalent : 동등한, 같은, ~에 상당하는
488 grotesque : 기괴한, 이상한, 어리석은
489 mark : 특징짓다, 특색을 이루다
490 amiss : 부적당한, 적절하지 않은
491 broach : 처음으로 입 밖에 내다, (하기 힘든 얘기를) 꺼내다

Hildegarde regarded him with scorn. She sniffed. "Do you think it's anything to boast about?"

"I'm not boasting," he asserted[492] uncomfortably. She sniffed again. "The idea," she said, and after a moment: "I should think you'd have enough pride to stop it."

"How can I?" he demanded.

"I'm not going to argue with you," she retorted.[493] "But there's a right way of doing things and a wrong way. If you've made up your mind[494] to be different from everybody else, I don't suppose I can stop you, but I really don't think it's very considerate."[495]

"But, Hildegarde, I can't help[496] it."

"You can too. You're simply stubborn.[497] You think you don't want to be like any one else. You always have been that way, and you always will be. But just think how it would be if every one else looked at things as you do — what would the world be like?"

---

492 assert : 단언하다, 강력히 주장하다, 시위하다
493 retort : 응수하다, 반론하다, 말대꾸하다, 반격하다
494 make up one's mind : 마음을 먹다
495 considerate : 사려 깊은
496 cannot help : ~하지 않을 수 없다 *help : 피하다, ~하지 않다, 못 하게 하다
497 stubborn : 완고한, 고집 센, 완강한, 불굴의

As this was an inane and unanswerable argument[498] Benjamin made no reply, and from that time on a chasm[499] began to widen between them. He wondered what possible fascination she had ever exercised over him.

To add to[500] the breach, he found, as the new century gathered headway,[501] that his thirst for gaiety[502] grew stronger. Never a party of any kind in the city of Baltimore but he was there,[503] dancing with the prettiest of the young married women, chatting with the most popular of the debutantes,[504] and finding their company charming, while his wife, a dowager of evil omen,[505] sat among the chaperons,[506] now in

---

498 an inane and unanswerable argument : 무의미하고도 답이 없는 논쟁

499 chasm : 깊이 갈라진 틈

500 add to : 더하다

501 gather headway : 전진하다

502 thirst for gaiety : 흥겨움(향락)에 대한 갈증

503 never a party of any kind in the city of Baltimore but he was there : 볼티모어 시의 어떤 종류의 파티든 그가 참석하지 않은 파티는 하나도 없었다
     ＊but : ~ 하지 않은

504 debutante : 처음 사교계에 나온 여성

505 a dowager of evil omen : 불길한 징조를 띤 노부인

506 chaperon : 샤프롱(사교계에 나오는 미혼 여성을 따라다니며 돌봐 주는 부인)

haughty disapproval,[507] and now following him with solemn, puzzled, and reproachful[508] eyes.

"Look!" people would remark. "What a pity![509] A young fellow that age tied to a woman of forty-five. He must be twenty years younger than his wife." They had forgotten — as people inevitably forget — that back in 1880 their mammas and papas had also remarked about this same ill-matched pair.[510]

Benjamin's growing unhappiness at home was compensated for[511] by his many new interests. He took up[512] golf and made a great success of it. He went in for[513] dancing: in 1906 he was an expert at "The Boston," and in 1908 he was considered proficient[514] at the "Maxine," while in 1909 his "Castle Walk"[515] was the envy of every young man in town.

---

507   in haughty disapproval : 거만한 태도로 못마땅해하며

508   reproachful : 비난하는, 책망하는 듯한

509   What a pity! : 불쌍해라, 애석하군

510   ill-matched pair : 어울리지 않는(잘못 짝지어진) 한 쌍

511   compensate for : 보상하다

512   take up : (특히 재미로) ~을 배우다(시작하다)

513   go in for : 마음을 붙이다, 열중하다

514   proficient : 능숙한, 숙련된

515   The Boston … Maxine … Castle Walk : 모두 댄스(스텝)의 일종

His social activities, of course, interfered[516] to some extent[517] with his business, but then he had worked hard at wholesale hardware for twenty-five years and felt that he could soon hand it on[518] to his son, Roscoe, who had recently graduated from Harvard.

He and his son were, in fact, often mistaken for each other. This pleased Benjamin — he soon forgot the insidious[519] fear which had come over him on his return from the Spanish-American War, and grew to take a naive pleasure in his appearance. There was only one fly in the delicious ointment[520] — he hated to appear in public with his wife. Hildegarde was almost fifty, and the sight of her made him feel absurd....[521]

---

516 interfere : 충돌하다, 방해하다, 간섭하다
517 to some extent : 어느 정도, 다소
518 hand on : 넘겨주다, 건네주다
519 insidious : 틈을 엿보는, 음험한, 방심할 수 없는, 모르는 사이에 작용하는
520 a fly in the ointment : 옥에 티
521 absurd : <형용사> 불합리한, 어리석은, <명사> 부조리

Chapter IX

One September day in 1910 — a few years after Roger
Button & Co., Wholesale Hardware, had been handed over[522]
to young Roscoe Button — a man, apparently[523] about twenty
years old, entered himself as a freshman at Harvard University
in Cambridge. He did not make the mistake of announcing
that he would never see fifty again,[524] nor did he mention the
fact that his son had been graduated from the same institution
ten years before.

He was admitted, and almost immediately attained[525] a
prominent[526] position in the class, partly because he seemed
a little older than the other freshmen, whose average age was
about eighteen.

But his success was largely due to[527] the fact that in the

---

522 hand over : 넘겨주다, 물려주다

523 apparently : 명백히, 외견상으로

524 he would never see fifty again : 다시는 50세를 보지(겪지) 못할 것이
다 *1860년 9월 생인 Benjamin은 1910년 9월 어느 날인 지금 50세의 생
일이 막 지났으므로 그에게 50세는 다시 오지 않을 것임.

525 attain : 얻다, 획득하다

526 prominent : 두드러진, 저명한, 탁월한

527 due to : ~ 때문에, ~에 기인하는

football game with Yale he played so brilliantly, with so much dash[528] and with such a cold, remorseless[529] anger that he scored[530] seven touchdowns[531] and fourteen field goals[532] for Harvard, and caused one entire eleven of Yale men to be carried singly from the field, unconscious.[533] He was the most celebrated man in college.

Strange to say, in his third or junior year he was scarcely[534] able to "make"[535] the team. The coaches said that he had lost weight,[536] and it seemed to the more observant[537] among them that he was not quite as tall as before. He made no touchdowns — indeed, he was retained[538] on the team

---

528　dash : 돌진

529　remorseless : 무자비한, 냉혹한

530　score : 점수를 기록하다, 점수를 내다

531　touchdown : 미식축구의 터치다운(6점짜리 공격)

532　field goal : 미식축구의 필드 골(골 포스트 사이로 차 넣는 골)

533　caused one entire eleven of Yale men to be carried singly from the field, unconscious : 예일 선수 11명 전체를 의식이 없는 상태로 하나씩 실려 나가게 했다

534　scarcely : 거의 ~가 아니다

535　make : <구어> (팀)의 일원이 되다, 성공적이 되게 하다

536　lose weight : 몸무게가 줄다, 살이 빠지다

537　observant : 관찰력이 뛰어난, 잘 지켜보고 있는

538　retain : 보유하다, 유지하다, 계속 사용하다

chiefly[539] in hope that his enormous reputation would bring terror and disorganisation[540] to the Yale team.

In his senior year he did not make the team at all. He had grown so slight and frail[541] that one day he was taken by some sophomores for a freshman, an incident which humiliated[542] him terribly. He became known as something of a prodigy[543] — a senior who was surely no more than sixteen — and he was often shocked at the worldliness[544] of some of his classmates. His studies seemed harder to him — he felt that they were too advanced.[545] He had heard his classmates speak of St. Midas's, the famous preparatory school,[546] at which so many of them had prepared for college, and he determined after his graduation to enter himself at St. Midas's, where the sheltered[547] life among boys his own size would be more

---

539 chiefly : 주로

540 disorganisation : 혼란

541 frail : 무른, 약한

542 humiliate : 창피를 주다

543 prodigy : 경이, 비범, 괴물, 불가사의, 비범한 사람

544 worldliness : 세속적임, 약삭빠름

545 advanced : 상급인

546 preparatory school : <미국> 대학 예비학교(대학 진학 코스의 사립학교)

547 sheltered : 보호된, 지켜지는, 세상의 풍파에서 격리된

congenial[548] to him.

Upon his graduation in 1914 he went home to Baltimore with his Harvard diploma in his pocket. Hildegarde was now residing[549] in Italy, so Benjamin went to live with his son, Roscoe. But though he was welcomed in a general way[550] there was obviously no heartiness[551] in Roscoe's feeling toward him — there was even perceptible[552] a tendency on his son's part to think that Benjamin, as he moped[553] about the house in adolescent[554] mooniness,[555] was somewhat in the way. Roscoe was married now and prominent in Baltimore life, and he wanted no scandal to creep out[556] in connection with[557] his family.

Benjamin, no longer *persona grata*[558] with the debutantes

---

548 congenial : 마음이 맞는, 성미와 맞는, 적합한, 쾌적한
549 reside : 거주하다
550 in a general way : 일반적으로, 대체로
551 heartiness : 진심
552 perceptible : 알아차릴 수 있는
553 mope : 의기소침해하다, 맥이 빠져 지내다
554 adolescent : 청소년의, 사춘기의
555 mooniness : 멍함, 얼빠짐 *moony : 꿈꾸는 듯한, 나른한, 얼빠진
556 creep out : 서서히 다가오다, 슬금슬금 기어 나오다
557 in connection with : ~와 관련하여, ~에 관한
558 *persona grata* : 호감이 가는 인물

and younger college set,[559] found himself left much alone, except for the companionship of three or four fifteen-year-old boys in the neighbourhood. His idea of going to St. Midas's school recurred[560] to him.

5   "Say,"[561] he said to Roscoe one day, "I've told you over and over that I want to go to prep school."

"Well, go, then," replied Roscoe shortly. The matter was distasteful[562] to him, and he wished to avoid a discussion.

"I can't go alone," said Benjamin helplessly. "You'll have to
10   enter me and take me up there."

"I haven't got time," declared Roscoe abruptly. His eyes narrowed[563] and he looked uneasily at his father. "As a matter of fact," he added, "you'd better not go on with this business much longer. You better pull up short.[564] You better — you
15   better" — he paused and his face crimsoned[565] as he sought

---

559   set: 한패(거리), 동아리, 사람들, 사회
560   recur: 다시 발생하다, 되풀이되다
561   say: 이봐, 저어, (삽입구처럼 예시하는 것 앞에서) 이를테면, 예를 들면, 글쎄요
562   distasteful: 싫은, 불쾌한
563   narrow: 가늘게 뜨다
564   pull up short: 당장 그만두다(멈추다)
565   crimson: 붉어지다

for words — "you better turn right around and start back the other way.[566] This has gone too far to be a joke. It isn't funny any longer. You — you behave yourself!"[567]

Benjamin looked at him, on the verge of tears.[568]

"And another thing," continued Roscoe, "when visitors are in the house I want you to call me 'Uncle' — not 'Roscoe,' but 'Uncle,' do you understand? It looks absurd for a boy of fifteen to call me by my first name. Perhaps you'd better call me 'Uncle' *all* the time, so you'll get used to it."

With a harsh look at his father, Roscoe turned away....

Chapter X

At the termination[569] of this interview, Benjamin wandered[570] dismally[571] upstairs and stared at himself in the mirror. He

---

566 turn right around and start back the other way : 당장 방향을 바꿔 다른 쪽으로 되돌아가기 시작하다

567 behave oneself : 적절히 처신하다, 예의 바르게 행동하다

568 on the verge of tears : 금방 울음을 터뜨릴 지경의

569 termination : 종말, 끝

570 wander : 헤매다, 어슬렁거리다

571 dismally : 음산하게, 우울하게

had not shaved for three months, but he could find nothing on his face but a faint white down[572] with which it seemed unnecessary to meddle.[573] When he had first come home from Harvard, Roscoe had approached him with the proposition

5 that he should wear eye-glasses and imitation[574] whiskers glued[575] to his cheeks, and it had seemed for a moment that the farce[576] of his early years was to be repeated. But whiskers had itched and made him ashamed. He wept and Roscoe had reluctantly relented.[577]

10   Benjamin opened a book of boys' stories, *The Boy Scouts in Bimini Bay,* and began to read. But he found himself thinking persistently[578] about the war. America had joined the Allied[579] cause[580] during the preceding[581] month, and Benjamin wanted

---

572 down : 솜털, 배내털, 부드러운 털

573 meddle : 만지작거리다, 간섭하다, 쓸데없이 참견하다

574 imitation : 모조품

575 glue : 풀로 붙이다

576 farce : 소극, 광대극

577 reluctantly relented : 마지못해 마음이 부드러워졌다(누그러졌다)

578 persistently : 계속해서, 끊임없이, 끈덕지게, 고집스럽게

579 the Allied : (제1·2차 세계대전 중의) 연합국

580 cause : 대의명분, (~을 위한) 운동

581 preceding : 앞의

to enlist, but, alas,[582] sixteen was the minimum age,[583] and he did not look that old. His true age, which was fifty-seven, would have disqualified[584] him, anyway.

There was a knock at his door, and the butler appeared with a letter bearing a large official legend in the corner[585] and addressed to Mr. Benjamin Button. Benjamin tore it open eagerly, and read the enclosure[586] with delight. It informed him that many reserve officers[587] who had served in the Spanish-American War were being called back into service with a higher rank, and it enclosed his commission[588] as brigadier-general[589] in the United States army with orders to report[590] immediately.

---

582 alas: 아아, 슬프도다, 불행한지고

583 minimum age: 최저 연령

584 disqualify: 자격을 박탈하다, 실격시키다

585 bearing a large official legend in the corner: 한쪽 구석에 커다란 공식적 장식 문장(紋章)이 있는 *bear: (눈에 보이게) 있다(지니다)

586 enclosure: 동봉된 것

587 reserve officer: 예비역 장교

588 commission: 위임장, 사령

589 brigadier-general: 준장

590 report: 출두(하다), (입대) 신고(하다)

Benjamin jumped to his feet fairly[591] quivering[592] with enthusiasm. This was what he had wanted. He seized his cap, and ten minutes later he had entered a large tailoring establishment[593] on Charles Street, and asked in his uncertain treble[594] to be measured[595] for a uniform.

"Want to play soldier, sonny?"[596] demanded a clerk casually.[597]

Benjamin flushed. "Say! Never mind what I want!" he retorted angrily. "My name's Button and I live on Mt. Vernon Place, so you know I'm good for[598] it."

"Well," admitted the clerk hesitantly, "if you're not, I guess your daddy is, all right."

Benjamin was measured, and a week later his uniform was completed. He had difficulty in obtaining the proper general's

---

591 fairly: 심하게, 꽤나

592 quiver: 떨다

593 tailoring establishment: 양복점 ＊establishment: 기관, 시설

594 treble: 새된 목소리

595 measure: 치수를 재다

596 sonny: <구어> 아가야, 애야(소년, 연소자에 대한 친근한 호칭)

597 casually: 태연히, 일상적으로

598 good for: 신뢰할 수 있는, 신용 있는, 지불할 수 있는

insignia[599] because the dealer kept insisting to Benjamin that a nice Y.W.C.A.[600] badge would look just as well and be much more fun to play with.

Saying nothing to Roscoe, he left the house one night and proceeded by train to Camp Mosby, in South Carolina, where he was to command an infantry brigade.[601] On a sultry April day he approached the entrance to the camp, paid off the taxicab which had brought him from the station, and turned to the sentry[602] on guard.[603]

"Get some one to handle my luggage!" he said briskly.[604]

The sentry eyed him reproachfully.[605] "Say," he remarked, "where you goin' with the general's duds,[606] sonny?"

Benjamin, veteran of the Spanish-American War, whirled[607] upon him with fire in his eye, but with, alas, a changing treble

---

599 insignia : 휘장, 배지, 표장
600 Y.W.C.A. : 기독교 여자청년회(Young Women's Christian Association)
     의 약칭
601 infantry brigade : 보병여단
602 sentry : 보초
603 on guard : 보초를 서는
604 briskly : 활발히, 기운차게
605 reproachfully : 비난하는 듯, 꾸짖는 듯이
606 duds : 옷
607 whirl : 갑자기 방향을 바꾸다

voice.

"Come to attention!"[608] he tried to thunder;[609] he paused for breath — then suddenly he saw the sentry snap[610] his heels together and bring his rifle to the present.[611] Benjamin concealed a smile of gratification,[612] but when he glanced around his smile faded.[613] It was not he who had inspired obedience,[614] but an imposing[615] artillery colonel[616] who was approaching on horseback.[617]

"Colonel!" called Benjamin shrilly.[618]

The colonel came up, drew rein,[619] and looked coolly down at him with a twinkle in his eyes.[620] "Whose little boy are

---

608 come to attention : <군사 용어> 차렷!

609 thunder : 큰 소리를 내다, 소리 지르다

610 snap : 딱 소리를 내며 부딪치다

611 bring his rifle to present : 받들어총(의 자세)을 취하다

612 gratification : 만족, 희열, 큰 기쁨

613 fade : 흐릿해지다, 아련해지다

614 who had inspired obedience : 복종을 불러일으킨 사람

615 imposing : 인상적인, 눈길을 끄는

616 artillery colonel : 포병 대령

617 on horseback : 말을 탄

618 shrilly : 새된 소리로, 높고 날카롭게

619 draw rein : 말고삐를 당기다

620 with a twinkle in his eyes : 눈을 반짝이며, 눈을 끔벅이며

you?" he demanded kindly.

"I'll soon darn[621] well show you whose little boy I am!" retorted Benjamin in a ferocious[622] voice. "Get down off that horse!"

The colonel roared with laughter.[623]

"You want him, eh, general?"

"Here!" cried Benjamin desperately. "Read this." And he thrust his commission toward the colonel. The colonel read it, his eyes popping from their sockets. "Where'd you get this?" he demanded, slipping the document into his own pocket. "I got it from the Government, as you'll soon find out!" "You come along with me," said the colonel with a peculiar look. "We'll go up to headquarters and talk this over. Come along." The colonel turned and began walking his horse in the direction of headquarters. There was nothing for Benjamin to do but follow with as much dignity as possible — meanwhile promising himself a stern revenge.[624] But this revenge did

---

621 darn : = damn. 빌어먹을

622 ferocious : 사나운, 포악한, 잔인한

623 roar with laughter : 크게 웃음을 터뜨리다

624 meanwhile promising himself a stern revenge : 그러는 한편, 엄중한 앙갚음을 해 주리라 속으로 맹세하면서

not materialise.[625] Two days later, however, his son Roscoe materialised from Baltimore, hot and cross[626] from a hasty trip, and escorted[627] the weeping general, *sans*[628] uniform, back to his home.

Chapter XI

In 1920 Roscoe Button's first child was born. During the attendant[629] festivities,[630] however, no one thought it "the thing" to mention,[631] that the little grubby[632] boy, apparently about ten years of age who played around the house with lead soldiers and a miniature circus,[633] was the new baby's own grandfather.

---

625 materialise : = materialize. 실현되다, ~에 형체를 부여하다

626 cross : 성을 내는, 찌무룩한, 까다로운, 성마른

627 escort : 호송하다, 호위하다, 함께 가다

628 sans : ~ 없이

629 attendant : ~에 따르는

630 festivities : (복수형으로) 축제의 행사, 법석

631 "the thing" to mention : 언급해도 좋을 '거리', 대화하기에 '적절한 것'

632 grubby : 지저분한, 더러운, 게으른, 칠칠치 못한

633 miniature circus : 서커스 미니어처(서커스 풍경, 인물 등을 축소해서 만들어 놓은 모형 장난감)

No one disliked the little boy whose fresh, cheerful face was crossed[634] with just a hint of sadness, but to Roscoe Button his presence was a source of torment.[635] In the idiom[636] of his generation[637] Roscoe did not consider[638] the matter "efficient."[639] It seemed to him that his father, in refusing to look sixty, had not behaved like a "red-blooded[640] he-man"[641] — this was Roscoe's favourite expression — but in a curious and perverse[642] manner. Indeed, to think about the matter for as much as a half an hour drove him to the edge[643] of insanity.[644] Roscoe believed that "live wires" should keep young, but carrying it out on such a scale was — was — was

---

634 cross : (마음이나 표정 등에) 떠오르다

635 source of torment : 고통(고민거리)의 원천

636 idiom : 숙어, 관용구

637 in the idiom of his generation : 그의 세대가 잘 쓰는 관용구(어법)에 따르면

638 consider : ~로 생각하다, ~을 ~으로 간주하다

639 efficient : 효율적인, 유능한, 실력 있는, (수단, 조처 따위가) 유효한 * 이 대목은 우리식의 속어로 '선수답다'는 의미로 봐서 도무지 '선수답지 못한' 부친의 생애에 대해 불만스러워하는 아들의 심리를 드러내고 있는 듯함.

640 red-blooded : 기운찬, 발랄한, 용감한

641 he-man : <구어> 사내다운 (사내)

642 perverse : 심술궂은, 뜻대로 안 되는, 성미가 비꼬인

643 edge : 가장자리, 변두리, 끝자락

644 insanity : 정신이상, 광기

inefficient.[645] And there Roscoe rested.

Five years later Roscoe's little boy had grown old enough to play childish games with little Benjamin under the supervision[646] of the same nurse. Roscoe took them both to kindergarten on the same day, and Benjamin found that playing with little strips of coloured paper, making mats and chains and curious and beautiful designs, was the most fascinating game in the world. Once he was bad and had to stand in the corner — then he cried — but for the most part there were gay hours in the cheerful room, with the sunlight coming in the windows and Miss Bailey's kind hand resting for a moment now and then in his tousled[647] hair.

Roscoe's son moved up into the first grade after a year, but Benjamin stayed on in the kindergarten. He was very happy. Sometimes when other tots[648] talked about what they would do when they grew up a shadow would cross his little face as

---

645 "live wires" should keep young, but carrying it out on such a scale was — was — was inefficient: "정력가"(활동가)라면 젊음을 유지해야 하기는 하지만 그런 수준으로까지(그 지경까지 어려지면서까지) 실행하는 것은, 정말이지, '비효율적'이다

646 supervision: 감독, 감시

647 tousled: 헝클어진, 단정치 못한

648 tot: 어린아이

if in a dim, childish way he realised that those were things in which he was never to share.

The days flowed[649] on in monotonous[650] content. He went back a third year to the kindergarten, but he was too little now to understand what the bright shining strips of paper were for. He cried because the other boys were bigger than he, and he was afraid of them. The teacher talked to him, but though he tried to understand he could not understand at all.

He was taken from the kindergarten. His nurse,[651] Nana, in her starched[652] gingham[653] dress, became the centre of his tiny world. On bright days they walked in the park; Nana would point at a great gray monster and say "elephant," and Benjamin would say it after[654] her, and when he was being undressed for bed that night he would say it over and over aloud to her: "Elyphant, elyphant, elyphant." Sometimes Nana let him jump on the bed, which was fun, because if you sat down exactly right it would bounce you up on your

---

649 flow : (세월이) 물 흐르듯 지나가다, 흘러가다
650 monotonous : 단조로운
651 nurse : 유모
652 starched : 풀을 먹인
653 gingham : 깅엄(줄무늬, 체크무늬의 평직 면포)
654 after : ~를 따라

feet again,[655] and if you said "Ah" for a long time while you jumped you got a very pleasing broken vocal[656] effect.

He loved to take a big cane from the hat-rack[657] and go around hitting chairs and tables with it and saying: "Fight, fight, fight." When there were people there the old ladies would cluck[658] at him, which interested him, and the young ladies would try to kiss him, which he submitted[659] to with mild boredom. And when the long day was done at five o'clock he would go upstairs with Nana and be fed on oatmeal and nice soft mushy[660] foods with a spoon.

There were no troublesome[661] memories in his childish sleep; no token came to him of his brave days at college, of the glittering[662] years when he flustered[663] the hearts of many

---

655 it would bounce you up on your feet again : 튀어오르게 해서 발로 다시 서게 하다

656 vocal : 목소리의, 음성의, 소리를 내는

657 hat-rack : 모자걸이

658 cluck : 혀를 차다

659 submit : 감수하다, 복종하다

660 mushy : 무른

661 troublesome : 귀찮은, 성가신, 곤란한

662 glittering : 번쩍이는, 빛나는, 화려한

663 fluster : 당황시키다, 안절부절못하게 하다

girls. There were only the white, safe walls of his crib[664] and Nana and a man who came to see him sometimes, and a great big orange ball that Nana pointed at just before his twilight[665] bed hour and called "sun." When the sun went his eyes were sleepy — there were no dreams, no dreams to haunt[666] him.

The past — the wild charge[667] at the head of his men[668] up San Juan Hill; the first years of his marriage when he worked late into the summer dusk[669] down in the busy city for young Hildegarde whom he loved; the days before that when he sat smoking far into the night[670] in the gloomy[671] old Button house on Monroe Street with his grandfather — all these had faded like unsubstantial[672] dreams from his mind as though they had never been. He did not remember.

He did not remember clearly whether the milk was warm

---

664 crib : (소아용) 테두리 난간이 있는 침대
665 twilight : 어스름, 땅거미 진
666 haunt : 괴롭히다, 나타나다, 머리에서 떠나지 않다
667 wild charge : 거친 공격
668 men : <주로 복수로> 부하
669 dusk : 땅거미, 해 질 녘
670 far into the night : 밤이 깊도록
671 gloomy : 우울한
672 unsubstantial : 실체가 없는, 공상적인, 사실에 의거하지 않은, 비현실적인

or cool at his last feeding[673] or how the days passed — there was only his crib and Nana's familiar presence. And then he remembered nothing. When he was hungry he cried — that was all. Through the noons and nights he breathed and over him there were soft mumblings[674] and murmurings[675] that he scarcely heard, and faintly differentiated[676] smells, and light and darkness.

Then it was all dark, and his white crib and the dim faces that moved above him, and the warm sweet aroma[677] of the milk, faded out[678] altogether from his mind.

---

673 feeding: 급식, 먹음

674 mumbling: 중얼거림

675 murmuring: 속삭임, 투덜거림

676 differentiate: 구분하다

677 aroma: 방향, 향기, 풍취

678 fade out: 서서히 모습을 감추다, 소실되다

작품 해설

1. 생애 과정 뒤집기와 정형화된 삶의 양식 비판

이 단편소설에서 작가는 '정상적인 생애 과정'을 극단적이고 우스꽝스럽게 거꾸로 뒤집는다. 주인공 Benjamin Button은 육신과 정신이 '노인'으로 태어나 아이의 상태를 향해 '늙어 가다'가 끝내 '무'(無)로 돌아가도록 설정되어 있다. 인생 과정에서 생물학적인 차원과 사회적 차원을 이렇게 극단적으로 뒤틀어 놓고 나면 '자연스러워 보이는' 과정이 달리 보일 수 있다. 즉, 이 과정에 '정상적인 생애'라는 규제적 범주를 앞세운 사회적 통제가 내밀하게 작동하는 양상이 드러난다. 다시 말해 범주화된 생물학적인 나이를 벗어난 생각과 행동들, 혹은 사회적으로 그렇게 여겨지는 것들은 '터무니없는 비정상'이자 '괴이한 고집'의 소산이며 주변 사람들을 불편하게 만들거나 두렵게 하는 것으로 간주된다.

예컨대 50세로 보이는 18세의 Button이 예일대 입학의 모든 형식적인 요건을 충족시키고 시험을 통과했음에도 불구하고 퇴짜를 맞는 장면을 떠올려 보자. 학부모처럼 보이는 Button이 신입생은 바로 자기라고 거듭 설명하는 극히 과장된 상황을 마주하고 입학 담당자는 더없이 황당해하며 끝내 화를 내고 만다. 그런데 그가 화를 내는 것은 우선

Button이 이렇게 도무지 믿기지 않는 나이를 대며 자신이 신입생이라고 우기기 때문이지만 그 이상으로 나이에 걸맞지 않게 '그런 나이'에 신입생으로 들어와 공부하겠다는 '생각' 자체가 괴이하다고 판단했기 때문이다.

하지만 오늘날에는 생물학적 나이를 떠난 '평생교육'이 이제는 '상식'이 되고 그런 삶이 '자연스럽고' 더 '가치 있게' 보이기까지 한다. 오늘날의 입학 담당자는, 예전의 그 입학 담당자의 경우와 비교할 때, 생애 과정에 따라 경직되게 설정된 사회적 역할들과는 다른 전제에 놓여 있기에 '제 나이'에 입학하는 학생보다 Button을 훨씬 더 크게 환영할 수도 있을 것이다.

2. 생애 과정 뒤집기의 매혹과 문제

'나이에 걸맞지 않은' 양상을 형상화하는 과정에서 조금 더 주목하게 만드는 게 있다면 '노년'에 대한 시선이다. 비록 이 작품에서 노년에 대해 노골적인 적대감이 형상화되었다고 보기는 어렵다. 하지만 태어난 이후 '노인' Benjamin Button이 다뤄지는 방식을 보면 '노년'이 가족적·사회적으로 얼마나 보잘것없는 것으로 취급되고 있는지 짐작 가능하다.

그런데 Button은 뒤집힌 생애 과정 덕분에 삶을 마감하는 시점으로 다가갈수록 더 뼈저리게 느껴질 수 있을 노년에 대한 경시를 일찌감치 '유년'에 지나친다. 게다가 '유년'이기 때문에 그런 경시가 딱히 뼈저릴 까닭도 없다. 그의 삶에서는 노력, 성취, 힘겨움 등의 낱말은 큰 비중을 차지하지 않는다. 예컨대 인기 있는 여성 Hildegarde의 마음을 사로잡아 결혼에 이른 것은 딱히 Button이 자신의 생에서나 그녀를 위해 어떤 특별한 노력을 기울였기 때문이라기보다는 그에게는 그녀가 그저 '부드럽고 그윽한 나이'(mellow age)라고 생각한 50세로 보였기 때문이다.

생애 과정 뒤집기의 매력을 좀 더 확장해 보면, 이미 노년으로 태어난 까닭에 성년에 이르기까지 노력을 통해 갖추고 성취해 가는 과정이 생략되었듯, 이와 동시에 Button의 삶에서는 삶의 일정 시점 이후 나이가 들면서 강렬해질 수 있는 삶에 대한 제반 고집과 집착에서 놓여나는 과정의 힘겨움도 생략된다. 생의 과정을 기억하되 그로부터 놓여나는 힘겨운 노력의 과정 자체가 불필요하다. 그 대신 시간이 경과함에 따라 기억 자체가 없어짐으로써 고집을 부리고 집착할 것 자체가 없어지는 '자연스러운 소멸의 과정'(normal ungrowth)으로 대체된다.

이렇게 성장하는 과정에서 무엇을 애써 성취할 필요도 없고 늙어 가면서 무엇을 애써 놓아야 할 필요도 없는 Button의 상태는 노인일 때나 유아일 때나 비유컨대 언제나 물을 흠뻑 빨아들인 스펀지와 같은 인상을 풍긴다. 구체적으로 말하면, 세상과 마주해 Button은 그 세상으로부터 무엇을 흡수하는 것 같지 않으며 반대로 자신으로부터 무엇을 짜내 덜어 내거나 하는 작용을 하는 것으로 느껴지지도 않는다. 이런 Button에게서 언뜻 생명력이 빠진 사물의 느낌이 들기도 한다면 지나친 과장일까.

이 작품은 생애 과정 뒤집기를 통해 자연스러운 생애 과정의 단계를 밑그림으로 깔고 그 위에 사회적 성장단계의 패턴을 그려 가는 과정을 한결 더 의식적이고 반성적인 것으로 사고하는 계기를 마련해 준다.